WHAT SWEET MADNESS

Afterward, she recalled the minute in which the dance stopped and she swept a final curtsey to him, raising a face alight with laughter to his. And the answering blaze that leapt into his hazel eyes.

For a breathless moment, they stared at one another, the laughter wiped from their faces. At last, Sir Jeremy broke the tense silence.

"I must be mad," he muttered, taking Clarissa by the shoulders.

She tilted her face toward his. "Madness, yes," she whispered, her arms reaching upward, drawing him nearer. "But—"

Her words were stopped as his mouth descended close to hers. "I've wanted to do this all evening," he said. And then he kissed her.

DEAR DECEIVER

ELIZABETH LYNCH

AVON BOOKS ✦ NEW YORK

DEAR DECEIVER is an original publication of Avon Books. This work has never before appeared in book form. This work is a novel. Any similarity to actual persons or events is purely coincidental.

AVON BOOKS
A division of
The Hearst Corporation
1350 Avenue of the Americas
New York, New York 10019

Copyright © 1995 by Elizabeth Lynch
Published by arrangement with the author
Library of Congress Catalog Card Number: 94-96777
ISBN: 0-380-78046-1

First Avon Books Printing: July 1995

AVON TRADEMARK REG. U.S. PAT. OFF. AND IN OTHER COUNTRIES, MARCA REGISTRADA, HECHO EN U.S.A.

Printed in the U.S.A.

RA   10   9   8   7   6   5   4   3   2   1

DEAR DECEIVER

1

London, October 1/88

Clarissa glanced out the sitting-room window, hoping for distraction and finding the dismals. The neat square should have looked elegant and cared-for, but winter hadn't arrived and fall hadn't made up its mind to go. Under a pewter colored sky and the eye of a bored nursemaid, the children from the house across the way poked dispiritedly about in the square's tiny park. Its shrubbery was bedraggled; stray droplets of drizzle clung to the grillework of the iron gate.

Clarissa turned to face a room gleaming with sunny hangings of yellow satin and warm from a fire crackling on the hearth. Even in its glow, she shivered as her eyes fell to a wrinkled piece of paper on an inlaid table.

The paper was a cartoon, cleverly drawn, crudely humorous. Its centerpiece was a young and beautiful female reclining in a wood, wearing a gauzy gown that clung closely to each delectable curve. She cast a pouting look over one shoulder toward a gaggle of swains, all in varying degrees

1

of slack-jawed lust. The caption read: "Titania And Her Suitors."

Staring down at the cartoon was a face identical to Titania's—except for its grave stillness, so different from the picture's flirtatious pout. Then, too, while pen and ink had captured the original's finely molded cheekbones and delicately curved mouth, they could not depict her glorious coloring: the dark blue of the large eyes, the rich reddish-gold hair that had earned her the young bucks' waggishly poetic nickname.

But the cartoon was certainly adequate. No one in polite society could fail to understand Titania's true identity, which was that of her grace Clarissa Harcourt, dowager duchess of Belfort, a widow for just about a year, a scandal for nearly five.

Lost in her own thoughts, she heard the brisk tap at the door with a start. "Come in," she said, her eyes still on the crumpled bit of paper.

Two women stood on the threshold. One of them, in a sober dove-grey dress, a cap perched over her mass of wavy dark hair, was clearly a servant, though the set of her chin and her expressive dark eyes were hardly subservient.

The other was many years older than either maid or mistress. "What in the world are you dreaming of, my dear?" this lady demanded. "Poor Martha knocked three times before you took notice of us."

Clarissa swung about with a smile of greeting. "How wretched of me, and you just back from Vienna!"

Unfastening her cloak, Lady Anne Talmadge swept into the sitting room with an assurance bred by years as a diplomat's wife. She was dressed for a call in a modishly cut gown of fine green wool, a plumed, broad-brimmed hat shading her sharp-featured but kind face. Her smile faded as she saw what had occupied Clarissa's attention. With a swiftly decisive movement, she snatched up the cartoon, her brows snapping together in a fierce frown.

"How on earth did this rubbish get into the house, Clary?" demanded Lady Talmadge.

"I've no idea."

"*I've* a very good idea," said Martha, to whom Lady Talmadge handed the paper with a grimace. Kneeling by the hearth, Martha fed the cartoon to the flames.

"There we go, a fine place for a nasty bit o' trash like that. You should have put it there from the first, Your Grace, instead of fretting over it."

Neither of the ladies, who had settled themselves into chairs by the window, evinced the slightest displeasure at this forthright speech; indeed, Lady Talmadge nodded approvingly.

"Just so, Martha. And I think I've a good idea, too, who brought it here."

"Some people, my lady," said Martha darkly, "aren't worthy to be called gentlemen, much less noblemen. And some *other* people"—here, an arrow-straight look at Clarissa—"aren't given near their due as lady of the house. I'll bring the tea directly, Your Grace."

Clarissa watched her go, smiling despite herself. "I believe Martha could debate Mr. Fox and not back down an inch."

"I believe so, too, particularly when she's right. Clarissa, something *must* be done about Belfort."

"Belfort—" Clarissa paused. "It's still so startling to me to hear Richard Harcourt called thus." She broke off again, glancing down at her black skirts.

Lady Talmadge's bright eyes were warm with sympathy, but she kept her voice brisk. "Oh, indeed, love, it's exceedingly difficult for me to hear, too. But Richard Harcourt is duke of Belfort now—

terrible as that is. How I *wish* your poor husband had had another cousin."

"Or a son?" Clarissa cocked an eyebrow wryly.

"Well, it would have made matters rather less complicated for you, but what's that to the purpose now, love?"

Their eyes met; they exchanged smiles, these veterans of a bygone battle—the now-hopeless fight to gain Clarissa uncritical acceptance in the bosom of polite society.

Ask any gathering of the *haut ton* an idle question about the dowager duchess of Belfort, and one would provoke a dozen comments, many contradictory, all vaguely uncomplimentary. Why, she had no position to speak of—her mother a baronet's younger daughter, her father a country clergyman. A forward miss, distressingly quick to speak her mind. A cold piece, unable to chatter commonplaces during a morning call or rout party. No, no—she was a terrible flirt. When pressed, the commentators could not give hard evidence of this. But it stood to reason. The gentlemen flocked around her; they always had, since she'd first set foot in London.

Such a very young bride she had been.

With *such* a husband—a sixty-year-old duke, the realm's most famous bachelor. How had she ensnared him? And where in the world, everyone wondered, had the old duke found this beautiful nobody?

He had found her, prosaically enough, near her aunt's house in Bath, where Clarissa had gone to live after the carriage accident that had claimed her parents' lives. She was walking her aunt's crotchety pair of pugs; the old duke had just arrived in town to take the waters and indulge in a bit of sport at the gaming tables. There had been a whirlwind courtship, a hasty marriage. And then the trouble had begun. . . .

"Are you so surprised at that drawing, Anne?" Clarissa's question forced Lady Talmadge back to the present. "I cannot say that I am."

Anne Talmadge looked thoughtful, but refrained from offering a reassuring denial. She turned instead to the tea tray set down by Martha, who left as quietly as she had entered.

"No, you are right, my dear," said Lady Talmadge, pouring with practiced grace. "I'm afraid your circumstances have always been irresistible to the gossips—starting with your husband himself! Such a dear, eccentric man, collecting enough paintings and sculptures to fill a palace, flirting with all the belles for *decades* and never marrying— then stealing away abroad with a bride no one had ever heard of!"

If only, she thought for the hundredth time, the old duke had presented Clarissa to society at the very start. But that was old Belfort for you, never a one to worry about appearances. And it couldn't be helped now.

"And then," said Clarissa wryly, "what should we do after a year but materialize in town—except that one of us was an invalid by then, and closeted with the medical specialists. How vexingly odd of us."

Blunt but true, thought Lady Talmadge. Clarissa could have done very little to allay the suspicion and ill will that had greeted her in London.

The duke's acquaintances had been outwardly solicitous—the poor man, losing the use of his legs after falling from his horse!

But the whispers had been as inevitable as spring rain. A May–December marriage! Why, no good could come of it—especially now that the poor husband was ill and the chit had all London as her hunting-ground. . . .

Anne, who had been abroad with Lord Talmadge, had come upon this interesting saga rather late in the day. She had not expected, from the breathless stories she heard, to find anything likable in the duchess Clarissa, who by then had fallen in with a wild set who played cards for high stakes, frequented masked balls, and raced in the park on wagers. Calling upon Clarissa out of politeness and curiosity, Anne had found to her surprise no vulgar upstart, but a frightened, green girl, surprisingly well read but woefully ignorant of the ways of the world. Anne's heart had been touched; she had taken Clarissa under her wing and done what she could to repair the damage done the young duchess's reputation.

"Poor Anne," said Clarissa now. "You have always tried to be wise for me. I'm sorry I've been such a slow pupil."

"Never slow," said Lady Talmadge. "Extremely stubborn, I grant you. And of course, at the start, far too trusting."

"I know," said Clarissa with a rueful smile. "*What* a fortunate thing that you arrived to take me in hand!"

Lady Talmadge shook her head at her friend. "Have I ever said how dreadfully sorry I am for the wretched time you had of it when you first came to town?"

"Yes, though you never had need to apologize," Clarissa said calmly. "You have always been all that is kind. Just as my Robert always was. As for the rest of the beau monde, they can go to the devil."

Lady Talmadge knew Clarissa too well by now to be surprised by this frankness, though she privately thought Clarissa's peculiar blend of beauty and bluntness was at the heart of her troubles with the polite world.

Men were drawn to her, but Clarissa had never behaved as an accredited Incomparable ought. She was lamentably uninterested in flirtatious games, and—difficult as it was for her suitors to believe— genuinely fond of her invalid husband. No gentleman could boast of success with her, but that had never prevented the more spiteful among them from claiming victories that never existed. Especially now that Clarissa was a widow, and unprotected . . .

Lady Talmadge's eyes wandered involuntarily toward the busily crackling fire, though the scurrilous cartoon had long turned into ashes. She poured them each another cup of tea, and forced herself to speak matter-of-factly. "There's no sense beating about the bush, Clarissa—your reputation hangs by the slenderest of threads. The gossip is much worse than before Talmadge and I left for Austria. And your odious cousin Richard, far from trying to squelch the nastiness, seems determined to encourage it."

"I know. He brought the wretched drawing into the house, of course. He left it in a sealed envelope by my plate at breakfast. How discreet."

"The blackguard!" Lady Talmadge exclaimed, in mingled fury and apprehension.

"It is worse than you know," said Clarissa. "Last week he offered me carte blanche."

"He—*what?*"

"I said," Clarissa repeated obligingly, "he offered me carte blanche. He said he would be most generous if I went along with the—ah—arrangement. I have a month to think it over, until he returns from the meet at Epsom. He appeared to consider it quite a compliment—'under the circumstances,' as he put it." She carefully folded her hands in her lap; they trembled slightly.

"Richard Harcourt is a knave and a rakehell, with not a scrap of honor to his name," said Anne, fighting hard to keep her voice level. "But I find it difficult to understand where even he would have the audacity—"

"It is not so very mystifying," said Clarissa. "I'm . . . well, to be perfectly plain, I'm trapped here."

"Trapped? That's nonsense. You must set up your own establishment instantly. Or travel—yes, that's it! You can tour the Continent, Clary, dear. It's the perfect thing. But you mustn't stay an instant longer in Belfort House with that blackguard."

"That's just it. I cannot go anywhere. It's because of the will."

"The will? My dear, I don't understand. Surely your settlement—"

Clarissa sighed. "Of course there is a settlement—but I cannot touch it until I have been a widow for at least eighteen months."

"But why on earth—"

"Oh, Robert meant it for the best reasons in the world! We had talked about it, you see. He worried what would happen if I were left on my own with a rich inheritance. He thought perhaps the wolves would be circling—" She gave an odd, broken little laugh. "He thought I should have a little time to think about what to do next, not be rushed into a second marriage with a fortune hunter. Oh, poor Robert, he couldn't possibly have known. . . ."

"Dear heaven," Anne whispered. "You've been left to Richard Harcourt's protection."

"Precisely. In another seven months, I will be independent again. But until then . . ."

"Well, then, you must come stay with Talmadge and me."

"Oh, Anne, don't you think I would love to do

just that?'' Clarissa sprang up from her seat and began to pace agitatedly. "But it's no good. Belfort would find a way to get at me.''

"Do you think he would be that outrageous?''

"I think he is that determined.'' Clarissa fixed her friend with a fierce, urgent look. "It has become very bad, Anne. I thought at first he was a rogue, of course, and would make some outrageous suggestion to me sooner or later. But I also thought that he would understand 'no' when I said 'no.' It's frightening—he cannot bear being thwarted. When he is in the house, he is always so close—always finding some excuse to take my arm, put his hands on my shoulders, touch my hair. . . . I bar my door at night, of course, but I feel so alone! All the servants here are his; he dismissed every one of Robert's and mine except for Martha, and I had to insist upon keeping her.''

"Whatever is within my power I will do for you, you know that,'' Anne said. "But if you will not come to stay with us, what then?''

"I have an idea.'' Clarissa leaned forward and spoke with hushed intensity. "I have some money saved—Robert always gave me more pin money than I needed. It's not enough to take a house here in town, but I think I could afford to live modestly in the country for a while. Just until the settlement takes effect. But I can't go back to Bath, or to my father's family. Belfort would look there right away.''

"I have it,'' said Lady Talmadge unexpectedly. "You must go to Helen.''

"Your sister in Yorkshire! What a wonderful idea!'' Clarissa's face darkened. "But, Anne, I can't take charity from her.''

"You won't have to. Helen and her husband have a tenant farm—just the house and a few acres, really—and it's been vacant for ages. They'd be grateful to you for taking it off their hands."

"It sounds perfect." Clarissa gave her friend's hand an urgent squeeze. "Oh, Anne, I hardly dare hope, but I think it might just work. Can we possibly make all the arrangements in a month?"

"Probably not, but what's that to the purpose? You can stay in York until it's all settled." Once presented with a course of action, Lady Talmadge disposed briskly of all obstacles. "Now, for heaven's sake, dear girl, stop pacing and sit down. We must devise a plan for getting you away without Belfort's noticing."

A few weeks later, Clarissa moved soundlessly down the wide, deeply shadowed hallway of the London town house, shading her candle with her hand. Reaching the library door, she turned the knob with practiced delicacy. It turned with well-oiled silence—Belfort House being the meticulously kept establishment that it was—and she pushed open the door to slip inside.

She had often made this nighttime journey to fetch a book to soothe her toward sleep, but of late, the visits had been rare. Clarissa kept strictly to herself after enduring evening meals with Belfort. Even tonight, knowing he was away, she found it hard to repress a shiver.

"Stop that," she said aloud, smiling involuntarily an instant later. There was, at long last, reason to smile. Anne had been as good as her word, devising plans for Clarissa's departure with the precision of a general. The details had been greatly complicated by the need to avoid the servants' watchful eyes, but Anne was equal to anything.

Only once had Lady Talmadge hesitated—at Clarissa's insistence that all the arrangements be made in her maiden name, and that not even Anne's sister know Clarissa's true identity. Anne had demurred—"How positively Gothic, dearest; I can't think it's truly needed"—but Clarissa had been firm that there must be nothing to trace her to Yorkshire. Anne had reluctantly agreed, and the farm had been hired on behalf of Mrs. Wyndham.

Moving slowly along the tall bookshelves that lined the room, she trailed a fingertip along the spines, some beautifully tooled leather, others ragged with age and use.

This was the only room in Belfort House she would truly miss. Her husband had found her affection for it vastly amusing. " 'Pon rep, a house crammed with paintings and porcelain—some of it demmed fashionable, too, if I say so myself—and my wife turns up her nose at it all to bury herself in books!"

She found what she sought: a volume of poems by Robert Herrick. Opening the book, she stared down at the inscription in the old duke's beautiful copperplate: *To my dearest Clary; may she ever remember to gather her rosebuds while she may.*

How like him that had been: ambiguous, affectionate, and slightly outrageous. He had been so even at their first meeting in Laura Place, when one of her aunt's pugs had decided it would be delightful to chase the duke's sedan chair, entangling the leash about the bearers' legs in the process.

The old gentleman had introduced himself and proposed to her almost before she had unknotted the wretched dogs' leads. "Have no fear," he had said airily. "I'm quite sane, you know. It's simply that when one achieves my exalted years, one can't waste time trifling, and beauty such as yours is beyond my power to resist. . . . May I know your name, dear lady?"

She had laughed; she hadn't been able to help herself, although it was an entire week before she believed he was serious. And she had told him no;

she liked him, but did not love him. The old duke swept it all away: "What's that to the purpose? You like me; splendid. I like you, too—how delicious to discover you've a brain behind that lovely face! Thousands of matches start with less. Now, stop being missish. You can marry me, see a bit of the world, have as many books as you like, and tell Aunt Dorothea to go to the devil, or you can walk those blasted pugs until you're a doddering old ruin like me. What's it to be?"

I was nineteen, Clarissa thought, shaking her head at herself. *I thought I was equal to anything. . . .*

A hand fell lightly upon her shoulder; she stiffened abruptly and gasped, barely hearing the voice above the pounding of her heart. "Startled, my dear? A thousand apologies."

She took a deep breath, closing her eyes for a moment. "Naturally, I was startled," she said evenly. "Surely, Cousin Richard, you don't expect a civil greeting if you make a habit of creeping up behind people."

"Touché, Cousin." Belfort's teeth were very white and even; his smile might have been quite attractive had it reached as far as his eyes. Clarissa did not smile back. She turned to face him, shrugging free from his grasp as she did so.

"This is quite a surprise," she said. "Did you not find the meet agreeable, Cousin?" She moved a few steps away, but Belfort remained uncomfortably close, blocking the way to the door.

"No, I didn't," he replied. "Damned dull sport." Picking up a volume at random, he hefted it experimentally in one hand. "I notice you did not call my arrival a *pleasant* surprise. Have I offended in some way?"

She stared at him silently, impassively, a trick she had used many times on gossipy hostesses. It reduced them in short order to a fit of nervous giggles. The duke, however, stared coolly back.

At length he turned peevish, to her satisfaction. Tossing the book to the floor, he flung himself down upon a sofa a few feet away. He was in his shirt sleeves, and his neckcloth was in disarray; Clarissa noted his heightened color and the feral brightness of his pale grey eyes. She knew he had been drinking; she was not at all surprised.

"I believe I'll bid you good night, Cousin," she said.

"I don't believe so at all," he replied, propping himself up on an elbow to look at her. "I *believe* I desire a word with you, Cousin."

Fear shot coldly down her spine—could he possibly have learned of her plans?

"A word, Your Grace?" It sounded like a squeak to her, but the duke seemed not to notice.

"Yes. About our conversation before I left town."

Ridiculously, relief swept through her. "Ah. That. Well, Your Grace, forgive my discourtesy, but I fear I must decline." *How idiotic*, she thought; *the man wants to make me his mistress, and I'm apologizing. . . .*

"Discourtesy," he repeated reflectively, reaching for the brandy decanter on the table beside him. Odd, Clarissa thought. She was sure many women found him boyishly handsome, with his aquiline features, fair, silky hair, and lean grace. He was only a few inches taller than she, but gave an impression of a swordsman's wiry strength. As a matter of fact, he was reckoned quite deadly with a blade, an attribute that for some ladies only added to his attractions. For herself, Clarissa had never considered him attractive. She had never been able to overlook the curious deadness of his eyes.

"You've been damned discourteous, dear Cousin Clarissa," he said, startling her from her thoughts. "And well you know it. You think I'm a low sort, don't you? Not quite up to the mark?"

Mistrusting the gentleness of his voice, she remained mute, mentally counting the number of steps it would take to reach the door.

"Tongue-tied, my dear?" He smiled again. "How sad. You usually have so much to say for yourself. Such a well-read, well-bred lady as you are. Oh. Well *read*, at any event. I don't believe I can swear to your breeding."

"You're drunk, Cousin," she said coldly. "I think it's best I retire."

"Not just yet." He rose to his feet as she eyed him warily. The shadows from her candle made his face difficult to read, but there was no mistaking the menace in his voice. "As I've said, I don't think you're much of a lady, and I don't think much of your airs. You were a nobody when my foolish old cousin found you, and you're a nobody still—with a fine gown and a fine title."

He had slowly moved closer to her as he spoke. "And a fine face, too," he said softly, and she could feel his breath on her cheek. "We mustn't forget that, must we? Old Robert was an extravagant fool, but his taste . . . was . . . excellent. . . ." He traced a finger down her cheek; she drew back sharply, with a strangled cry. His mouth tightened.

"A little late in the day to be playing the prude, don't you think?" he snapped. "I know all about you." His fingers dug into her shoulders; he pulled her closer to him despite her struggles. "All the town knows what a sly little baggage you are; you needn't play the pure miss with me—"

She tried to scream; he lowered his head swiftly, smothering her mouth with a brutal kiss, gripping the back of her neck with one hand as the other moved with terrifying swiftness to the neckline of her dressing gown. Desperately, she tried to twist away from him, hearing, over the sickening thud of her heart, the sound of ripping cloth. This must not happen, she thought; it cannot—

"Damn you!" the duke swore. She was released abruptly, and shot a dazed glance at the door. There stood the butler, openmouthed, his night-shirt tucked hastily into his trousers, a candle in his hand.

"Your Grace's pardon," he stammered. "I heard a noise from below; I feared it was thieves. We'd no idea Your Grace was home—"

The duke began another furious outburst, but Clarissa forestalled him. "That's perfectly all right, Coates," she said swiftly, ignoring the butler's dis-believing stare. "His Grace arrived home unex-pectedly. No doubt he wishes you to prepare his rooms now."

Holding her torn dressing gown together with one hand, she grabbed her book and made her es-cape without daring to glance back.

In her room, she turned the key in the door, drew a chair in front of it, and leaned against the wall to gather her strength. Her breathing came in ragged gasps.

Two days, she thought. *In two days I will be gone, and not a moment too soon.*

2

Yorkshire, early November

Once again the fire in the study had been allowed to go out. Sir Jeremy Sutcliffe discovered this at six one chilly morning when he entered his sanctum, fresh from a bracing wash with the cold water from the ewer in his bedchamber. Ready for a day of introspection and productivity, he hoped to complete the third chapter of his history about a brief, unsuccessful attempt by the Romans to establish a holding in Thorndale, the corner of Yorkshire in which Thornbeck House now stood.

The first sight to greet his eyes was the grate, with its layering of cold grey ashes. He yanked open the heavy moss-green curtains; pale light from the moors beyond the window filtered into the room. For a moment he stood meditatively looking out the window, a tall, powerfully built man in his mid-thirties, sensibly attired in buckskin breeches and a plain, well-cut blue coat. Then he pulled the bell cord.

The knock on the door came with reasonable speed.

"Come in," Sir Jeremy said curtly.

Mickle eased his way through the crack in the door. "Would you be needing something, Sir Jeremy?"

Sir Jeremy, who was quite fond of the old retainer, raised one black eyebrow and nodded toward the fireplace.

Mickle, following his gaze, frowned in chagrin. "That'd be Betty, sir. Time and time I've explained to her, the master's fire must be banked for the night. You must be fair starved with the cold—"

"Perhaps someone else could see to it," Sir Jeremy suggested. "Betty seems to have some difficulty remembering." Mickle looked doubtful. "See here, Mickle," Sir Jeremy continued mildly. "I know you're about to explain to me that Betty is the junior housemaid and the study is her especial pride, and that we can't have Alice attending to it because Alice is first housemaid and Betty's elder sister besides, but that isn't the point, any of it."

"I was about to suggest no such thing," Mickle said, looking hurt.

"Just explain to them that the fire mustn't go out. It doesn't matter who does it. And have my tea sent up."

Mickle nodded, and went disconsolately to the door.

"Oh, good God," Sir Jeremy said. "Cheer up, man. I'm not about to sack the lot of you."

"Very good, Sir Jeremy," Mickle replied formally.

Jeremy watched his butler's straight-backed retreat, reflecting ruefully upon the trials of having servants who remembered what one had looked like in short pants. Shrugging his shoulders, he sat down at the massive desk, a fine mahogany specimen that had been, to the best of his recollection, his late father's only extravagance. The Sutcliffes tended toward prudence and away from fashion. Thornbeck House was furnished comfortably but plainly, with sturdy pieces that had outlasted generation upon generation: oaken chests, Tudor chairs, and the imposing refectory table (rarely used nowadays) in the formal dining hall.

Upon the desk were scattered leaves of paper, some blank, others heavily scribbled upon, an assortment of inkpots, and a rack holding quill pens, along with a few piles of books—histories, dictionaries, grammars in Latin, Spanish, and Portuguese. To the uninitiated eye, it was a disaster, but to Jeremy, the clutter had its own sublime meaning, and Betty was under strictest orders to leave it undisturbed. Since Betty's cleaning forays into the study were markedly unenthusiastic, this was not a difficult rule to enforce.

Squeezed into one corner of the desk top was a pile of letters; Jeremy reached for it with a resigned sigh. He had been remiss about going through his correspondence over the past week. But he was planning to ride into York. He had best review the letters in case he needed to post any replies in town.

He riffled through the stack efficiently. A few tradesmen's bills were remanded to a small brass tray at his elbow to await his weekly meeting with Stainewick, his bailiff. A missive from a Cambridge don in response to his query on the construction of Roman fortifications he put aside, with a wistful glance, for more leisurely reading.

That left two letters. One was an invitation to dinner from his friends the Petherstones at Aysgarth Manor, five miles away. Along with the Viscount Stafford and his lady, who dwelt seven miles west in Palladian splendor at their showplace, Castle Stafford, Helen and William Petherstone were the pillars of the dale's high society.

Helen Petherstone wrote with studied casualness that the party was to be quite an informal, comfortable gathering, simply family and—perhaps—the little widow who was their new tenant at Metcalfe Farm.

Jeremy smiled wryly. William and Helen Petherstone were two of his dearest friends, but Helen's powers of dissembling were lamentable. Had this indeed been an ordinary gathering, she would have urged his acceptance with her customary exuberance: "Please don't send your regrets, dear boy—the ride will do you good, and despite your best efforts even you cannot remain closeted with the Romans days on end. Most unhealthy . . ."

No, restraint in Helen was usually a sign of intrigue. Specifically, matchmaking. Well, she would have her work cut out for her—the last thing Jeremy wanted to do was to sit in the Red Room of Aysgarth Manor, making conversation over the roast beef with some featherheaded London twit. He would have cried off in a minute, were he not sure William would rescue him after a suitable interval with a game of chess in the library. With a resigned sigh, Jeremy dashed off a note of acceptance.

The last letter bore the address of his London solicitor. This admirably brief communication advised him that the quarterly rent had been paid in full by the tenant of Sir Jeremy's town house in Arlington Street, said sum being promptly deposited in Sir Jeremy's name with his bankers, awaiting his wishes should anything further be required, yrs. very truly, etc. etc.

Sir Jeremy folded the letter, his brows set in a frown unexpectedly harsh for such an innocuous piece of news. He opened one of the elegantly carved drawers of the desk and placed the letter at the top of a neat stack of similar letters, all bound with a red grosgrain ribbon. This drawer was otherwise empty except for a miniature in a gilt frame, which Jeremy picked up, balancing it a moment in the palm of his hand.

It was a portrait of a woman, dark-haired and vivid. The subject's compelling vitality had unfortunately eluded the artist, but he had captured well enough the charm of her wide black eyes and full-lipped mouth, the allure of the cloud of raven curls. By any standard, the face belonged to a beauty, but it gave curiously little pleasure to Sir Jeremy, who was about to replace it when a cough at his elbow caused him to swing about in his chair.

"What's this?" he said, feigning sternness. "I thought you'd be asleep, mouse."

"No," came the laconic reply from the dark-haired child who stood by Sir Jeremy's chair, carefully balancing a small tray containing a pot of tea. Sir Jeremy relieved her of this burden, clearing a place with his elbow to set it upon his desk. "Have you gone into service, then?" he asked her.

"Well, Mickle said I could help."

"Mickle probably couldn't bear to say no to you, little minx."

"A minx? What's that?"

"Never mind."

Mickle had arrived with the rest of the breakfast tray. "She got here safe and sound, I see, Sir Jeremy," he said, beaming.

"Yes, but why is she hefting pots of hot tea about the house, Mickle?"

"It's powerful hard for Cook and me to say no to Miss Susannah, once she has it in her mind to do something."

"I know," murmured Sir Jeremy, with a rueful glance at his daughter, who, oblivious, was inspecting the clutter on the desk top.

Mickle grinned, and withdrew.

The room was growing pleasantly warm, a sleepy-eyed Betty having arrived to make up the fire. Susannah continued her perusal of Sir Jeremy's desk, lifting stacks of paper, pausing a moment for a closer look at a brass inkwell. Seeing disaster looming all too clearly, Sir Jeremy cleared his throat. She uncurled her fingers from the inkwell, and turned round to face him.

"You still haven't told me what got you up so early, sweet," he said.

"To see you before you go away," Susannah explained, with an air of surprise. Her clear grey-green eyes, startling against long, dark lashes, were identical to her father's.

"It's only for a little while, to York. I'll be back by evening, I promise."

She scanned his face intently, and gave a sudden, brilliant smile. "Good. Mrs. Crowerby will make something special, then. I'll ask her—very nicely," she added, seeing Sir Jeremy's warning glance.

He shook his head at her. "Don't drive Cook to distraction while I'm gone, now. And make sure you mind Miss Harte and Nurse."

"Miss Harte is silly sometimes," said Susannah. "But I will mind her." She had an unusual, surprisingly husky voice. Just turning nine, she was a thin, wiry child, small for her age, and her habit of making dry pronouncements in that deep little voice often drew a look of startled amusement from visitors who encountered her for the first time.

Sir Jeremy admonished his daughter to show more respect for her governess, but reflected that Susannah had summed up the situation with characteristic directness. He feared she was outgrowing Miss Harte far faster than he had anticipated. But where was he to find another governess willing to come to the remoteness of Thornbeck House?

Putting aside that coil for the moment, he moved to pour himself some tea, but stopped suddenly. Susannah was turning the gilt-framed miniature over in her hand.

"This is Mama," she said. It was not a question.

He checked, with an effort, his impulse to take the miniature away from her. "That's right."

"She was pretty."

"So are you, mouse."

"Did she live here?"

"No. I've told you. We lived in London. It was a long time ago."

"Before I was born," Susannah agreed, looking slightly awed at the thought of such distant times. "Have I been to London, Papa?"

"You were born there," Sir Jeremy said, watching his daughter as she ran a tentative finger over the face in the miniature.

"Is she in heaven, Papa? Nurse says to pray for her, but does that mean she's not in heaven?"

"Of course it doesn't," Sir Jeremy said stoutly. "But, you know, it's quite all right to pray for her, regardless. I'm sure she prays for you, too."

Susannah was much taken with this notion. "Really, Papa? Do you think she sees me?"

Her head was bent over the miniature, and she could not see how his expression darkened before he replied. "I don't know for certain, mouse," he said. "I'm sure she thinks of you, though." Gently, he took the miniature from her grasp, and put it away in the drawer. "And now I think Miss Susannah Sutcliffe should be off to eat her breakfast."

Susannah looked mutinous, but edged toward the door all the same. "You won't leave without saying good-bye, Papa."

"Never. Be a good girl, now, and perhaps there'll be a surprise for you when I get back."

An odd expression flitted across her face; she

looked as if she wished to say something more, but she did not. She only reached up to kiss him on the cheek, and disappeared in the direction of the kitchens.

Sir Jeremy smiled after her, and returned to his lukewarm tea and his books. He thought he might finish a few more pages before he set off.

By early that afternoon, on what happened to be her ninth birthday, Susannah Sutcliffe was hiding in the hayloft of the Thornbeck House stables and listening to two extremely cross people attempting to find her.

"Miss Susannah!" That was Miss Harte's voice, always a bit shrill, now gone reedy with anxiety. "Come out this instant."

"She'll have nowt o' that," said Nurse, with grim satisfaction, her dialect broadening, as it always did when she was vexed. "Happen we'll have to drag her out by that black hair o' hers."

Susannah scowled, her dark brows drawing together in a rather formidable line. She did indeed have a long mane of thick, unruly curls, which for obscure reasons regularly incurred Nurse's wrath. "Black as Satan," Nurse would mutter, giving Susannah's hair a tug with the brush that brought tears to the child's eyes. "And just as contrary."

Miss Harte, for the most part, paid little attention to the color or condition of Susannah's hair, except to lament her charge's propensity for losing her ribbons. Charged with teaching Susannah her letters, good deportment, and the pianoforte, Miss Harte was too distracted to worry much about her pupil's appearance, so long as it was presentable. But she had a trick of watching Susannah, sometimes, with an anxiousness in her eyes. It was likely to emerge when Miss Harte was tired and peevish, after her charge had asked her yet another unanswerable question about that day's lesson.

"Oh, child," she said once, the Look creeping across her face. "It really isn't ladylike to be so inquisitive. And it's so important that you turn out properly."

Turning Out Properly, it seemed to Susannah, must be one of her principal aims, along with Acting Like a Lady and Keeping a Civil Tongue in One's Head. Of the three, the first remained mysterious, the second was difficult, and the third a constant trial, with one exception. She had learned very early that questions about her mama were not civil, although why was not clear, since Mama had been dead since Susannah was a baby and certainly couldn't be a trouble to anyone.

"Am I very like my mama?" she had asked Miss Harte one day.

"La, I don't know, child," the governess had answered, distractedly sorting through the music on the pianoforte. "Perhaps so, but I couldn't say for certain, for I never knew Lady Sutcliffe. Ah, here it is! Now, no more chatter, for we have a lovely little song to learn."

"Am I like my mama?" Susannah asked Nurse a few days later, during the nightly ritual of hair brushing and braiding.

"No, tha'rt not, Miss Susannah," said Nurse. "Tha's got thy father's eyes. And her ladyship was a pretty, flighty thing."

Susannah digested that silently a moment. "Then I am not pretty?"

"No, and be glad of that," said Nurse. "Vanity is a sin. Better not to remind thy father of her, anyway. He'll hear nowt said about her these eight years past."

That was not precisely true, Susannah thought as she lay on her stomach in the hayloft. Papa answered her questions about Mama sometimes, as he had that morning. Although he always sounded so strange and unhappy when he talked about her—

"Miss Susannah!" Nurse sounded grim indeed. Susannah curled her body more tightly into the hay, digging her hands deeply into the pockets of her grey woolen dress. "Come out, now, and nowt of thy trickery, or I swear I'll tell Sir Jeremy how wicked tha's been."

That almost brought Susannah down from the hayloft, even with the knowledge that Papa wasn't expected back for hours. Susannah couldn't bear to think of the sorrow in her father's face when he learned of her misbehavior. Papa loved her, but then, he didn't know how wicked she was, as Nurse frequently pointed out.

"Wicked," Susannah whispered, trying the word out, watching her breath stir the hay next to her cheek. "Wicked wicked wicked."

Susannah's father spent most of his time shut away in his study. This left Susannah in the care of Nurse and Miss Harte, whom she did her best to avoid, seeking out Mickle and Cook. They were far more comfortable to be around, and besides, Cook sometimes could be cajoled into letting Susannah knead bread dough or bring Papa his tea tray. It was Susannah's secret plan to persuade Cook to tutor her in the mysteries of the kitchen, so that perhaps one day she might be able to run away to work in a great house, thus escaping the clutches of Nurse and Miss Harte for good.

Susannah smiled to herself, remembering Papa's good-natured teasing when she'd brought the breakfast tea. She always asked Mickle to let her do so—otherwise it was hard to catch a glimpse of Papa before he began working.

Ever since she could remember, Papa had been

reading in foreign languages and writing history. Occasionally their friends Mr. and Mrs. Petherstone would tease Papa about his bookish ways. Mr. Petherstone said once that Papa hadn't always been an historian—he had worked once in the Foreign Office. But references to life before Thornbeck House were rare, especially from Papa.

Still, he could discuss many other things, such as where it would be profitable to fish that day, or the best way to train a puppy to mind when called, or precisely why one needed to wear a hat out of doors. Susannah loved him for the level way in which he considered her opinions, with none of Nurse's abruptness or Miss Harte's patronizing.

She lay very still in the hayloft, thinking perhaps her pursuers had left. But no, Miss Harte was speaking again.

"It is so vexing. Thank heaven Sir Jeremy's gone to town today—I could scarcely face him with this latest disaster! Perhaps Cook has seen her." And at last Susannah heard their footsteps fade as they moved out of the stable.

When she was certain they were gone, Susannah eased out of her corner with a long sigh. It was her birthday, and she was hiding because no one in Thornbeck House had remembered, not even Papa. Well, he couldn't have helped having to go into York that day. It was babyish, she told herself firmly, to mind so. But it hurt all the same to go through the day with everyone acting as though there were nothing extraordinary about it.

So she was going away. Thornbeck House would hardly miss her for the day. Bundled next to her in the loft were her heaviest cloak, a knitted cap and mittens, and a portion of bread and cheese. She intended to be out for a long while.

She let herself cautiously out of the stable's side door; the yard was deserted. Susannah struck out to the east, toward the far border of her father's property, where she knew of several delightful hiding places. As she pushed through the gate and into the open fields, she looked up at the sky, which was cloudy as ever but a duller, more leaden grey than before. She lifted her face to the wind and fancied she felt a new, sharper edge to it. Snow weather, Papa would have said. She was sure she had at least several hours before it started.

3

About five miles away, at Aysgarth Manor, Helen Petherstone uncovered a tray in the sitting room. "Baked eggs, bread and butter, tea? Splendid. I don't know how we'd go on without you, Mrs. Ivesby."

Mrs. Ivesby shrugged her ample shoulders. "I'm sure I don't know, Mrs. P., for you and the master wouldn't eat a thing I didn't make you eat. I've some nice scones today. Happen you'll try them, Mrs. P.?"

Helen laughed, and shook her head. "No, not today. You fed me too well at breakfast."

"You had nowt but tea and toast this morning, Mrs. P., as I know very well," Mrs. Ivesby muttered darkly, but she knew better than to argue. Her mistress, watching her departure with a comical grimace, was by no means emaciated, although she had a naturally wiry build and enough restless energy to maintain it. Her strong, clear features and straightforward manner marked her unmistakably as Lady Talmadge's older sister. But where Anne was impeccably elegant, Helen was cheerfully practical—always ready to dust a cupboard or, as on that day, clean a batch of silver. Her salt-and-pepper hair was partly covered by a neat lace cap; she wore an old-fashioned merino gown, swathed at that moment by an apron.

Silver polishing, as it happened, was not the housekeeper's idea of how Mrs. Petherstone should spend the morning, but Helen pointed out frequently that the Manor was hardly grand enough for such airs. Still, Mrs. Ivesby was far too precious a domestic jewel to offend, and Helen always pacified her by taking luncheon in leisurely style.

Since Helen was by nature impatient with relaxing, this was a generous concession, as she observed to her husband.

"I fear Mrs. Ivesby doesn't quite view it that way, my dear," said William Petherstone, glancing up from his book. "I imagine she's congratulating herself at this moment on the good turn she's done you."

"She probably is," Helen said ruefully, untying her apron. "William, do look up from your Gibbon long enough to have a baked egg. We won't be forgiven if we don't finish this."

"Why, I'm only sitting restfully, as Mrs. Ivesby would have us do in the afternoons. I'm quite the model pupil."

"Yes, you are, aren't you?" Helen surveyed her husband fondly, making a mental note to darn the small hole in the sleeve of his blue broadcloth coat. Like herself, he was in his fifties and a trifle short-sighted. Unlike herself, he was a bit thick-waisted, with ruddy cheeks, thinning grey hair, and sharp grey eyes behind steel-rimmed glasses.

In contrast to her younger sister, Helen had had little inclination for city life. She had gone to London for her Season, dutifully spent the required months attending rout parties and formal dances, then promptly returned to Yorkshire and William, her childhood sweetheart. Twenty-five years later, they had raised a daughter, married now and living in Scotland, and a son, currently in India—"making his fortune," as Mr. Petherstone would say, "or perhaps unmaking it, but we shall see."

Helen glanced out the window as she poured the tea. "A dreary day, and no mistake," she said. "I do believe it will snow."

"Do you think so, my dear?" William was moved to look up from his book again. "Well, I did think it looked rather ominous this morning. I hope young Sutcliffe comes safely home from York before much longer."

"Oh, did you see Jeremy this morning? I didn't know he called here."

"He didn't; I chanced to meet him as I was riding out to Metcalfe Farm. I told him not to worry about that invitation to dinner for tomorrow if the weather takes a bad turn."

"True enough. If it does get bad, I do hope he'll be sensible and stay home, much as I'd like to have him." She paused. "Did you see Mrs. Wyndham today, then?"

"Naturally. I thought it best to look in on her, make sure she's well provisioned in case the storm proves nasty. No problem there—she's a most sensible young lady. I told her she'd best stay close to home, and she agreed."

"Oh, William," Helen said mournfully. "I had such plans for tomorrow."

"Yes, I saw the gleam in your eyes as you were planning your party. But we simply can't have them collapsing in snowdrifts, you know."

Helen subsided into restless thought. A pity about the dinner party. She had been utterly charmed with the widow Wyndham—such a lovely girl, so unexpectedly graceful and well spoken. She'd expected someone rather colorless and frail. Whatever had Anne's letter said? Oh, yes—"I am sad to say that London has not agreed with her constitution."

Far from being a querulous invalid, Mrs. Wyndham was quite presentable—friendly and charming, though with a slight air of gravity Helen found entirely appropriate, considering her widowhood and recent ill health. A perfect prospect for Jeremy Sutcliffe, who simply must not be allowed to shut himself up in Thornbeck House a day longer.

"My dear." She started at her husband's voice. William—wonder of wonders!—had looked up from his book, and was regarding her keenly. "You have got your intriguing look on."

"Have I indeed?" Helen tried, unsuccessfully, for an effect of bland innocence.

"Yes," came the uncompromising answer. "Not that seeing it requires any extraordinary insight on my part. An eligible young widow, an invitation to young Sutcliffe, and *voilà!* I'm sadly disappointed, love. You used to be far more subtle. Matchmaking, indeed!"

"It isn't matchmaking." Helen suddenly found the view from the window absorbing. A few snow flurries blew aimlessly about, borne by frequent chilly gusts. "I'm only being neighborly."

"Neighborly!" William shut his book. "What a rapper, my lass! Your Mrs. Wyndham would see through you in an instant. Not to mention young Sutcliffe."

Helen could not help laughing. "What an odious thing to say! She's not 'my' Mrs. Wyndham. And anyway, it's time *your* young Sutcliffe thought about marrying again. He's no longer a lad, as you persist in calling him."

"I haven't heard him objecting," said William mildly. "But I yield you the point, my dear. He's certainly no lad—and he's old enough to choose his own wife."

"A hit!" said Helen.

Her husband nodded with mock graciousness. "At all events, I don't think they'd make a congenial dinner party," he continued. "I'm sure Jeremy accepted only out of regard for you—he was unaccountably disagreeable when I told him about Mrs. Wyndham's coming up from London. If he weren't nearly a son to me, I'd say he was surly. Of course, he doesn't approve of Londoners in general, and he made a rather cutting remark about doubting she'd like country life once she'd had a true taste of it."

"How extraordinary," Helen murmured. "Not like Jeremy at all."

"No, and not a promising beginning for your schemes," William said. "Ah, well. I rather doubt Jeremy will marry again very soon, if at all. You know that as well as I, my dear."

"More's the pity. If it hadn't been for that silly woman—well, I won't speak harshly of her, after all this time, but when I think of what a dear boy he was, and how utterly *cynical* he's become—"

"There, now," said William. "No use bringing up old troubles, it's been seven—no, eight years, hasn't it? And Jeremy's fine with little Susannah."

"Yes, isn't he?" Helen looked thoughtful. "She's an odd little thing. So serious."

"Her father's daughter, I suppose."

"Well, yes, although Jeremy was never quite so *grim* before that woman—oh, never mind. I do worry about Susannah, though. I never cared much for old Nurse, and although Miss Harte is a decent enough creature, she has very little imagination. The poor child seems lonely."

"Surely Sutcliffe would attend to it if something were truly amiss," her husband said.

"Perhaps," Helen said doubtfully. "I don't doubt he loves her dearly, but he seems so very distracted sometimes by his . . . blasted books! Like you," she ended sweetly, crossing to stand behind her husband, who had shifted in his chair to look out the window again. "What in the world are you—Oh!"

The flurries had turned into a steadily falling curtain of snow. Already the sweep of the manor's front drive was draped with an inch-thick mantle.

Mr. Petherstone shook his head. "Tricky weather, this time of year. Wouldn't want to be caught on the moor in a storm like that."

Helen shivered. "Lord, it's cold! I'll ask Ivesby to build up the fire in here." She turned to her husband, a gleam in her eyes. "And if we're to be cooped up together in a storm, may I challenge you to a hand of piquet? I intend to reclaim my losses from our last go-round."

Driving in from York that evening and cursing the weather under his breath for perhaps the fiftieth time, Jeremy Sutcliffe cut a far-from-dashing figure. Much could be forgiven him under the circumstances, of course. But even allowing for the devastation wrought by the swiftly falling snow and his consequent bad temper, Sir Jeremy could never have been mistaken for a dandy; the greatcoat and battered crowned hat had long since seen better days. Any lingering confidence in Sir Jeremy's sense of style would have been quickly banished by a look at his hopelessly sensible equipage, a sturdy gig drawn by an equally sturdy dapple-grey mare.

Sir Jeremy concentrated on guiding the mare over the deceptively innocent-looking lane, its ruts and dips distorted now by a blanket of snow. From time to time, his thoughts wandered treacherously to dreams of the library at Thornbeck House, complete with a roaring fire and a glass of whiskey by his easy chair, a vision powerful enough to momentarily slacken Sir Jeremy's hands upon the reins. The mare recalled him quickly to attention with a warning jostle.

It was with a sigh of relief that he made the final turn into the drive leading to Thornbeck House; the stolid mare picked up its pace at entering a path so familiar that the snow was a mere irritation. Home at last, thought Sir Jeremy gratefully. Home at warm, snug, brightly lit Thornbeck House.

Brightly lit! As the gig drew nearer the house, he frowned with growing puzzlement and annoyance, taking in the lanterns blazing at either side of the massive doorway, the windows aglow with branches of candles, every curtain drawn back.

"What the devil?" he said to the mare, who sensibly ignored him. "I suppose I should be touched by their concern, but what the devil ails them?"

A broad shaft of light struck out across the snow as the great door swung open and Mickle emerged—also unusual, since Mickle was far more likely to be tucked away in his quarters before a roaring fire than standing sentinel at the gates. Tossing the reins to Kit, the stableboy, Sir Jeremy began to congratulate Mickle for his promptness, when an even more unusual sight stopped him in mid-sentence.

Following Mickle was an oddly assorted entourage, beginning with Nurse, a thick fringed shawl cast about her black bombazine dress, her mouth folded grimly; and Miss Harte, hands tightly clasped and nose reddened, from weeping or the cold he could not tell. Behind them shrank two housemaids, bearing yet more lanterns, tinderboxes, and flint. No one would meet Sir Jeremy's suddenly penetrating gaze.

"What the devil is the meaning of all this?"

Mickle took a deep breath, squaring his thin shoulders. "You mustn't think we've been lax, Sir Jeremy. We've been searching high and low since this afternoon, and there's a party gone out now to the west, and young Kit is going to the village to round up more volunteers—"

"Volunteers?" Sir Jeremy echoed blankly. "Searching for what?" His eyes fell upon Miss Harte, whose mouth worked in a silent attempt at speech, but she merely moaned, burying her face in her handkerchief. A horrible suspicion, pushed aside a moment earlier as unthinkable, returned to Sir Jeremy with icy force.

"Mickle," he said, his voice dangerously soft. "Tell me what is amiss. Now."

"It's . . . it's Miss Susannah," came the stammered answer, and to Sir Jeremy it seemed as if the entire world were dropping away in great pieces about him, leaving nothing but Mickle's fearful eyes blinking swiftly up at him behind fogged spectacles, and Mickle's halting voice.

"She's g-gone, sir. Missing. Since this afternoon. We—I mean, Nurse and Miss Harte and myself, we think she ran away to play on the moors—she does that sometimes, Sir Jeremy, but she's been gone for hours. In the storm, sir."

The storm was annoying but not alarming, Clarissa decided as she placed another book on the newly installed shelves in what she was calling the sitting room at Metcalfe Farm. The larder was full, and they had plenty of firewood. A lamp cast a warm, flickering glow upon the room; a gust of wind rattled a windowpane, causing Clarissa to glance briefly at the darkness beyond the window.

Her main concern had been the welfare of young Rob Fothergill, who helpfully performed odd jobs and kept the small barn in order. But that afternoon, practical Rob had sized up the darkness of the sky and coldness of the air, then secured the outbuildings, before setting off for his father's farm on the other side of the village.

"Might I do owt else for thee, missus?" he'd asked Clarissa, in the broad accent she and Martha were just starting to understand. When she shook her head, he continued, "Well, then, I'd best pike off to my dad's."

Rob had left in plenty of time to avoid even the first snowflakes, to Clarissa's relief. Now she had only boredom to worry about, and there was far too much to do for that to be a problem.

Metcalfe Farm was grand for a farmhouse, but worlds removed from Belfort House, and that perfectly suited Clarissa. Plain, stone, and square-built, it boasted a small porch sheltering the white-painted front door, three rooms downstairs and three rooms up. A narrow flagstoned hallway led from the front rooms to the kitchen; at either end of the house, steep, winding staircases led to the bedrooms above.

Clarissa and Martha had made up two bedchambers upstairs, the third being given over to a jumble of trunks and boxes. They had achieved a kind of orderly clutter in the sitting room, where Clarissa planned to receive visitors.

"Not that we'll be having many callers," Clarissa observed to Martha now.

"Really?" asked Martha, running a cloth over the mantel above the fireplace. "I should think you would welcome a few, Your Grace. I mean, ma'am," she said conscientiously, recalling her mistress's new identity.

"Don't be nonsensical," Clarissa said in surprise.

"Well, you can't bury yourself away, ma'am," Martha said. "You'll be bored silly in a week."

"How can you say that?" Clarissa demanded.

"Have we not had *excitement* enough in the last few months?"

Martha shook her dust rag into the hearth. She moved to the window with a bucket and began on the small, dust-dim panes. "Well, ma'am," she said over the rhythmic swish of the cloth, "that black-guard at Belfort House gave you nothing but grief, and you're well shed of him. But it's past now, and you might be wishing to consider what happens next, like—" Here Martha paused.

"Yes?" prompted Clarissa sweetly.

Martha set her jaw firmly, and plunged ahead. "Like another husband, Miss Clary! You're too young yet to stick one foot in the grave. There, I've said too much, but I'm not sorry."

Martha stalked down the passageway to the kitchen, where she had a kettle of mutton stew on to simmer.

Clarissa bit her lip and returned to her books. She wasn't shutting herself away. It simply wasn't true. She had, at first, been awed by the sheer grandeur of the countryside; everything in the dales seemed drawn on a vast, intimidating scale. But she was not, repeat *not*, hiding.

And she did *not* want another husband.

Dear old Belfort had not been a bad husband. What, then, troubled her? Was it what her Aunt Dorothea had distastefully termed "the marriage act"? Clarissa, considering this, gave a little shake of her head. The old duke had made it clear at the outset that theirs was to be no bloodless marriage of convenience. And he had been all consideration, as courtly and fastidious in amorous matters as in all else.

Had she wanted more? She could not say.

Even after his accident, when the duke had painfully tried to set her free in all but name, she had found she could not play the light o' love. *I might*

as well have, for all the good it did me, she thought
with black humor. *Sometimes I wonder why I did not.
Am I cold, I wonder?*

Turning abruptly away from her task, she went
to the kitchen. Martha was at the table, setting out
bowls of stew.

"You need a shawl, Miss Clary," she said auto-
matically.

"So do you," Clarissa said, grinning in spite of
herself. She fetched two from the pegs on the wall
by the door and handed Martha one. "Let's cry
peace, shall we?"

Martha smiled. "Yes, ma'am." Another gust of
wind whistled by the walls of the farmhouse as
they sat down to eat. "Nasty storm, this. Likely
we'll be cut off for a bit, ma'am. I shouldn't wonder
if the roads are blocked by morning."

"You're probably right," Clarissa said, buttering
a slice of bread With her oppressive mood lifting,
she suddenly felt quite hungry. "Oh, well. It just
means we'll have to finish straightening out the
front room—"

The sound froze both of them in their seats.

"Merciful heavens," said Martha. "Whatever
was that?"

Clarissa shook her head, straining to hear. After
a few moments she caught it—an odd kind of rustle, then a thump, near the door that led to the
kitchen yard.

"It sounds almost like an animal," Clarissa said.
"A dog, perhaps. It couldn't be anything else,
could it?" But her skepticism was halfhearted.
Even as she spoke, she was undoing the bolt, and
swinging open the stout, white-painted door with
an ease that surprised her.

As a result, she almost fell over the bundle on
the step. The darkness was so complete that at first

it seemed she had found a loose bale of cloth. Then Martha hurried over with a lamp.

"Dear God, it's a child," Clarissa breathed, hastening to gather up the limp, small form. "How in the world did it get here?"

"She, Miss Clary," corrected Martha, as Clarissa carried the child into the warmth of the kitchen. "And I wouldn't be worrying about that now. We'd better get her warm and dry, ma'am. I don't like the looks of her at all, I don't."

It was midmorning the next day before the snow stopped altogether Throughout the night, the searchers had set out from Thornbeck House. Carrying lanterns, they slogged doggedly through the mounting drifts, calling Susannah's name, but after the first few hours everyone, Jeremy included, fell prey to unspoken despair.

The early morning light saw Jeremy riding, or attempting to ride, down one of the old packhorse trails leading away from the Thornbeck grounds. Such tracks, used by tinkers and traders from time immemorial, webbed the dale, and Jeremy thought Susannah might have chosen to explore them. But in the alien, white-shrouded landscape, he began to think this idea foolish. The going was frustrating, and the utter silence was beginning to work an uneasy effect on him. He reined in and paused to get his bearings. He was approaching a fork in the pathway: one track looped back toward the village, the other toward Metcalfe Farm and Aysgarth Manor.

Thinking of the search parties already making their way toward the village and Aysgarth, Sir Jeremy decided to head for the farm. He thought it unlikely he'd find Susannah at Metcalfe Farm, for he'd never had much to do with the previous occupants. But it had to be worth a try. Perhaps Helen's new tenant had seen Susannah before the storm broke—if the woman hadn't been busy having hysterics.

Doubtless the Londoners would be no help at all. Probably hadn't even had the sense to prepare for the storm, Jeremy reflected gloomily. In all likelihood he'd find the widow frozen in her bed, silly thing, and be no closer to finding where Susannah was, if she was alive.

The cry resounded with the force of a whip cracking in the freezing air, as a dark figure stepped suddenly from behind a tangled clump of trees. It all happened in a few seconds—the horse's rearing fright, the figure's upraised hands, his own frantic efforts to bring his mount under control. He wheeled the gelding smartly about, cursing all the while. When at last the horse stood quivering at the side of the track, he looked about, furious. Seeing nothing, for a fleeting moment he wondered if the entire incident had been some ghastly apparition.

A groan from the far side of a snowdrift chased the thought away.

Sprawled near the stone fence was a slightly built youth, barely into his teens, from the looks of him. Jeremy tethered the gelding to a tree, strode over, and hauled the lad up.

"Are you all right?" he asked. Receiving a shaky nod from the boy, Jeremy promptly lost his temper.

"What the devil were you doing?" he yelled, unceremoniously depositing his companion on his feet. The boy leaned against a tree, gasping. "Do you like the notion of being crushed by a horse's hooves?"

He was taken aback by the furious flash of blue eyes, which were all that was visible of the boy's face under his hat and muffler.

The boy muttered something.

"Speak up, boy."

"I said," enunciated the boy, pulling the muffler slightly downward, "that if you hadn't been so ham-handed on the reins there wouldn't have been an accident."

"Let us just say," Jeremy said evenly, "that if it weren't for my *ham-handedness* you'd be lying there with a broken neck instead of leaning against that wall, delivering commentary on my horsemanship."

The boy gave an unmistakable snort.

"And furthermore," Sir Jeremy continued coldly, "a stripling like you has no business blundering about without a thought as to where you're going. You might have been killed a minute ago." Bleakly, he thought of his own child, and was swept with a sudden anger at this careless youth's disregard for his own safety. "Where do you live?" he demanded. "I don't believe I've seen you before in these parts."

The boy's eyes fell. "I'm visiting east of here," he said. "I've an errand. Urgent."

"Oh, urgent, is it?" Jeremy said. "Perhaps you'd care to enlighten me."

"No, I wouldn't!" The boy's outraged hauteur amused Jeremy in spite of himself. This lad really was young—and damned near squeaking. Jeremy decided to relent.

"Look here," he said, in what he hoped was a fatherly way. "I don't know just what kind of lark you think you're kicking up"—the boy bridled, and Jeremy raised a hand to continue—"and I'm not sure I want to know. Just get yourself back home, and we'll forget this happened. You'll be far better off at your own fireside."

"I see, sir," the boy said docilely.

Sir Jeremy looked at him, hard. "I meant what I said, mind."

"I *see*, sir."

"Right, then."

Sir Jeremy went to the horse, unlooped the reins, and climbed back into the saddle. The boy stood as if rooted to his place by the wall.

"Safe home, boy. Don't dawdle," Sir Jeremy told him. The boy gave a grunt. What a callow young idiot, Jeremy thought. Deserved to have the wind knocked out of him. Jeremy set his heels to the gelding's sides and was off. Just before he started up the next rise he reined in and glanced back. The young scapegrace, as he suspected, was striding off, cool as you please, not east, in Jeremy's wake, but on his original course. Jeremy opened his mouth to shout after the lad, when an extraordinary sight silenced him.

From underneath the worn felt hat, a bright, thick braid of red-gold hair was slipping, bit by bit. Before Jeremy's surprised gaze, it uncoiled itself with sinuous grace, until it swung smoothly to and fro, reaching just below the waist of its oblivious owner.

"I'll be damned," Jeremy said.

The gelding gave an impatient snort. Sir Jeremy shook his head, and started off again. There was no time for that particular mystery just then. He had a good deal of riding and searching to do before he reached Metcalfe Farm.

Two hours later, Clarissa trudged wearily back toward Metcalfe Farm, realizing with a pang of guilt that for the last half mile she had concentrated more on the thought of a hot drink and a warm bed than on how their young charge was faring.

It had been a long, anxious night for Clarissa and Martha. Almost immediately they had seen that their castaway was out of her head with fever. Fortunately, both of them had had plenty of experience with simple nursing. They had sponged her down again and again, spooned an herbal posset down her throat, and wrapped her thickly with blankets, hoping to break a sweat out. But it was evident they needed a doctor, and Clarissa had set out to seek the Petherstones' advice as soon as the weather cleared.

At Aysgarth Manor, the Petherstones had greeted Clarissa's news with a combination of fear and relief, explaining that they were positive they knew her mystery patient.

"It's little Susannah Sutcliffe, as I live and breathe," exclaimed Mr. Petherstone.

"Thank heaven," added Helen.

Clarissa had listened to the story of Susannah's disappearance, at first with sympathy, then with dawning indignation, wondering how the household at Thornbeck House could pay so little heed to a child that she was missing for hours before anyone thought to inquire.

But a mixture of manners and sheer fatigue had kept her silent. It had been a wearying walk to the Petherstones', made more so by her frightening encounter with that horrible, bad-tempered rider, and she had not realized the toll it had taken until she tried to make her adieus.

"Oh, you can't go back, my dear!" Helen Petherstone had exclaimed in distress. "Stay, do, and let Mrs. Ivesby make you a posset. William will see to everything now."

Indeed, Mr. Petherstone (with uncharacteristic briskness) had sent one servant off to Thornbeck House and another for the doctor. Clarissa had let herself be persuaded to rest for an hour, but then had insisted upon returning to the farm. Slowly she had retraced her path in the chill afternoon light, with a basket packed by Mrs. Ivesby.

Now she finally caught sight of the farmhouse's

rough grey walls, and tears of relief sprang unexpectedly to her eyes. She shook her head at herself and opened the door.

"Our reinforcements are on the way," Clarissa called. She paused.

Voices were drifting from the sitting room. One was definitely Martha's; the other a man's, irritable and low. She shrugged out of her coat and scarf, tossing her braid over her shoulder, and went to investigate.

Martha was talking to someone whose back was to Clarissa, but who at first glance looked oddly familiar. Martha was definitely annoyed, holding herself stiffly upright and answering a question with meticulous politeness.

"I'm not presuming, I'm sure, your honor," Martha was saying. "I only think it best to wait till we know more—" She broke off, seeing Clarissa.

"Good news," Clarissa began. "The doctor—" She stopped abruptly, momentarily transfixed by the blaze of recognition in the stranger's grey-green eyes as he swung about to face her.

Clarissa looked speechlessly up at him. She was not a tiny woman, but he was very tall—and big, with broad shoulders and long, powerful legs. For a dazed moment, she refused to believe that the scowling stranger of the lane had found his way into her sitting room. But there was no mistaking that dark, hawk-featured face, the sweeping black brows lowered formidably over keen, startlingly light hazel eyes.

"What are you doing here?" Clarissa demanded, oblivious to Martha's astonished look.

"I might ask the same of you," he retorted, continuing to stare at her.

A blush rose in her cheeks; she was suddenly aware of her unsuitable appearance, the shabby breeches and coat unearthed from an old trunk upstairs. "You're that rude man with the monstrous grey horse," she said without thinking.

"You have the advantage of me," he said coldly. "But the light is beginning to dawn at last." He gave her a brief bow. "Mrs. Wyndham, is it not? It seems I am in your debt."

"In my debt?" she asked cautiously. "Then you're not the doctor?"

"No," he said baldly. A knock sounded at the front door; Martha hurried off to answer it. "If I'm not mistaken, that's our friend Dr. Tolliver now." He smiled faintly at her puzzled frown. "Allow me to properly introduce myself, ma'am. In addition to being the person you have so flatteringly described, I'm Jeremy Sutcliffe of Thornbeck House, at your service—and much obliged to you for your care of my daughter. But I've no intention of inconveniencing you further. We'll be removing to Thornbeck House as soon as I can make arrangements."

"That's ridiculous!" Clarissa exploded. "She's entirely too ill. Even you must see that, sir."

"Even I?" Sir Jeremy sounded dangerous, and Martha, who had returned, intervened, her interested gaze shifting from one angry face to the other.

"By your leave, Sir Jeremy, ma'am"—she had a warning glance for Clarissa—"the doctor is upstairs with the child now. Perhaps he'll know what's best to be done."

"Just so," said Clarissa, with a wrathful stare at Sir Jeremy. "Martha, please go upstairs and see if the good doctor requires anything."

Martha looked askance, but knew better than to argue with that particular look. With a reluctant curtsey, she departed again, leaving Clarissa and Sir Jeremy facing each other in uncomfortable silence.

Clarissa, returning his intense scrutiny look for look, noted that her guest had not bothered to take off his greatcoat, which hung in sodden folds about him. His dark hair, tied into a queue with a plain black riband, was somewhat disordered, and as he ran a hand through it with an exasperated sigh, she could see why. Suddenly Clarissa noticed the weariness in his eyes, and the lines of fatigue etched at the corners of his firm mouth.

"Please, Sir Jeremy, sit down," she said quietly. "I can bring you some tea. Or we have brandy, if you'd rather."

"No need to trouble yourself," he said stiffly, but he sat down by the fire opposite Clarissa. He drew off his riding gloves, crushing them together in one fist.

"I believe the doctor came as quickly as he could," Clarissa offered, feeling a need to break the edgy silence. "I do hope he will know what to do—"

"Tolliver is an excellent doctor," her guest snapped. "As good as or better than any overpaid London sawbones, though I'd hardly expect you to believe that."

The man was impossible! "Really?" Clarissa said sweetly. "Just what do you imagine I'd believe?"

"I have a fair idea," Sir Jeremy said bitingly. "No doubt you consider us a hopeless clutch of ignorant bumpkins."

Fighting her rising outrage, Clarissa paused before replying. "Sir Jeremy, your feelings are most understandable. I meant no criticism of the doctor. But I truly think that to move your little girl now will do more harm than good."

"Oh you do, ma'am?" he replied, stung. "What other learned medical opinions would you like to share with me?"

Hot color rose to her cheeks. "As you well know,

I'm not an expert, and of course I'll do whatever the doctor advises," she said.

"I'm most gratified to hear it, ma'am. It greatly relieves me to know you are not a managing sort of female."

"I'm delighted to set your mind at ease, Sir Jeremy," Clarissa flashed back. "Although had I not had a streak of *managing female* in me, your daughter might well have died last night."

Her words hit him on the raw. "I have already expressed my gratitude to you for that, ma'am," he replied with constraint. "You have been kindness itself, but my daughter belongs at home."

"So she might run away again?"

It was purely a guess, and a ruthless one at that. But the shot went straight home. His shoulders slumped wearily, and he passed a hand absently across his forehead, clearly at a loss.

"She told you she ran away?" he asked abruptly.

"No. It was wrong of me to say that," Clarissa said uncomfortably. "She's said very little, actually, since we found her. She's been very sick." She glanced away, briefly, from the look on Sir Jeremy's face. "I supposed she'd run away—perhaps on a lark, as children will do sometimes. I wondered how in the world she came to wander about in such weather . . ."

She stopped, embarrassed.

"Actually, you wondered how she came to be so neglected," Sir Jeremy said dryly.

She found herself studying his sodden riding boots with great interest. "I'm sure you and Susannah's mother must have been terribly worried," Clarissa temporized.

"She has no mother," he said. The sentence dropped harshly into the room.

"Oh, I am so sorry," Clarissa said, at a loss.

The shadows were lengthening in the parlor, and

the firelight flickered fitfully across his face as he stared into the flames, unconsciously slapping his gloves against the palm of his left hand. His expression was guarded as he lifted his eyes to hers again.

"It was a long time ago," he said. "A rather old wound, so there is no need to trouble yourself. . . . So you think I'm an ogre, Mrs. Wyndham?"

"Hardly that, sir," she stammered, taken aback by the swift change of subject.

"Don't let us mince words, Mrs. Wyndham. Especially after you have been so admirably forthright."

"Very well, then, if you must hear it," Clarissa said recklessly. "I confess I find it curious, sir, that a child of Susannah's age from a good home should be wandering the open countryside by herself. Has she no one to look after her?"

"She has an army to look after her!" Sir Jeremy glared at her.

"Apparently an army was not quite sufficient."

"By God, ma'am, you're self-righteous! It seems you are an expert in medicine *and* child rearing. Is there anything else in which you would care to instruct me?"

Politeness was forgotten; both had unconsciously drawn upright in their anger, and it was at this dagger-drawing point that Martha ushered Dr. Tolliver into the parlor.

"So this is the intrepid Mrs. Wyndham," said the doctor, a stout, greying man of middling height who tactfully disregarded the hostility between Clarissa and Sir Jeremy. "Well, madam, you and your Martha are to be commended. Had you not acted so sensibly, the child might not still be with us."

"But now, Doctor?" Clarissa asked, aware of Sir Jeremy's sharp intake of breath. "How is she?"

"Not entirely out of the woods yet, though she's quite strong for her size," the doctor replied. "She has a nasty cold, with more than a touch of lung congestion—but I don't think it's likely to turn to pneumonia, thanks to your prompt attentions. The fever's down, without a doubt, but she's certainly been pulled about a bit. I'll be leaving a cordial for her to take twice a day—a restorative, you understand. Have to build her up. The most important thing is to keep her quiet."

"Sir Jeremy and I had been discussing the possibility of removing her to Thornbeck House," Clarissa ventured delicately, earning a sardonic look from her guest.

"Out of the question, my dear Mrs. Wyndham." The doctor was polite but firm. "She's in no condition to be moved, at the present, and I would want her to be a good deal stronger before I'd risk exposing her to another chill. You see the danger, I hope."

"Yes, I see now," Clarissa murmured. "How thoughtless of me."

"Mrs. Wyndham is far too gracious, Doctor," said Sir Jeremy, bowing ironically in her direction. "It was my idea."

"Quite understandable," Dr. Tolliver said. "But it's impossible just now, I'm afraid. Give her some time, sir. Your daughter has quite a lot of strength for her size. She'll be right as rain before you know it."

Sir Jeremy grasped the doctor's hand, and shook it vigorously. "I'm more indebted to you for that news than I can say, Tolliver. How long do you think it will be before she's up and about?"

"Well, I couldn't say precisely, but in all likelihood she'll be her old self in a week or so." The doctor reached for his hat and wound a woolen muffler about his neck, missing the chagrined look that passed between Sir Jeremy and Clarissa. "And now, I've another patient to call on. Never fear, Sir Jeremy! You've an amazingly hardy little girl upstairs." With a brisk wave, he took his leave.

Sir Jeremy went upstairs to bid Susannah goodbye, although he had to content himself with a brief look-in, since she was finally in a deep, normal sleep. He touched her ruffled dark hair with a gentle finger.

"Rest up, sweetheart," he whispered. "We'll get you home again soon."

Straightening, he saw the widow in the doorway, her carefully composed expression unreadable. Resentment stabbed at him again. Confound her, did she mean to guard Susannah against him?

"Until tomorrow, Mrs. Wyndham," he said. "At nine o'clock precisely." At her inquiring look he added gravely, "I thought perhaps you'd welcome warning of the ogre's approach."

He left without waiting for a reply, other than her indignant gasp. That should hold her, he decided with grim satisfaction. What an infuriating woman she was. Sharp-tongued and altogether too sharp-eyed.

Riding home afterward, Sir Jeremy had plenty to think about. He did have to admit the widow was not what he had expected. The hoyden in breeches he'd encountered on the packhorse track was hardly his notion of a London-bred society lady. With that red-gold braid hanging over her shoulder, she'd looked like a combination of urchin and schoolgirl. No schoolgirl, though, could have mustered the blazing contempt of those large, dark blue eyes, flashing at him with thinly veiled hostility—which, come to think of it, was probably too kind a word. She'd been furious.

Furious—and beautiful, he thought, remembering the widow's arresting, expressive face, with its high cheekbones and mobile, full mouth. He suddenly wondered what it would have been like to stop the argument by kissing those unconsciously inviting lips. . . .

Sir Jeremy gave an exasperated shake of his head, as if that could clear the widow's image from his mind. The last thing he was about to do was fall into a mooncalf rhapsody over a fair face, town-bred or no. He knew from harsh experience that accredited beauties had their limitations.

No, he would put the bothersome Mrs. Wyndham out of his mind for now. He had a great deal to consider, starting with what to do about Nurse and Miss Harte.

Thornbeck House had never looked more inviting, or more solid, than it did as he cantered up the drive. Odd, he thought, how reassuring the world seemed, now that he had found Susannah again. And the staff, crowding behind Mickle to greet Sir Jeremy by the great main door, was equal to his uplifted mood—with some notable exceptions, he saw, as he gazed about the circle of eager faces.

"Where are Nurse and Miss Harte?" he asked.

The faces dropped; suddenly, it seemed, nearly everyone remembered urgent errands elsewhere. Only Mickle remained, uncomfortable before Sir Jeremy's ironic gaze.

"Well, Sir Jeremy," Mickle began, "Nurse be in her room. She were powerful affected by Miss Susannah being missing."

He forbore to add that Nurse had spent several hours ranting to everyone and no one that "that imp of Satan," "that daughter of Delilah," had finally brought ruin on Thornbeck House. Nurse had, after all, served the family longer than Mickle himself. Maybe she was going off her head, as he sometimes suspected, but he wasn't about to point that out.

"Miss Susannah is safe enough for now, so Nurse may be easy on that account," Sir Jeremy said. He frowned suddenly. "Where's Miss Harte, Mickle?"

Here Mickle looked unhappy indeed. "Gone, sir."

"*Gone?*"

"Yes, sir. She were even worse off than Nurse. Took to her room with hartshorn, and we saw nowt of her the rest of the day. But one of the maids heard her saying as how she couldn't forgive herself for Miss Susannah's being lost. And then she just left."

"How, for God's sake?"

"Seems she had Kit saddle up the grey mare, and they rode into the village. Then she found a carter to take her to York, God's truth, Sir Jeremy. We none of us thought she had it in her. But she told me she was going to wait in York until she could take a stage south. She left you a letter, too."

Mickle felt about in his pocket and produced a somewhat crumpled missive, which he handed over silently. Sir Jeremy took it, grimacing slightly at the overpowering scent of lavender that arose as he broke the flimsy seal. The letter was a convoluted mix of apologies, excuses, and martyrdom, and concluded with the news that Miss Harte, never having found her situation in Yorkshire agreeable anyway, was taking advantage of a recent offer to teach deportment at a friend's seminary for young ladies in Bath.

Sir Jeremy crumpled the letter.

"So," he said. Mickle, finding neither the syllable nor the look on his employer's face very promising, hastily asked whether Sir Jeremy wanted his supper laid out in the dining parlor.

"I won't be dining tonight," Sir Jeremy replied. "Bring a bottle of brandy to my study, will you?" He stalked down the corridor, slammed the door of his scholarly retreat, and glowered at its disorder. Mickle nervously arrived a few minutes later with the brandy, which he set upon the last remaining clear space on the desk, and hurried out.

Sir Jeremy watched his servant's agitated progress with a sour grin, and took a deep draught of the brandy. A fire had been laid in the grate—at least *some* household necessities were being attended to in the confusion—and he gazed into it now, willing forgetfulness from the flames and the brandy. It worked for about five minutes, before the memory of the young widow's clear blue gaze and nettlesome questions returned to him.

"I confess I find it curious, sir, that a child of Susannah's age should be wandering the open countryside . . ."

"Damn you, mind your own business!" Sir Jeremy told the fire furiously, and retreated into the brandy glass again.

4

A few days later, Helen Petherstone ventured over the newly cleared roads to Thornbeck House with a batch of her most reliable and restorative cordial for Nurse, along with some of Mrs. Ivesby's famous bannocks. Her greeting from Sir Jeremy was edgy, to say the least.

"Enchanted, ma'am! Braving rude weather, and bearing gifts to boot! Mickle, take the basket to the kitchen and tell Cook to send some tea up."

"My pleasure, sir!" sniffed Mickle, who felt this reception too flippant for Mrs. Petherstone.

"Jeremy, you've no shame," said Helen, settling into a wing chair by the fireside.

"Yours does seem to be the majority opinion," Sir Jeremy replied dryly. "I have that on good authority."

The sardonic twist to his mouth stopped Helen's laughter in its tracks. "Good authority?" she echoed. "And who might that be?"

"Why, none other than your charming tenant, Helen," replied Jeremy in a tone that made it clear he found Mrs. Wyndham far from charming.

"I collect the two of you quarreled?"

"That's putting it mildly." Jeremy's eyes blazed

with remembered wrath. "I found your little widow meddlesome, quarrelsome, and too sharp-tongued by half!"

"That sounds harsh, Jeremy," Helen said diplomatically. "She did take care of Susannah, you know. I think that was very kind of her."

Jeremy exhaled an exasperated sigh. "I'm not forgetting that. But neither am I a docile schoolboy, to sit still for a lecture on fatherly duties."

"She—lectured you?" Helen said, totally at sea.

"By God, yes!" Sir Jeremy paused. "I fear I lost my temper," he admitted. "I'd been half mad with worry for Susannah, and to find her so ill . . ." He trailed off.

"Naturally, you were upset," Helen said gently.

"Upset!" Sir Jeremy gave a harsh laugh. "Well, I made a proper apology, you may be sure. I've faults enough, but shouting at females is not one of them. Usually."

"Nor is being a bad father," Helen said firmly. "It was a trying day for both of you, and I'm sure you'll make a fresh start." She ignored Sir Jeremy's skeptical glance. "Don't regard it! It seems you have more pressing matters on your mind—such as what are you going to do when Susannah comes home?"

He sighed. "It's a devil of a coil, ma'am," he said frankly. "I've advertised for a governess in the York and London papers, but Lord knows when I'll hear something."

"Then, too, about Nurse—" Helen began delicately.

"Oh, don't spare me!" Jeremy smiled wryly. "I know well enough that Nurse is getting too far on in years to keep a sharp eye on Susannah."

Helen folded her hands in her lap and gazed thoughtfully out the drawing-room window. "If Susannah were not so *active*, perhaps . . ."

"No use crying over that." Jeremy laughed. "Ah, well, there's nothing for it but to scrape along as best we may. I'll have Betty play nursemaid for now. It's not the best of solutions, but what the devil am I to do?"

At that moment, Helen saw in a flash exactly what Jeremy should do. It was a solution so obvious, so *right*, she couldn't think why she'd overlooked it. But, of course, she had to introduce it just the proper way—

Mickle stepped onto the drawing-room threshold. "Mrs. Wyndham to see you, Sir Jeremy," he said.

"The very thing!" Helen exclaimed, clapping her hands and forgetting entirely her resolve to be subtle.

Clarissa, a basket over one arm and a heavy dark cloak over her shoulders, paused in the doorway. A wool scarf of brilliant blue had covered her hair; she unwound it now, and bright tendrils escaped the severe knot gathered at the nape of her neck. Brows raised, she looked inquiringly from Mrs. Petherstone to Sir Jeremy, who had risen from his chair.

"No," said Sir Jeremy.

"Pardon?" Clarissa said.

"Your pardon, Mrs. Wyndham. I was addressing our friend, here. No, Helen."

"Well, whyever not?" Helen demanded. "How stupid of us not to have considered it earlier! Mrs. Wyndham would be just the thing."

"No, she would not!" said Sir Jeremy with suppressed violence. "You don't know what you're suggesting, Helen."

"I know perfectly well what I'm suggesting. Depend upon it, Mrs. Wyndham is the answer."

"Mrs. Wyndham," said Clarissa with some asperity, "desires to know what exactly she is the answer to."

"Don't mind us, dear!" Helen said, laughing. "We've been considering what to do when little Susannah comes home, and it occurred to me—"

"Helen's intentions were admirable, but unfortunately impractical," Sir Jeremy said. His cool hazel eyes locked with Clarissa's. "Please, Mrs. Wyndham, sit down," he said politely. "Your walk must surely have tired you."

After a moment's consideration, Clarissa nodded curtly and took a seat. "What were you about to say, ma'am, before you were so rudely interrupted?"

"Only that Susannah needs someone to take her in hand until a new governess is found," Helen told her. "Can you quite bear the idea of playing schoolmistress for a while?"

"Playing schoolmistress!" Clarissa turned toward Sir Jeremy, who stood tall and grim-faced near the fire. "Am I to suppose that you favor the notion, sir?"

"Not in the least," Sir Jeremy said bluntly. "Ah—that is, I have no intention of imposing upon you so shamefully."

To her annoyance, a blush rose in Clarissa's cheeks. How infuriating the man was. Most unsettling, in fact. She covered her reaction by turning to the fire, holding out her hands.

"How very thoughtful of you, sir," she said tartly.

"But ninny-headed," said Mrs. Petherstone. "Oh, don't fly into the boughs, Jeremy! Be sensible!"

His fierce rejoinder silenced, Jeremy folded his arms across his chest and glared at her.

Mrs. Petherstone turned a disarming smile upon Clarissa, who was looking every bit as thunderous as Sir Jeremy. "Forgive me, dear, for volunteering

you so brashly. But Susannah really needs someone, not just to watch over her, but to give those
keen wits of hers a challenge! And she gets on so
wonderfully with you."

Clarissa was silent for a moment, considering.
Governessing? How absurd! And yet, poor little Susannah—why should she suffer for her father's
pigheadedness? Glancing over at Sir Jeremy, she
smiled dazzlingly, raising her chin.

"Susannah is a delightful child. It would be no
trouble," she said sweetly. "If Sir Jeremy is agreeable, of course."

Sir Jeremy raised a quizzical brow. *Expects me to
turn ogre again, does she?* "It would be most un-
handsome of me to refuse such generosity," he said
blandly, gratified by the startled look in her eyes.

"Famous, then! It's all settled," said Mrs. Petherstone, who seemed not to notice anything amiss.
"I expect you and Mrs. Wyndham can arrive at a
time for the lessons, do not you, Jeremy? Now, do
let me offer you a ride to the farm. I'll just pop
upstairs to inquire after Nurse, and we'll be on our
way."

Silence reigned for a few moments in the wake
of Helen's departure. Glancing down at her clasped
hands, Clarissa felt Sir Jeremy's eyes upon her.

"This is rather outside your usual pursuits, I expect," he said.

"And what do you imagine are my usual pursuits?" asked Clarissa, nettled.

"Suffice it to say I don't think governessing is
among them," Sir Jeremy replied dryly.

"I assure you, sir, my parents did not neglect my
education," she said stiffly, but let it lie. She had
no intention of regaling Sir Jeremy with the story
of her youth, or any other stories, for that matter.
Recollecting her basket, she reached down.

"I had forgotten. Here is a note from Susannah;

she sends her love. And there are some herbal teas and therapeutic jelly for Nurse."

"Thank you," said Sir Jeremy, reflecting wryly that Nurse was likely to be quite spoiled with all this cosseting.

Clarissa handed him the basket. For a moment, his long fingers covered hers; the warmth and strength of his touch did something strange to the pit of her stomach.

"It's—it's nothing, sir," she managed. "By the bye, Martha swears by the jelly as a restorative remedy for chest colds, as well as rheumatism."

He flashed a sudden grin at her. "You might do well to save some for yourself," he said. "I fear you'll need some sort of restorative after a few lessons with my daughter."

Clarissa smiled involuntarily. "I'm not such a poor creature, sir."

"That's as well," said Sir Jeremy, reverting to brusqueness with disconcerting speed. "You'll be left to your own devices, ma'am. I spend most mornings in my study, writing. The afternoons I reserve for estate business. I don't wish to be distracted by domestic or educational crises."

Pompous ass, Clarissa thought, regretting her smile. "I'll arrive after breakfast and depart by teatime. I will do my best not to disturb you."

"You can still cry off, you know."

Her head snapped up. "Not for the world," she said.

His look of exasperation made her feel inestimably better.

"Permit me to escort you to the carriage." He offered her his arm. After a second's hesitation, she took it.

In the courtyard, the flagstones were treacherously slippery under their feet. Mickle, who had just aided Helen into the Petherstone carriage, stepped carefully aside as they approached.

"I bid you good day, sir," Clarissa said quickly, letting go of Sir Jeremy's arm. "Pray don't trouble yourself further—"

Her words broke off in a gasp as Sir Jeremy's hands fell to her waist. Through the folds of cloak and woolen gown she felt the warm strength of his hands, pressing briefly but intimately against her. With one smooth motion, he lifted her into the carriage before she could say a word, depositing her beside Helen with surprising gentleness.

Color flooded her cheeks; he bowed ironically.

"No trouble in the least, Mrs. Wyndham."

"Are you quite well, Mrs. Wyndham?" asked Helen, as the carriage drew away. "You seem distracted."

"I'm perfectly well," Clarissa said.

But just as they reached the bend that would remove Thornbeck House from their view, she glanced over her shoulder, hating herself for the impulse. He still watched them, a tall figure in the courtyard, hands on his hips, dark hair ruffled by the icy breeze. Clarissa quickly turned away.

London, mid-December

Snow was falling lightly over the city, a sight that drew the Duke of Belfort's drab from the untidy jumble of cushions by the fireside to press her face against the window with a tipsy smile.

"Oh, it does look that pretty, sir," she said.

Belfort said nothing, having no desire to encourage her prattle. Lying back against the mass of cushions, he simply watched her, highly amused with himself at this latest dalliance, a scrubbing-wench from his very own kitchens.

She made a fetching enough sight, the firelight

outlining her lush body clearly through the ridiculous negligee that was plainly her idea of a fine lady's boudoir attire. But it was a nice body, at any rate—long, well-turned legs, slender waist, full, firm breasts. Only when she opened her mouth was the effect spoiled. She'd told him she was a country girl from Devon, and he believed it: the soft West Country burr hadn't vanished entirely from her low, husky voice, her chief charm next to a mass of reddish-gold hair. Her name was Tansy.

He didn't really know why he'd brought her to the suite of rooms he kept in Half Moon Street, where he'd housed a succession of high-flyer mistresses who were placed several cuts above the likes of Tansy in the ranks of the demimonde. Only a few weeks earlier, he'd endured a tempestuous final parting with his latest, a Drury Lane tragedienne much admired for her Cordelias and Ophelias.

He stirred restlessly, shifting his eyes from Tansy to the miniature resting on a small table near the window.

His late cousin's wife, damn her lovely eyes, smiled serenely back at him. The miniature was a copy of the full-sized portrait that still hung in its place of honor above the drawing-room fireplace at Belfort House. It gave him some small satisfaction to keep Madam Clarissa's likeness there in Half Moon Street, where he took his pleasures. Had things gone differently, he might have installed her there—how piquant would that have been!

As it was—and how he hated this weakness—he wondered where she was now, what she was doing.

She had vanished as though the earth had swallowed her. Neither bribes nor threats could pry anything from the Belfort House staff, and he knew, with furious certainty, that their silence stemmed from ignorance, not loyalty. How well the bitch had covered her tracks!

She had gone to none of the obvious places—not to the pathetic house in Bath, where that old beldame of an aunt had told his agent she'd heard nothing, and good riddance to the shameless baggage. (That, at least, had afforded Belfort sour amusement.) She was not in Somerset, with her father's people. Nor was she in Brighton, nor in any of the other fashionable enclaves, pretending to be on a healthful retreat. Nor had anyone matching her description been observed purchasing a passage at the docks—though he knew she might well have managed to disguise herself, clever minx that she was.

Always so clever, with those fine, steady eyes, that cutting tongue, and the books; always a book in her hand and a look on her face that told him plainly she thought herself far too fine for dalliance. Particularly with him.

He was still mad for her, of course.

He said nothing to anyone. The gossip and the betting-book entries had subsided weeks ago, but even in the thick of the storm after Clarissa's abrupt disappearance from the public eye, Belfort kept his own counsel. For anyone disinclined to accept his curt explanation that the dowager duchess had retired to the country for an indefinite period, Belfort had only a raised eyebrow and silence.

Now no one asked, or seemed to care, except for him—and Travers, a thick-set, ruddy-faced man of indeterminate age for whom "agent" was rather too refined a description. Belfort had first encountered him several years before as a porter in a smokily disreputable gaming hell, and from time to time had found his services useful in persuading reluctant gambling partners to make good on their vowels.

Now, he directed Travers to turn his peculiar talents toward finding Clarissa. Each month, Belfort issued Travers a certain sum to pursue inquiries, and each month Travers came back empty-handed.

At their last meeting Belfort had let Travers know his displeasure at this state of affairs, but unlike so many in his employ, Travers was not intimidated. Travers was used to working with characters far less posh than His Grace, and said so.

"And the way it stands, Yer Grace, you'll do far better to stay nice and keep things quiet than to risk a hue and cry over wherever that poor pretty can have got herself to. For it'd be terrible embarrassing if it were to come out that she's just plain run off, 'stead of rusticating ever so nice in the country, now wouldn't it?"

Nevertheless, Travers played fair, and told His Grace frankly that, while there wasn't any use in threatening him, there didn't seem to be much use in spending more blunt, either.

"There isn't a bloody clue. I've tracked down every rumor, drunk or sober, and come up empty. It's plain to me she's slipped the country altogether. She could be anywhere or nowhere, and that's a fact—unless you've heard something more solid, or know someone who has."

Thinking about that last meeting, Belfort smiled thinly. There was such a someone, he'd have bet his title on it—Lady Anne Talmadge, whom, in a weak moment, he had engaged in conversation at Vauxhall.

She had been cool, amused.

"And how is the dowager keeping herself, Belfort? In good health?" she had asked him.

He'd murmured an innocuous reply, but knew from the coldness in her eyes that his expression conveyed something else entirely. They had said very little after that. But as he led her back to her acquaintances among the other wives of the diplomatic circle, he had said: "Your concern for the dowager is admirable. I must tell you, however, that I know well how to order my family's affairs. You do understand."

There had been no mistaking the sardonic tilt to her smile. "Perfectly, Your Grace."

At the window, Tansy looked shyly over her shoulder at him.

"Come here," he said. Her skin was really quite exquisite, soft and almost velvety. Even her hands were only slightly roughened; she hadn't been in service long enough for her fingers to redden and body coarsen. She was very still as he untied the sash of the frilly wrapper; experience had taught her to be watchful of his quicksilver moods, which could shift from playfulness to cold command in the blink of an eye. Leaning back against the cushions, he made her stand before him as the gown slid around her ankles, watching her with his odd-colored eyes that gave nothing away. Though the room was slightly chilly, she knew better than to wrap her arms round herself. Languidly, he reached out a hand to take hers, tugging her down to him.

"Ah, you're a beauty, Tansy," he said, cupping one of her breasts, his thumb sliding slowly over the dark pink nipple, making her suck in her breath. "A rose sprung from the scullery, eh?" His other hand was tangled in her bright hair, hurting slightly, pulling her head down to his. Covering her soft gasp with his mouth, he had a sudden flash, as often happened with little Tansy, of another time, another woman with bright reddish hair. Except her eyes were not doe brown, but a flashing, contemptuous blue. And instead of curving her body silkily into his, she was stiff, unyielding, struggling to raise her arms to strike and scratch. . . .

Unconsciously his grip had tightened on Tansy; her pained exclamation brought him back. "Quiet," he muttered roughly, pushing her onto her back, pinning her mouth with his again, nudging her legs apart with his knee. "You're here to please me, aren't you?"

"Yes, oh, yes, sir . . ."

"Then spread your legs and be still, damn you."

After he was finished, it was quite a while before she ventured to speak again. She took a few sips from the cup of wine he proffered, sitting cross-legged upon the cushions, her wrapper pulled untidily about her. Her eyes followed his gaze, which had wandered once more toward the miniature on the table near the window.

"She be so pretty, Her Grace—" He swung around, facing her with cold anger, and she quailed. "Meaning no disrespect, sir, oh, no! She were such a kind lady, she were, it were a pleasure to serve her. Not that I saw her very much before she took her journey to the north country—"

"*What* did you say?"

She froze. "N-nothing, sir, I'm . . . I'm sorry to be blathering on . . ."

"Her Grace is in Wiltshire, at Belfort Park," he said slowly. "What makes you think she would journey north?"

"Nothing! I mean, nothing, sir, it were just something I heard, I'm sure I don't know a thing . . ."

"Are you? Tell me what you heard, my dear." His voice had become deeper, gentler, almost soothing. Tansy relaxed, and spoke with more confidence.

"Well, sir, it were weeks and weeks ago now, of course, and I can't tell you the words exact. I was busy polishing up the carvings in the upstairs hall.

Her Grace's door wasn't shut proper, and I heard Her Grace's woman talking about being sure to pack this and that. Warm clothes, like. Because of being in Yorkshire, and all."

"Yorkshire, you say?" The voice was still gentle, but Tansy instinctively shrank from the sudden leap of predatory excitement in his eyes, the tightening of his hands about her waist. "Where in Yorkshire?"

"I don't know," she faltered, a cold sense of apprehension settling upon her. "Martha found the door ajar and saw me standing outside, and she were that angry, she shooed me off properly . . ." She raised her brown eyes pleadingly. "I'm sorry if I did wrong in listening, sir! I couldn't help that the door was open."

"Yes, it was naughty of you, wasn't it, Tansy?"

Swiftly he reached downward, nipping her bottom with a vicious pinch. She cried out involuntarily. "But you'll make it up to me, won't you, darling?"

He'd speak to Travers in the morning.

5

Thornbeck House, December

"**M**rs. Wyndham, I can help!"

Intent upon coaxing a highly strung orange kitten from its perch atop a tall bookcase, Clarissa turned to see her pupil in a precarious position as well, having decided to aid the rescue effort by setting a rickety stack of books upon a chair and climbing on top of them.

"Oh, heavens," Clarissa said, but mildly; she was used to Susannah by now.

"Thank you very much for helping, but"—she gently but firmly helped Susannah down—"we're probably scaring poor Gillian with all this attention."

Seeing disappointment darken Susannah's expressive face, she had a sudden inspiration. "I have an idea! Why don't you run to the kitchen and ask Cook for a dish of cream? No doubt we can coax Gilly down that way."

"Oh, that's very good!" Susannah said excitedly. "Gilly's bound to get hungry sooner or later."

"True indeed," Clarissa said wryly to herself as

Susannah scampered off. Food was Gilly's ruling passion.

The kitten's occasional tantrum aside, governessing was proceeding smoothly enough, Clarissa thought, opening a primer to review the day's lesson. Susannah was extremely bright, quick to learn, and just as quickly bored. Devising ways to channel the child's considerable energy was a challenge Clarissa found interesting and surprisingly fun.

She was forced, however, to rely upon some unorthodox methods—as Sir Jeremy had discovered one day when, drawn by the unaccustomed noises from the schoolroom, he came upon a particularly vigorous game of Cavaliers and Roundheads.

"Are we under siege, Mrs. Wyndham?" he had asked from the doorway. Clarissa had been barricaded behind an upended chair, as Susannah gleefully advanced from a position of strength near the pianoforte.

Intent upon the game, Clarissa had looked up, startled, into hazel eyes gleaming with amusement. "Not at all, Sir Jeremy," she had replied, with as much dignity as possible from behind her makeshift barricade.

"But we *are* in a siege!" Susannah had explained with relish. "Mrs. Wyndham is the Cavaliers, and I am the Roundheads, and the chair is the wall around York. I'm besieging it."

"Most interesting," Sir Jeremy had observed, raising one dark brow.

"Yes, isn't it?" Clarissa had said brightly. "We are studying the Civil War, with particular regard to battles in Yorkshire." She paused. "I'm sorry not to have asked before: was there anything you required of me?"

"Anything—" Sir Jeremy had blinked. "No. Forgive me for interrupting the, er, history lesson. I'll leave you to it."

Thinking over the encounter, Clarissa sighed, tapping her quill against the blank page of her copybook. Embarrassing as it was, the incident had served to thaw the constraint between Clarissa and her reluctant employer. Their occasional conversations were actually rather pleasant now, for Sir Jeremy was exceedingly well read, and his observations held a glint of dry humor that Clarissa found most appealing. What was more, he did not regard her interest in matters of the mind as unnatural. For Clarissa, accustomed to conversations in which little was asked of her besides looking lovely, talking to Sir Jeremy was a delightful novelty, and one she wished would occur more often.

But in general, Sir Jeremy kept his distance. Susannah usually breakfasted with him, but he was nearly always closeted in his study by the time Clarissa arrived to begin lessons. Or else he was out riding about the estate with the bailiff. It was almost as if he were avoiding her—which, of course, was a ridiculous notion, she told herself firmly.

At any rate, he would have to talk to her that day. They had agreed to meet once a month to review Susannah's progress, and the time for the first meeting had come.

Thinking of Susannah, Clarissa shook her head with a rueful smile and rose. That child had been gone for far longer than required to fetch a dish of cream.

In the kitchen, Susannah had quite forgotten about rescuing Gilly and was engrossed in helping Cook knead a batch of bread dough. Clarissa paused unseen in the doorway to watch, smiling. She understood Susannah's liking for this warm, large room, with its clean flagstone floor, neatly stacked crockery, and shadowy ceiling, with oaken beams darkened by generations of cookery. And it was impossible to dislike the passionate, if quicksilver, intensity Susannah brought to all her projects. Her dark brows were set in a slight frown of concentration as she worked the dough with floury hands.

Feeling herself observed, Susannah looked up swiftly, in a characteristic movement that, to Clarissa, made her resemble a startled sparrow. Her expression changed to guilty awareness.

"Oh! Gilly! Mrs. Wyndham . . . I'm sorry, I truly meant to fetch some cream, but—"

" 'Tis all my fault, Mrs. Wyndham," Cook interposed. "I got to talking to the lass and lost all track of time."

Shaking her head at them, Clarissa was beginning to reply when a rusty voice behind her interrupted.

"Ah, art shirking thy lessons again, Miss Susannah? Tha's a fine handful for Mrs. Wyndham, no mistake."

Nurse advanced stiffly into the room, clad in her customary black bombazine, its severity softened by the brightly patterned shawl about her shoulders. Her presence had an immediate effect on Susannah; it pained Clarissa to see the light die from Susannah's eyes. The child's shoulders slumped disconsolately, and she began to untie the oversized apron that covered her dress.

Even as she watched Susannah, Clarissa was aware of Nurse's alert dark gaze. Clearly, Nurse considered this a test.

"Thank you for your concern, Nurse," Clarissa said with quiet firmness. "But there's no need to worry, Susannah was just on her way back to the schoolroom, were you not, Susannah?"

Susannah nodded vigorously, draping her apron over a chair and heading for the door.

"I'll be up directly, and in the meantime, you may begin the grammar lesson I've set out for you. Oh, and Susannah"—Clarissa gently stopped her pupil from her dash out the door—"don't forget the cream."

Susannah flashed a quick smile in response to this sally, and took herself off.

"Have a care with that lass, Mrs. Wyndham," said Nurse, looking after Susannah with displeasure. "She'll charm thee, but she's a right sly one, and no mistake."

Clarissa's lips tightened. "I'm obliged for your advice, Nurse," she replied coolly.

"But tha knows better, is that it, mistress?" Cocking her head to one side, Nurse gave Clarissa a knowing smile. "I've been with the Sutcliffes since before tha was born, and I know a fair bit myself."

"Of course," Clarissa said. "And I know a fair bit about teaching. I expect I'll manage."

"Oh, aye." Nurse gave a dry cackle. "Eh, never heed it anyway—happen Sir Jeremy will be finding a real governess before long."

Cook, who had been silently kneading another batch of bread dough throughout this exchange, looked up at that.

"Were tha wanting thy tray?" she said to Nurse. "It's all ready for thee; I'll fetch it."

Nurse knew she was being dismissed, and did not like it, but she knew better than to challenge Cook in Cook's own domain. Regally, she took the tray and stalked from the kitchen, bidding Clarissa a curt good-day.

Cook and Clarissa stared after her, wearing identically glum expressions.

"Never heed her, Mrs. Wyndham," said Cook, unconsciously echoing Nurse. She dusted off her hands on her apron and reached for a kettle, simmering on the hob. "Happen tha'd care for some tea? It won't be a trouble."

"It sounds nice, but I should get back to the schoolroom," Clarissa said regretfully.

"Ah, sit thee down," Cook said kindly. "Tha works hard, and Miss Susannah'll not stir for a good half hour, just to prove she's behaving. Here, sup, then, lass." Clarissa accepted the steaming mug with gratitude.

"Nurse!" Cook shook her head. "Tha mustn't heed her—she was the same with the last governess. She's a proud one, our Nurse, and powerful jealous of anyone else who takes an interest in the Sutcliffes. She's been at Thornbeck House—"

"Since before I was born, I know," Clarissa said.

"Lord love thee, mistress, since before *I* was born." Cook laughed. "She was nurse to Sir Jeremy. It's no wonder she puts on airs now and again."

"Oh, I can see plainly enough she'd walk through fire for a Sutcliffe," Clarissa said. "But I don't understand the way she acts toward Susannah. It seems Nurse feels she has a duty toward her, but she doesn't really like her very much."

"Not *like* her . . ." Cook appeared to demur at first, but then her round face turned thoughtful. "Well, tha might be right at that, Mrs. Wyndham. It's not what Miss Susannah does, either, though the Lord knows she gets into her scrapes. It's that she looks so like her mother."

"Whatever does that mean?"

"Nurse didn't care much for Lady Sutcliffe. Not many did." Cook looked uncomfortable.

Clarissa knew she shouldn't pry, but curiosity won out. "Well, what was Lady Sutcliffe like?"

Cook considered this, shaping bread dough into another loaf. "I can't rightly say," she said hesitantly. "She came to Thornbeck House but three

times at most, so I didn't know her. I remember
she was beautiful—like Miss Susannah's going to
be, hard though it is to see sometimes! And she
seemed right lively, always laughing and joking
with Sir Jeremy, but—"

"But?" Clarissa prompted, all pretense of disin-
terest dropped.

"But she was—eh, I don't know. Cold, like. Not
like you, for instance, thinking to ask about Betty's
cold this morning. She didn't seem to have much
thought for folk. She . . . she didn't have much
thought for Sir Jeremy, either."

"Oh." Clarissa badly wanted to ask more, but
they had finished their tea, and Cook rose to her
feet.

"Eh, I'm talking too much, lass, and me with this
bread to finish." Her eyes met Clarissa's in friendly
understanding. "I wish I could tell thee more, mistress, but there's not much to tell. Sir Jeremy and
his lady lived a London life back then; we never
saw them here, as I've said. He only came back
since—" Cook paused, a bit awkwardly.

"—since she died, yes," Clarissa said thoughtfully. Cook looked at her for a moment, then down
at the neat row of shaped loaves set out to rise. An
uncharacteristically troubled look darkened her
usually cheerful face.

Clarissa bid her good-day, and started toward
the schoolroom. She wondered why Cook had
looked at her so strangely just then.

Later that afternoon, Clarissa squared her shoulders and knocked firmly upon the heavy oak door
of Sir Jeremy's sanctum. Dead silence was the reply
from the study, so she knocked again, even more
loudly. The sound seemed to echo in the drafty corridor, and Clarissa drew her shawl a little more
closely about her shoulders. Still no response. Won-

dering whether she should summon Mickle and a footman to break down the door, she was preparing for a third knock when Sir Jeremy swung the door open and stood for a moment regarding her, his hand on the door frame. He wore informal country clothes: olive-green coat, grey vest, buckskin breeches, and top boots.

Clarissa lowered her raised fist to her side, feeling foolish.

"We had an appointment, I believe," she said, in her best coolly courteous manner.

"My apologies for not answering immediately," he said, matching her tone. "I tend to lose track of my surroundings when I'm working." He stepped aside to usher her into the room.

Never having crossed its threshold before, Clarissa looked about the study with lively curiosity. Like most of the rest of Thornbeck House, it had a warm appeal. Maybe it was the house's Tudor proportions, Clarissa thought. The casement windows, with their thick, leaded panes, added a certain something. So did Sir Jeremy's desk, with its wildly eclectic disorder. She could see a magnifying glass perched precariously upon a stack of books; a ruler, pencil, and measuring compass rested atop what appeared to be a carefully rendered building plan of some sort. Her gaze lit with sudden interest upon a volume of what looked like poetry in Portuguese, but before she could inquire about it, Sir Jeremy spoke.

"Is your curiosity satisfied, Mrs. Wyndham? Does the ogre's lair live up to expectations?"

She bit her lip in annoyance. "I didn't mean to be rude," she said. "And it's hardly an ogre's lair."

"It isn't? I'm devastated to disappoint you, Mrs. Wyndham," he said, showing her to a seat near the fire and taking the wing chair opposite.

She tipped her nose in the air. "No doubt you've

a delightful dungeon tucked away somewhere."

He threw back his head and laughed, surprising her. "Your faith in me is gratifying, but I must again disappoint you. Thornbeck House was built rather late in the day for dungeons. Although we do have a priest's hole."

"A priest's hole!" Clarissa's eyes brightened. "Where?"

"Oh, in one of the upstairs bedchambers. It was a heady adventure for me the day I discovered it, I can tell you. I wasn't much older than Susannah, at the time."

"And does Susannah know about it?"

"Good God, no!"

Clarissa could not help laughing at his horrified expression.

"You may smile, madam," Sir Jeremy continued severely, "but I assure you, nothing terrifies me more than the thought of my daughter's having access to a secret chamber. Just imagining the schemes she could hatch there has me quaking in my boots."

"Well, how poor-spirited of you," said Clarissa, trying and failing to suppress a grin, "when it could be such a marvelous history lesson for her."

"At present, Mrs. Wyndham, I prefer she take her lessons from books—or the occasional schoolroom siege," he added, cocking an eyebrow at her fleeting blush. "And speaking of Susannah's lessons—"

"Of course," Clarissa said hastily, wanting to conclude her business with this unaccustomed goodwill still between them. She untied the tapes of the portfolio she had brought with her. "I've brought a few of her compositions and drawings, to give you some idea of what we've been doing. It's difficult to tell entirely, of course, without being there in the schoolroom, but—"

"I'm sure these will do admirably, Mrs. Wyndham," Sir Jeremy said, his dark head bent over the papers.

Silenced, she watched him scan Susannah's work, unable to tell anything from his expression. *Well*, she thought, *if he's displeased, good riddance. Let him go along as best he can until a new governess arrives, which I doubt will be soon.*

"She writes well," he said abruptly, startling her from her thoughts.

"Indeed she does. She's quite articulate for a child of her age."

"Speaking from your vast experience?"

Clarissa's back straightened against the brocaded upholstery of her chair. "My own teaching experience isn't vast, as you so kindly point out," she said. "But I certainly saw enough of my father with his pupils—" She broke off, stopped both by the feeling that she was saying too much and by the memories that flooded back of the shabby vicarage in Somerset, the sun slanting across the clean, worn boards of the schoolroom floor, the row of little boys at their lessons.

"You were saying, Mrs. Wyndham?"

She sighed. She had to explain. "My father was a clergyman, Sir Jeremy. His living was not, shall we say, generous, so he was obliged to take in day pupils to make ends meet. And he had very modern notions; he didn't think females should be denied education. I took lessons alongside the boys, until—"

Sir Jeremy studied her averted face a moment, before gently prompting: "Until . . . ?"

"They died in a carriage accident, he and my mother. I was sent to live with my great-aunt. I was fifteen."

"I see. I'm sorry."

"Oh, you mustn't be," Clarissa said, looking up

swiftly. "It was a very long time ago."

"An eon, I expect," he replied, a corner of his mouth quirking upward. "How old are you, Mrs. Wyndham? Twenty-two?"

"Nearly twenty-five," she said coolly. "Hardly an infant, Sir Jeremy."

"Not an infant, then, but unusually erudite all the same. You surprise me."

"I do wish you'd stop saying that," Clarissa said wearily. "I am not a frivolous nitwit, sir."

"No, indeed," he replied with some irony. "A most unusual variant of London lady."

"Speaking from your vast experience?" Clarissa could not resist.

"Touché, ma'am. But in point of fact, I do speak from experience," said Sir Jeremy, his face turning grim. "I've seen more than I care to say of the sort of woman who finds intrigue amusing and loyalty a dead bore, for whom a husband is a necessary evil, or perhaps just a complaisant screen for her ... outside entanglements, shall we say? Or do I shock you?"

"No, sir; I told you, I am not an infant." But inwardly, Clarissa was shaken. With an effort, she continued to speak casually. "I do find it distressing, however, that your opinion of London ladies is so poor. Not everyone is like that."

"Ah, have eight years made such a difference, then?" Sir Jeremy smiled at her, dark brows raised in patent disbelief. "I never go to town, but I hear the gossip—the fruits of being a diligent correspondent! The players may change, but the play's the same. Can you say that Georgiana Cavendish and the set at Devonshire House are not as profligate as ever? And what of Her Grace of Belfort, the one they call *the fair Titania*? A model of propriety, I'm sure."

Clarissa's heart gave a sickening lurch. To cover

her start, she made much of rearranging the papers in the portfolio lying open on the desk. "Well, sir," she said, tension lending asperity to her voice, "I submit that one must be equally harsh with the male of the species."

Unexpectedly, he laughed. "Well put, if a trifle radical. But then, you apparently had a radical upbringing."

"I thank you for the compliment," Clarissa said pointedly.

"Not at all. You've made a powerful impression on my daughter, you know. She is forever explaining what 'Mrs. Wyndham says.' And I've seen the books in your parlor; the Virgil intrigued me, as did the volume of Mr. Burns's poetry. You've eclectic tastes, Mrs. Wyndham."

"You flatter me, sir," said Clarissa. The thought of those keen grey-green eyes inspecting her possessions and drawing conclusions was unaccountably disturbing.

"Surely you know me well enough by now to realize flattery is not my strong suit, Mrs. Wyndham." He stacked the papers neatly inside the portfolio and retied the tapes. "Well, everything seems satisfactory. Let me assure you, by the bye, that I'm making every effort to secure a governess. Until then, I'm very much in your debt."

"It's no trouble, truly," Clarissa said. "Don't regard it."

"Nevertheless, I do." He handed her the portfolio, and rose as she did. "Will you be staying to dine, Mrs. Wyndham?"

"Thank you, no; I must be off to the farm. Martha sets our table like clockwork."

"Then you must permit me to take you home. I'll have Mickle order the gig around."

"There's no need to trouble yourself, honestly,"

said Clarissa quickly. "I'm quite accustomed to the walk."

Sir Jeremy threw her an impatient look. "Mrs. Wyndham, don't argue. It is no trouble. If it will ease your conscience, I have a journal to bring to William Petherstone, and Metcalfe Farm is certainly on the way. There is no reason to object, unless you cannot bring yourself to sit in a carriage with me."

"That's nonsense, of course," Clarissa said weakly.

"Good. It's settled, then."

Jolting along in the gig toward Metcalfe Farm beside Sir Jeremy, Clarissa still couldn't understand his insistence upon escorting her home. She had to admit it was a welcome favor, though. It had been a long, eventful day, and she was glad to ride in a silence broken only by the dapple-grey mare's steady breathing and the rhythmic pounding of hooves upon the frozen ground.

There had been two more snowfalls since the storm that had greeted Clarissa's arrival, neither more than a light dusting upon the packed-down blanket of white that already shrouded the dale. The sweeping expanses of slopes and hills loomed in chilly splendor, dotted with a slender tracery of black, bare trees. Late-afternoon sunlight struck broad swaths of snow, turning them a pale but fiery gold.

"I shouldn't imagine this is what you're used to," Sir Jeremy said.

She twisted round toward him, drawing the folds of her heavy cloak a little more tightly against the keen, eddying wind.

"What isn't?" she asked. "If you mean the dales, you're right. They're nothing like the place where I grew up."

"London?"

"No, Somersetshire," she said, catching herself an instant too late. *Oh, what does it matter?* she wondered wearily. She was tired of swaddling herself in sober, unobtrusive gowns of gray and brown, of measuring information in careful spoonfuls.

He glanced over at her, a slight frown darkening his face. "Is something wrong?" he asked.

Clarissa forced a friendly smile to her lips. "No, I'm fine. A little tired, that's all . . . Tell me, sir, have you always lived here?"

His eyes narrowed thoughtfully, but he let it pass, answering easily enough: "Almost always. I was born here, of course. There have been Sutcliffes at Thornbeck since the Conqueror's time, though the manor house is more recent. It was begun by one of my ancestors who did rather well at the court of Henry the Eighth. Managed to get most of it finished before he fell out of favor, clever fellow."

She laughed. "Is that when he put in the hiding place?"

"Who knows? It was hardly a time of undivided allegiances here, and my family did their share of maneuvering, from what I can tell. We've been loyal and Church of England for the last four generations, though, so we're quite secure now."

Clarissa gazed ahead of her at the dapple grey, stolidly picking its way along the packed-down road. "It must be very dear to you. Thornbeck House, I mean."

He considered this, mildly startled. "Yes, I suppose. I can't imagine living anywhere else."

"Not at *all*?" Clarissa tried, from politeness, to hide her surprise, but did not succeed entirely.

He glanced over at her, smiling slightly. "Do you object, Mrs. Wyndham?"

"Well, of course not; it is hardly my affair, after all."

"No, I suppose not."

Annoyed, she decided to be blunt. "My meaning, sir, was that your home is lovely, but it seems to me that a gentlemen with means and an inquiring mind—both of which you apparently possess—might wish to see more of the world."

"Oh, might he?" Sir Jeremy laughed shortly. "For your information, my dear ma'am, the wider world does not hold the charms for everyone that it so obviously does for you."

Taken aback by his almost savage tone, she burst out without thinking: "However did you manage to live in London?"

The change in his expression was amazing; his profile took on a taut, hardened look as he stared down the road unfurling before them.

"I managed well enough," was all he said.

"I'm sorry," she said, dropping her eyes to her grey-mittened hands. "I didn't mean to pry, truly."

He seemed to make an effort to shake himself from his dark mood. "It's I who must apologize, Mrs. Wyndham; it was a natural enough question."

For lack of anything else to break the awkward silence, she remarked, "Susannah told me you worked for the Foreign Office."

"I did. It was a long time ago."

"Oh."

Clearly, Sir Jeremy had no intention of elaborating, and it was with some relief that she saw they were rounding the final sharp bend before the road dipped toward Metcalfe Farm. A thin plume of smoke drifted lazily upward from the kitchen chimney, and Clarissa warmed to the thought of supper before a roaring fire.

As Sir Jeremy drew the gig into the farmyard, she glanced up at him, still slightly wary. But his expression was clear of the bitter anger of just a few minutes before; his gaze was once more veiled.

She coughed slightly, gathering her skirts in preparation for climbing down.

Noting her movement, he sprang lightly down, looping the reins over a stone post and striding around to Clarissa's side of the gig as she watched with trepidation.

"Well, I must say, I'm most obliged to you for your kindness, Sir Jeremy. But there's no need to help me down, it's too much bother; I can—"

He ignored her, reaching up to grasp her by the waist and swinging her down as if she weighed no more than Susannah. Then he chuckled, and the sound sent an odd, fleeting weakness into Clarissa's knees. He bent his head so that they were nearly eye to eye; she caught her breath at the sudden intensity in his light eyes.

"Mrs. Wyndham," he said, a hint of mocking laughter in his voice, "I'm quite capable of deciding for myself when you're a bother."

Stiffening with indignation, she was mortified to realize his hands were still about her waist, holding her in an implacable grip. An angry retort formed on her lips; her hands went to his chest to push away.

Suddenly the mockery faded from his eyes. He tightened his grasp, drawing Clarissa gently but inexorably closer, his head bending lower toward hers. She forgot her indignation, spellbound by a rush of sudden awareness: his gleaming, intent hazel gaze; the scratchy texture of the greatcoat; the warm strength of his chest beneath her gloved fingers; his faint scent of sandalwood. She tilted her head back, her lips parting slightly, knowing she must move, must do something to stop this madness, and knowing she was utterly unwilling to break the spell as they drew closer together—

The creak of the farmhouse door sounded like a warning trumpet. Sir Jeremy's hands dropped abruptly; Clarissa sprang away from him as if from a coiled snake.

"You're home at last, Miss Clary!" Martha said cheerfully, a voluminous worsted cloak swirling about her, a basket in her hand. "I was just about to see to the hens—Oh! Your pardon, Sir Jeremy!"

He gave her a curt nod, then turned to lift his hat to Clarissa. "You'll excuse me, Mrs. Wyndham. I must be going." Barely giving her time to nod, he swung himself up into the gig, slapped the reins smartly against the affronted dapple grey, and clattered out of the farmyard.

"Well, that's strange," Martha said, staring after him with no little annoyance. "He's in an odd temper today, and no mistake. And you riding all the way from Thornbeck House with him, Miss Clary . . . Miss Clary?" She turned an inquiring gaze upon Clarissa, who was silently watching the gig, by now a swiftly diminishing shadow in the distance.

After a moment Martha raised her brows, but held her peace. "Come, Miss Clary," she said. "Best get inside. It's freezing out here, and your tea's waiting."

6

Three days later

The two figures moved into the bright sunlight from the sheltering archway in the stone wall surrounding the herb garden that had once been the pride and joy of Sir Jeremy's mother. Making their way toward the lane that led to Metcalfe Farm, they were etched in sharp relief against the snowy fields—the smaller one skipping, the taller one walking with unconscious purposefulness, a covered basket swinging easily from one hand.

The smile faded slowly from Sir Jeremy's face. He turned away from the window as his daughter and her temporary governess rounded the bend that took them out of sight of Thornbeck House. Jerking his chair away from his desk, he sat down and reached for a stack of papers, nearly upsetting his inkwell. With a muffled curse, he set it out of harm's way and got down to the business of reviewing the notes for his latest article, a comparison of building techniques in two Roman forts.

"For God's sake," he muttered into the tranquil silence of the study. Not for the first time, he wondered what the hell had gotten into him that day at Metcalfe Farm.

Well, it was a moot point now, he thought ruefully. His fragile truce with Mrs. Wyndham had been thrown into disarray since that ride together over the moors. Since then, she had strictly avoided him. As had he her.

But more often than he cared to admit, he had taken to watching for her. He had gotten into the habit of waiting at the window in the morning to see her coming up the drive, straight-backed and graceful, a writing tablet and books bundled under one arm and a friendly smile for Mickle, who was always there to greet her. Sir Jeremy liked her punctuality. God help him, he even liked her eccentric educational ideas.

Still, he wished he knew more. After all, he'd entrusted his daughter to her care, Sir Jeremy told himself firmly. It was only right that he ask the questions necessary to fully understand her character.

What had her late husband been like, for instance?

And why did that evasive look descend into her eyes whenever she talked about herself? He disliked that look. It was too uncomfortably reminiscent of another beautiful, not entirely candid woman.

Sir Jeremy sighed, shuffled his papers for a third time, and began, with a grim determination, to read his notes again.

"Stay there, drat you!"

Martha, tying a length of red ribbon round a tenuously arranged armful of evergreen boughs, fixed them with a fierce stare, as if she could will their compliance.

"Ah, the joy of the season," said Clarissa, looking up with a wry smile from her accounts. A frown settled upon her brow as she stared again at her work.

"Is it the cheese and butter we buy from the Fothergills?" Martha asked anxiously. " 'Cos I can bargain him down, no doubt."

Abandoning her attempt to tot up a wavering row of figures, Clarissa looked surprised. "No, no, it's just that I'm woolgathering hopelessly—" She broke off. "Bargain with John Fothergill? Whatever do you mean?"

"Well, seeing as Mrs. Fothergill went to her reward seven years or more ago, the poor man's been fending for himself."

"He looks well enough to me," said Clarissa, picturing young Rob's father, a thick-muscled, taciturn, and unfailingly polite man she saw most often with a cheerful collie trotting by his side.

"'Course he's well, ma'am," said Martha, a slight and not-unbecoming pink shading her cheeks, to Clarissa's interest. "But his jacket's in a terrible state, it is. Most likely he'd be happy to trade some of the butter and cheese in return for a bit of mending."

"Now I see," said Clarissa gravely. "Will you be dreadfully disappointed if I tell you we're really still quite comfortable, if not fabulously rich? Even so, you can offer to take care of Mr. Fothergill's coat—it seems a compassionate act—"

"No more of your nonsense, Miss Clary!" Martha said, attacking a pair of pewter candlesticks with a soft cloth. A speculative gleam Clarissa knew well came into her eyes. "I'll take myself off now, and stop distracting you."

"Oh, you aren't distracting me, and well you know it," said Clarissa glumly, setting her pen carefully aside so as not to smudge the page.

"The folk at Thornbeck House, then?"

Clarissa didn't pretend surprise. "Susannah, for one."

"No trouble there, surely? She's a taking little thing."

Clarissa toyed with her pen, sighing. "I like Susannah very much," she said at last. "But I know I'll be leaving her one day, and I hate to think of disappointing her."

"Will you, Miss Clary?"

"Well, I should think she'd feel *some* regret," Clarissa said.

"No, no," said Martha impatiently. "I meant, will you be leaving, ma'am?"

Clarissa stared at her. "Well, of course. By May, at least, depending upon how quickly the settlements are made—"

Martha cleared her throat.

"Mightn't it also depend a bit on Sir Jeremy, begging your pardon, ma'am?"

"Just what do you mean by that?" demanded Clarissa, forgetting entirely to rebuke Martha for impertinence.

"I mean," said Martha with the martyred air of one burning her bridges behind her, "that he seems to take . . . an interest in you, like."

"No, he doesn't," said Clarissa swiftly. Then, after a pause: "No more than he should for someone looking after his daughter. I think you should stop indulging in whimsical fancies about Sir Jeremy."

"I don't think it's whimsy, Miss Clary," said Martha stubbornly. "I saw the way he looked at you the day he drove you back from Thornbeck House."

Aware of the heat rising in her cheeks, Clarissa bent her head over her account book. "You're mistaken. There was nothing particular in his attentions. He is courteous, and grateful I'm taking care of Susannah, and that is all." *And if he'd any notion who I really am, he'd never let me in the house.* "Please don't speak of it again."

"Very well, Miss Clary. I didn't mean to give offense," said Martha She retreated to the kitchen, thinking all the while that Miss Clary was really a terrible liar.

The following Sunday dawned chilly but clear, leaving the district's residents no excuse for neglecting services at St. Osbert's, the small country church in the heart of the dale.

It was with particular impatience, therefore, that Rupert Viscount Stafford paced across the gleaming black-and-white tiled floor of the nobly proportioned entrance hall of Castle Stafford. Watching him, her expression torn between amusement and impatience, was his wife, whose proportions were equally noble.

"Stop that, do!" said Lady Stafford at last, shaking her head at him, so that the ostrich plumes curling over the brim of her hat trembled with indignation. "Won't bring her downstairs any faster."

"It keeps me from going upstairs to fetch her down myself," muttered Lord Stafford, who made up in wiry toughness what he lacked in stature.

"Not to be thought of," said Lady Stafford. "Wouldn't do any good. The age, you know. Forever taking a pet over this or that. Best leave her be. She'll be down any time now."

"She had damn—dashed well better be," said Lord Stafford. He threw an irritated glance toward one of the graceful, tall windows that had helped earn Castle Stafford its reputation as a north country temple to Palladian glory. Outside, a groom held a fine and restless pair of matched bays in check; his long-suffering gaze met and held his lordship's.

Lord Stafford swung away from the window.

"Charlotte, you will oblige me by explaining just what the *devil* it is that keeps a girl dressing for two hours!"

The viscountess considered the question calmly and shrugged her ample shoulders. "Couldn't say, my dear," she said apologetically. "Never took more than a half hour myself."

"Quite right, too! And don't whine to me about petticoats and dress hooks! I can say with certainty—" He broke off, beet red and furiously aware of Lady Stafford's serene gaze. Whirling round, he strode to the wide staircase that swept away from the far end of the hall. "Amabel! Come down this instant or your mother and I are on our way without you, mark my words! *Amabel!*"

"There's no need to shout, Father," said a composed voice from the gallery above him. A quiet rustle of skirts, a soft footfall on the velvet carpet of the topmost stair, and Lord Stafford found himself scowling into the cool green eyes of his only child.

"I'm perfectly ready to go," said the honorable Amabel Stafford.

Dipping into the Book of Job, the Reverend Mr. Horton preached with passion and length on the text: "Take heed, regard not iniquity, for this hast thou chosen rather than affliction."

Clarissa, shifting her posture discreetly in response to her left foot's falling asleep, wondered what the good reverend would make of her own particular affliction, the new Duke of Belfort. A mistake: Belfort's image, which she resolutely avoided conjuring up nowadays, banished her peace of mind. She sighed sharply, unthinkingly, earning a frown from the reverend and a look of mild concern from Helen Petherstone, seated beside her.

Clarissa's sigh also attracted the attention of Sir Jeremy, who glanced over from his pew across the aisle in time to catch her troubled look before it faded. Meeting his eyes, Clarissa quickly recomposed her features into a tranquil mask. But she knew from his look of silent inquiry that he was not fooled. She averted her gaze, letting it rest upon the backs of the Staffords, occupying their pew for the first time since her arrival in Yorkshire.

The sermon concluded with a flourish; the organ wheezed into life as the congregation rose to sing a final hymn. Clarissa prepared herself for a quick, unobtrusive exit. Her plans were foiled, however, by Lady Stafford, lying in wait on the porch.

"There you are!" said the viscountess, abruptly terminating a chat with Mr. Horton to advance purposefully upon Clarissa. "Mrs. Wyndham, I presume? Forgive the informality. Country manners, hey? Pleased to make your acquaintance, all the same. Come into the fresh air."

Borne inexorably off by the viscountess, Clarissa cast a desperate look around for Martha, who had taken up a seat at the rear of the church with the farming folk and servants. But Martha had most inconveniently vanished, very likely to enjoy the company of John Fothergill.

Clarissa followed the viscountess through the arched door. In the churchyard, the brisk, cold air swirled around them, whipping Lady Stafford's cheeks into alarmingly high color.

"Wanted to get you into the light," explained the viscountess, surveying Clarissa with the ruthless attention she reserved for her daughter and prize hunters. Evidently she approved of what she saw, for after a moment she nodded vigorously. "Excellent. London, I hear?"

In tribute to Lady Stafford's economical phrasing, Clarissa gave an even briefer than usual explanation of retiring to the country for her health. This earned her a reappraising look from the viscountess, followed by another decisive nod.

"Agrees with you, whatever you're doing," she said. "Eyes bright, color good. No sign of cough. Fine fettle. You're widowed, I hear?"

Pausing to absorb the abrupt change of tack, Clarissa nodded.

"Pity. My condolences. Still, you've years ahead of you. And you're out of black gloves, that's something. Plenty of fish in the sea. Not *this* sea, mind, unless it's young Sutcliffe."

As Clarissa hastened to assure Lady Stafford that under no circumstances did she consider Sir Jeremy anything resembling aquatic life, metaphorical or otherwise, they turned to watch him at the far end of the churchyard, where he exchanged pleasantries with the viscount and Miss Amabel, who was tilting her head upward to Sir Jeremy with a dazzling smile that was returned in kind.

Observing this, Clarissa felt her fingers curl inside her gloves with a fervor she firmly blamed on the cold. Fortunately, Lady Stafford appeared to notice nothing amiss.

"Fine figure of a man," observed the viscountess. "Bruising rider. Plenty of bottom. Had a promising career in the Foreign Office, too, before he decided to rusticate," she added, clearly as an afterthought. "Half the chits in the district in love with him at one time or other. Mind, I've my hopes he and Amabel will make a match of it."

Clarissa glanced sharply at Lady Stafford, who continued with oblivious enthusiasm. "Bloodlines are good—and they've known each other all their lives. Pity he's never gotten over that wife of his, though. Always thought she was bad ton, myself, but there you are; it's neither here nor there. All one can hope is that he'll be wanting to marry again soon to get an heir for Thornbeck House. Well, heigh-ho!"

Abandoning what had suddenly become a fascinating conversation, she briskly took Clarissa's arm and led her over to meet the other Staffords.

Brusquely disposing of the social niceties, Lady Stafford got down to business—first, however, sharply admonishing her husband to release Clarissa's hand. "No need to disturb the poor girl's circulation, Rupert!"

"No, indeed, Papa," said the Honorable Amabel in her light, well-modulated voice. "I hear Mrs. Wyndham is here for her health; we must help her regain her bloom, mustn't we, Sir Jeremy?" And she nodded demurely toward him.

"Beg pardon." The viscount coughed, reddening. Taking pity on him and fueled by a spark of annoyance at his daughter, Clarissa reassured him with her most charming smile.

"You've heard of the Christmas ball at the assembly rooms in York?" said Lady Stafford to Clarissa, who nodded. "Planning to attend, I hope?"

Having learned that no one planned to attend the Christmas ball in York before receiving the viscountess's stamp of approval, Clarissa said gravely, "I would be honored."

"Excellent. A week from Friday. Don't fail us, mind. Amabel! Rupert!"

Calling the viscount and Miss Stafford competently to heel, Lady Stafford swept off toward the carriage drawn by the splendid bays. Her family followed—the viscount in a schoolboy sulk, Miss Amabel with leisurely dignity after a final faint smile for Sir Jeremy.

"What a diverting pair!" said Clarissa, giving in to amusement as she watched them go.

"I see you found Stafford's attentions engaging enough."

Called back to rude reality by the sarcasm in Sir Jeremy's voice, Clarissa shot a cool glance upward at him. "Undoubtedly. But I should be too terrified of Lady Stafford to encourage him, of course."

That provoked a genuine smile from Sir Jeremy, despite his sworn intention to keep a civil distance. "A wise judgment," he said gravely. "In addition to hunting like an Amazon and keeping the most annoying toy spaniels in the West Riding, Lady Stafford rules social matters with an iron hand."

"I'm in a quake," said Clarissa, smiling quite unconsciously back at Sir Jeremy.

"So you should be, my girl," he said severely. "Lady Stafford has been known to scuttle the social aspirations of rudesbys who don't properly appreciate her taste in horses, dogs, and riding habits. Fortunately, she appears to have taken you under her wing. You'll be asked to the Castle Stafford ball, never fear."

"Wonderful!" said Clarissa. "What ball is that? I thought my social ambitions were quite realized with attendance at the Christmas dance."

"Hardly," said Sir Jeremy crushingly. "One *must* attend the Castle Stafford ball. It's in May, of all times, and is Lady Stafford's way of sorting the wheat from the chaff, socially speaking. No city riffraff. No nabobs. Can't have it." His imitation of the viscountess's forcefully bitten-off sentences was too much for Clarissa, who dissolved into laughter.

"She's dreadful, isn't she?" said Clarissa, when she could speak. "I meant it when I said she terrifies me."

"Ah, you seemed to face her courageously enough," Sir Jeremy said. A brief silence fell between them; Clarissa dropped her eyes, suddenly self-conscious.

"What troubled you during services?" he asked abruptly.

Her gaze flew to his before she could stop herself. "Nothing of consequence. I'm ashamed to admit it, actually—my foot fell asleep."

His eyes narrowed in thoughtful assessment, taking in her averted gaze, the nervous tapping of her fingers against her prayer book.

"I wish you could bring yourself to trust me," he said.

Clarissa bit her lip. She wished she could, too, but she remembered too well his bitter words about the flighty Titania. "What nonsense, sir. I find you—I find you extremely trustworthy. Please don't make too much of what happened." She adjusted her gloves. "I must go. I've kept Martha waiting too long already."

"No, you haven't," said Sir Jeremy. "She's gone with Susannah and the Fothergills into the village for a bit. I believe they're looking in on Sarah Potter, John Fothergill's old mother-in-law."

"Oh." Clarissa looked about her, flustered.

Sir Jeremy kept his expression carefully neutral. A casual observer never would have guessed that he was struggling with a strong desire to gather her in his arms.

Instead he said shortly, "It seems we must fetch them back. Allow me to escort you."

Blinking at his curt tone, Clarissa nodded and walked beside him. She kept her eyes fixed stubbornly ahead of her, but his nearness was impossible to ignore as he opened the gate and let them out of the churchyard. They set off down the track leading to the village, a narrow lane thickly bordered by trees, whose bare branches trembled slightly as they passed.

Breaking what seemed to her a strained silence,

Clarissa inquired about Sir Jeremy's search for a new governess.

"I've had three possibilities," he said. "Unfortunately, two were put off by the isolation of the situation, and the third, who seemed promising, decided to accept another position."

"Oh, dear," Clarissa said. "I don't envy you your task, sir. Finding just the right person will be difficult. Susannah truly needs someone with a—a challenging turn of mind."

He glanced down at her. "You understand her quite well."

She smiled, suddenly shy again, but replied: "Oh, she's not a difficult child to understand, really—she just wants to learn everything at once." She paused, then went on with a hint of mischief: "Rather like her papa, actually. I shouldn't be surprised at all if she develops your facility with languages."

"Perhaps she will, though the Lord knows it hasn't done her papa much good," Sir Jeremy replied dryly. As Clarissa was frowning over that remark, he added, "It sounds as if you might find yourself missing your governessing duties a little, after all."

"Well, Susannah is . . ." Clarissa paused, searching for the right words. "She's an easy child to grow fond of."

Without realizing it, they had come to a halt at a bend in the track. The wind picked up suddenly, playing with the hem of Clarissa's cloak; she shivered involuntarily.

"You're cold," Sir Jeremy said, with a hint of contrition. Quite unthinkingly, he reached for her hand. "No, you're freezing. It's time we gathered the rest of our parties together and started back."

As his hand clasped hers, Clarissa's reply died in her throat, and she looked up in surprise to encounter a startled look upon Sir Jeremy's face. Her color rose before the expression in his grey-green eyes. *This will not do*, she thought.

A scattering of crows burst from the trees by the side of the road, squawking noisily overhead. Clarissa started, pulled her hand violently from Sir Jeremy's grasp—and promptly lost her footing upon an icy patch. She slipped and would have fallen but for Sir Jeremy, who caught her swiftly, pulling her up and back around to face him. For a second longer than necessary, he held her against his chest. She felt a light, swift touch upon her hair, so light she thought she might have been imagining it. Quickly, but more carefully this time, she drew away.

"Lord, how clumsy of me!" She laughed shakily. Drawing away awkwardly, she rearranged her hood with trembling hands.

"We shouldn't delay getting to the village, I think," she said unsteadily.

"We won't," replied Sir Jeremy, his voice strained. "But, Clarissa—"

She shook her head, though her heart gave an unreasoning leap at his use of her name. "No," she said, the force of her voice coming as a shock as she tried to make words of her jumbled thoughts. "We're terribly late. Susannah and Martha will be wondering what has become of us."

Drawing a ragged, impatient breath, he looked as if he were about to remonstrate with her. The urgent entreaty in Clarissa's dark blue eyes stopped him, but his neutral tone came with an effort.

"As you wish, Mrs. Wyndham. We had better be on our way."

7

Susannah had promised to be on her best behavior, to do exactly as she was bid, and for heaven's sake to stay out of Mrs. Ivesby's hair. In return, she had permission to stay the night of the Christmas ball under the Petherstones' roof with Martha.

Mrs. Wyndham was to put on her ball dress at Aysgarth Manor before riding into York with the Petherstones. Having learned of this, Susannah had seen in a flash how delightful it would be for her to visit Aysgarth the evening of the ball as well.

So obvious to Susannah were the advantages of this plan that she had looked on in astonished dismay as her father's brows knit in a frown usually reserved for bad news from Stainewick.

"Was this Mrs. Wyndham's idea, Susannah?"

"N-no." Susannah faltered. "It—well, it was me. I mean, I thought of it. But I asked Mrs. Petherstone—very nicely—and she said it sounded like a lovely idea."

Papa muttered something that sounded to Susannah like "Much obliged, Helen," and fell silent for a moment. Susannah watched him anxiously.

"Please let me go, Papa. It isn't so very far, and it's the Petherstones. . . ."

"I know that, mouse. But you mustn't be imposing on the Petherstones—or on Mrs. Wyndham, for that matter."

"Mrs. Wyndham *thought* you might say no 'cause it would be a bother for her," said Susannah mutinously.

"How astute of Mrs. Wyndham," Papa said.

"But it won't be a bother, Papa! Mrs. Wyndham said I would be a great help. She said I can help her decide which ribbons to wear, and how to dress her hair, and so on."

"And so on?"

Susannah still couldn't tell from Papa's look whether he was pleased or displeased, but the lightening of his tone encouraged her.

"You wouldn't understand, Papa, it's *fashion*," said Susannah loftily, and felt a mixture of indignation and relief when Papa's frown disappeared at last and he began to laugh.

"No, you're right, mouse, I wouldn't understand, thank the Lord. Well, if Mrs. Wyndham and Helen Petherstone don't object, I can't find fault in your staying the night. But"—he gave Susannah a quelling look—"mind your manners. And don't vex Mrs. Wyndham."

"Oh, I won't. I'm looking forward ever so much to seeing her all dressed up, aren't you, Papa?"

Sir Jeremy cleared his throat, and commented that Mrs. Wyndham always dressed nicely enough.

"Of course," Susannah said scornfully. "But this is different. This is a ball. And ladies always look so beautiful for a ball, don't they? That's what Cook says. She says Mama always looked just beautiful. . . ." A hint of a frown crept back into Sir Jeremy's eyes. Hastily, Susannah sprang up from

her chair and ran to kiss his cheek. "Oh, thank you
ever so much for letting me go."

She whirled away, out of the study, leaving Sir
Jeremy seated at his desk, lost in thought.

Amabel Stafford, never the most easygoing of
employers, was a terror to dress for an occasion,
for all she had barely emerged from the cocoon of
her select Cheltenham seminary. The process always began quite early, and was not for the fainthearted. Parkins, her maid, found herself wishing
she had not been too proper to accept the tot of
rum jokingly offered her two hours earlier by Ned,
the second footman. She could have used that rum,
she thought, watching Miss Amabel ruthlessly dis-
card a sixth gown and unblinkingly appraise a seventh.

Amabel's admirers (a surprisingly large crowd,
considering that she had not yet had a full-fledged
London Season) often likened her to a moonbeam,
or a water sprite. These comparisons suited the
pale delicacy of her coloring and the fragile, cameo-
like perfection of her features. But Amabel thought
these images tiresome. Behind her dreamily ethereal exterior was a determination that once carried
her through the remainder of a hunt in which she
had been tossed nastily from her chestnut mare.
After hitting the ground with a heavy thud and
seeing stars, Amabel had spent just a minute of
stunned, outraged silence before rising with only a
touch of unsteadiness, shaking out her skirts, and
coolly remounting.

Something of that same determined look
gleamed in Amabel's gaze as Parkins held up the
seventh dress, an exquisite concoction of sea-green
satin. This, she rather thought, was the one.

"And in the hair, my lady?" ventured Parkins,
whose well-honed instincts told her the choice had

been made at last. Having carefully arranged the
folds of the gown over a wicker dress form, she
held up for approval a graceful arrangement of
three pale grey ostrich plumes, secured with a knot
of pink ribbon.

A slight frown of concentration momentarily
flawed Amabel's flowerlike face. Her first impulse
was to endorse Parkins's suggestion, but suddenly
and decisively, she shook her head. Exquisite as
they were, the plumes were just a trifle flashy. And
Amabel felt certain that flashiness was not the way
to pique the interest of Sir Jeremy Sutcliffe.

"I don't want those," she said. "Just those green
ribands through the curls, I think. And you can secure them with that pearl clip Mama gave me."

Just as well, Amabel told herself. She'd have to
wear her pearl strand that night anyway, she knew,
since Mama wouldn't have permitted any jewels
more sophisticated. What a bore it was, being on
the marriage mart.

With any luck, that wouldn't be the case much
longer.

Judging from his dress, which was neither
shabby nor flashy, the man cantering down the
York road on a placid roan mare could have been
a country doctor, or perhaps a prudent tradesman.
A sharp-eyed observer might have questioned the
great care he took to ensure that his hat was
jammed low over his brow and the knitted muffler
pulled up high over his lower jaw. But the day had
been cold, and, with darkness approaching, was
getting colder yet. Small wonder he was keeping
bundled up.

There was little else memorable about him. His
encounters with the locals in taprooms, in the occasional village, were brief and unremarkable.

Indeed, it was hard to fathom what his business

was, had anyone been wondering about it. In some of the places through which he had passed, a stranger had no reason for arriving, unless he was lost—which this particular stranger seemed to be rather often, although he never appeared to be very upset about it. He would ask a few general questions about the neighborhood, spinning them into a pleasant conversation. Eventually he would recall himself with a start, halting the agreeable exchange with an apologetic shrug and asking for directions to the main road.

Now the stranger seemed at last to be back on the right path, for he was trotting toward York by the smoothest and most direct route possible. Oddly, this gave him little pleasure. In fact, had anyone been within earshot, he would have been heard cursing under his breath.

It would all have seemed very strange, had anyone thought to consider it.

Clarissa stared into the mirror, a troubled frown creasing her brow momentarily—but not too quickly for Martha to notice.

"Are you worried about that dratted clip, Miss Clary? I can pin it down better."

"No, no, it's in tightly enough," Clarissa said hastily, a hand flying up to the diamond-and-sapphire ornament nestled securely (with the help of some painfully well-placed hairpins) in her fiery curls.

"There's no need to fret, ma'am," chimed in Jenny, one of Helen's maidservants. "You look fair lovely, and that's a fact."

"Well, thank you!" Clarissa turned from the mirror to smile at Jenny and Martha.

Jenny blushed, bobbed a curtsey, and excused herself.

Martha was less easily mollified. For the best

part of an hour, she had watched Clarissa stealing worried glances into the mirror.

"All right, then, what is it?" she demanded as soon as Jenny was gone. "It can't be the dress or the hair—pity knows we've been fussing with them long enough."

"Oh, no!" Clarissa reassured her hastily. "It was only . . . Well, this is the first time I've been in full ball dress since—since before Belfort died."

"Well, you needn't let that trouble you, Miss Clary," said Martha reasonably. "Wasn't it His Grace's own self that said you weren't to wear widow's weeds for him? Begging your pardon, but I always wondered that you wore them as long as you did."

"There was enough gossip, as it was, without that matter's being raised," muttered Clarissa, turning to inspect herself in the mirror with a final, critical look. "And anyway, it was only right."

"But that's not all that worries you, is it, Miss Clary?" asked Martha quietly as Clarissa's voice trailed off.

"No, it's not," said Clarissa slowly, turning in front of the mirror with slow, almost reluctant movements. "Ball dress," she said suddenly, the frown creeping across her face again. "It's so . . . conspicuous. I wonder if it might have been more prudent to stay at home. . . . Oh, I'm being nonsensical. Never mind! I think just a tiny stitch here, where this rosette is a bit loose, and I'll do nicely enough."

They were interrupted by a sudden commotion: The door swung open to admit Susannah, bearing a sumptuous evening cloak of rose-colored velvet and exclaiming breathlessly: "This is from Mrs. Petherstone, she says she thinks it will look ever so nice with your dress, Mrs. Wyndham, and—*oh!*"

She skittered to a dead stop in the center of the

room. As Martha looked on, suppressing a smile, Clarissa turned carefully round, a suitably grave expression on her face.

"Will I do?" she asked Susannah.

"Mrs. Wyndham, you're—like a *queen!*" Susannah gasped. "You'll be the most beautiful lady at the ball."

"Will I?" Clarissa laughed. "Well, we'll see! But I certainly will be the most *conceited* lady at the ball, with all the extravagant compliments being thrown my way!"

Martha, busying herself with gathering up comb, brush, and hairpins as she tidied the dressing table, thought that Miss Clary had never looked better. The rich sapphire velvet of her gown was a vivid foil for her red-gold hair, intensifying the dark blue of her eyes. The bodice clung smoothly to her slim waist, and soft ruffles of snowy lace edged the neck and elbow-length sleeves, threaded with a deep pink ribbon that matched the silver-embroidered underskirt of the gown. Pinned to the frothy lace corsage at her bosom was a magnificent sapphire-and-diamond brooch, a gift from the old duke. It matched the delicately wrought collar round Clarissa's neck, as well as the ornament pinning back the sweep of her hair, which was dressed in loose curls that tumbled over her shoulders.

Clarissa gathered up gloves, cloak, and reticule.

"If you two are quite finished advising and correcting, I shall be on my way," she said.

Sweeping an exaggerated curtsey that produced a delighted giggle from Susannah and a heavenward glance from Martha, Clarissa whisked herself out the door.

Sir Jeremy took a sip from the glass he held gingerly to his mouth and barely restrained a grimace. Insipid punch was only one of the many irritating by-products of the Christmas subscription ball. Joining it on Sir Jeremy's private list of iniquities were giggling debutantes, rapacious dowagers, and the polite fiction that conversation with one's partner was achievable during the figures of a country dance.

He suppressed a cough and retreated with practiced unobtrusiveness to the shadow of an alcove, just outside the sight line of Lady Stafford and the Honorable Amabel, who had swept in with the viscount and were scanning the ballroom with hawk-like intensity.

Sir Jeremy shook his head. What damnably stupid affairs these were. Overheated, overcrowded rooms. Empty chitchat. He had never cared for any of it, not even in London, where the company had been more impressive, the music more accomplished, the women incomparably more elegant—especially Caroline, who would have found this affair hopelessly provincial.

Images of his wife sprang, strongly and clearly, into Sir Jeremy's unwilling mind. Caroline, raven-haired, sparkling-eyed, and riveting, tossing her head back to laugh in the uninhibited, throaty way that in any other woman might have seemed vulgar, but in her was outrageously charming. Caroline, moving, straight-backed and graceful, across polished dance floors, through the most complicated of figures, flicking a glance over her shoulder at him, inscrutable and somehow playful at the same time.

Well, Caroline had been born for the social whirl, unlike himself. Oh, he had hardly been a recluse—had had, in fact, his own lively circle of friends—but his idea of a congenial evening had never meshed with Caroline's. Politics had bored her; so did talk of travel, science, or history. "Whigs and bluestockings!" she had snapped at him once, after he'd tried to persuade her to accompany him out one evening. "I think not, love."

A tightness crept into his mouth of which he was entirely unaware. Yes, he had had his political friends, she her . . . amusements. What might have happened had he put his foot down, declared their civilized married life a heap of rubbish, taken her back to Yorkshire for good? Might any of it have turned out differently? Might not—

"Jeremy, lad! There you are! Rejoin the living, man."

With a start, Jeremy turned to find William Petherstone at his elbow, a wry smile on his lips and two punch cups in his hands.

"If that's more damned punch, don't bother," said Sir Jeremy. "I've done my duty for the evening."

"What do you take me for, dear boy?" asked William, insulted. "It's claret, and as soft a wine as ever I—ah, an ignorant pup such as yourself can't be expected to appreciate such things. But try it anyway."

Sir Jeremy, efficiently disposing of his punch in an ornamental urn, accepted gratefully.

"You're a wonder, Will," he said.

"No, just an old hand at these affairs. I had Ivesby stow the claret in the coach before Helen came down. Drink up; there's a second bottle."

Sir Jeremy laughed, and took another appreciative swallow.

"My deepest thanks," he said. "This nearly makes the evening tolerable."

"Oh, it's not as bad as all that," said William pacifically. "Count your blessings. Look over there; see Battlebourne's son—the one who's home on leave from the army? The matchmaking mamas have been stalking him all evening. Must make the poor devil wish himself back in India."

"Good God," said Sir Jeremy, following Mr. Petherstone's gaze.

"Just so, dear boy. I think he'll contrive to slip away eventually—a most resourceful lad; Cornwallis thought the world of him, his father tells me—but there are at least two more matrons lying in wait."

"A truly sobering spectacle." Sir Jeremy laughed suddenly. "Thank God they've given up on me, anyway."

"Most of 'em," said William, uncharacteristically cryptic.

"Lord, Will. I'm past all that; been so for years."

"You do yourself an injustice, lad." Mr. Petherstone took a second to savor another sip of claret. "Even the invincible Lady Stafford leaves well enough alone."

"Does she?" William's pensiveness was replaced by a gleam of mischief. "Perhaps. But the daughter's another matter."

"Amabel?" Sir Jeremy said scoffingly. "She's a schoolgirl."

"That's what you think," replied William. "It's none of my affair, but it's my considered opinion that the Honorable Amabel is prodigiously hard to deflect, once she wants something."

"And just what is it you think she wants?" Sir Jeremy asked in a rather ominous tone.

"Oh, I don't pretend to know that, Jeremy, lad!" William grinned. "I don't even pretend to know what's in Helen's mind, let alone the Honorable Amabel's. And speaking of Helen . . ."

Jeremy bowed deeply as Mrs. Petherstone sailed up to them, regal in plum velvet and some of her mother's fine old Alençon lace. She shook her head at him, but there was laughter in her voice.

"Skulking in corners!" she accused as Jeremy straightened. "I thought you weren't so poor-spirited. Mark my words, it's best to plunge right into these affairs, get into the thick of it."

"Now, Helen," interposed her spouse, "Jeremy and I were just enjoying a quiet cup of, ah, punch. The poor lad needed reviving, after trotting through some of those country dances. Strenuous affairs, these."

"Fiddlesticks!" said Helen, rapping Sir Jeremy's knuckles lightly with her fan. "You haven't danced a step tonight, I'll warrant."

"That's unjust," Sir Jeremy said virtuously. "I stood up for a quadrille with Lady Kendall."

"Oh, Selina." Helen dismissed that elderly bastion of polite society with a shrug. "Of course you stood up with her; you aren't an utter barbarian, after all."

"You flatter me," Sir Jeremy said.

"I know," said Helen, ignoring her husband's cough. "Well, if you want to glower here in your corner all night, I suppose—Oh, do see! There's young Captain Battlebourne with our dear Mrs. Wyndham. How nice."

"I must say she's in excellent looks tonight," said William.

Sir Jeremy said nothing. No words occurred to him as he drank in the sight of Clarissa in her vivid blue gown, smiling up at that presumptuous pup Battlebourne. The candlelight flashed upon the sapphires at her throat, danced across the flower-shaped ornament in her hair. As she sank into a graceful curtsey before Battlebourne at the beginning of the set, one of her red-gold curls fell lightly onto the creamy expanse of shoulder emerging from her filmy lace stole. His fingers itched to sweep that curl back, to linger against the delicate, shadowed hollow beneath her collarbone.

As if the intensity of his gaze had been a call, Clarissa glanced in his direction. Then, pointedly, she swept her head back toward young Battlebourne, who guided her smoothly into the next figure.

Sir Jeremy drained the last of his cup with utter disregard for the quality of William Petherstone's excellent wine.

"Excuse me, Helen, William," he said, placing the cup on a tray borne by a passing manservant.

"Not at all, dear boy," William said. "Off to take Helen's advice?"

Sir Jeremy bowed to Mrs. Petherstone. "When have I not taken your admirable wife's advice, William?"

"Many times," murmured Helen, but it was to thin air: Sir Jeremy was already making his purposeful way toward the dance floor.

"Now, what's gotten into the boy?" said William, watching in disbelief as Sir Jeremy solicited the Honorable Amabel's hand for the next set.

"I certainly can't say," said Helen. She heaved a satisfied sigh. "But it all seems most promising. I think this calls for a bit of a celebration. Would you spare me some of that claret, husband, dear?" She laughed at William's look, which mingled chagrin and reluctant admiration. "Or have you and Jeremy drunk it all?"

Catching her breath on one of the crimson-upholstered chairs at the edge of the dance floor, Clarissa struggled with a puzzling mixture of pique and longing.

By any standard, she could have considered her first appearance in Yorkshire society a success. Her inner disquiet had made her restlessly gay, bent on sparkling at this slightly old-fashioned affair in a way she had never bothered to sparkle at modish soirees in town. And she found herself genuinely enjoying the evening. She had charmed the dowagers (including the gentle but fearsomely correct Selina Lady Kendall), exchanged friendly chitchat with a clutch of young matrons, and danced demurely with old General Twickenham, who hadn't stood up for a reel in years. Compliments abounded on her dress, her hair, the ravishing sapphires. Every unattached male in the room was jostling for a place on her dance card.

Except, of course, Sir Jeremy.

Had she not happened to see Sir Jeremy whirling Amabel Stafford through a fast-paced reel, had she not met Amabel's look and caught the unveiled flash of spiteful triumph there, the evening might possibly have been perfect.

Clarissa had no doubts as to young Miss Stafford's ambitions; she only wondered what Jeremy's intentions were.

He really should marry again, she remembered Helen Petherstone saying. *He's far too young to live like a hermit.*

Hermit indeed, Clarissa thought sourly, watching Sir Jeremy bend his head slightly to murmur something in the ear of the dashing young Lady Roxbury, who was very married but also a hopeless flirt. He certainly didn't appear so that evening.

"Mrs. Wyndham." The voice was patient but amused. "Here's your punch. If you still want it."

She looked up with a start into Captain Battlebourne's inquiring blue eyes. Murmuring an apology, she accepted the glass he offered.

"I'm afraid I was woolgathering," Clarissa told him.

"Well, don't look so stricken; it isn't a hanging offense, last I heard." He settled easily into the chair beside her; Clarissa laughed and sipped her punch. Captain Nathaniel Battlebourne was a paragon of escorts: polite, good-looking, an excellent dancer, and an easygoing, well-informed conversationalist. He made Clarissa laugh as she hadn't in months, with amusing but affectionate anecdotes about his large family—particularly a scapegrace younger brother who was attempting to cut a fashionable dash in London, to the despair of their long-suffering mother.

"You're from London, ma'am," the captain had implored Clarissa. "What can you tell me to set my poor mother's mind at ease?"

"About cutting a fashionable dash?" Clarissa had replied, half-appalled, half-amused by the question. "Nothing at all, I'm afraid!"

"How does it happen," he was asking now, "that a lady as charming as yourself should suddenly spring upon us?"

" 'Spring,' sir?" she returned, her tone carefully light. "You make me sound like one of those fearsome Bengal tigers you were talking about a while ago."

"Well, I meant nothing of the sort," he said, laughing. "I meant that in our rather quiet corner of the world one doesn't see new arrivals very often, particularly with so little fanfare. In fact, Miss Amabel Stafford was remarking upon the very thing just a few moments past."

"Oh, was she?" This tidbit was hardly comforting.

"Naturally, she was," the captain said carelessly. "Recollect we've little else to talk about! Still, you haven't answered my question. Where in the world have you been hiding?"

Drat the man's persistence—and his choice of words! "I've hardly been hiding," she said. "But I have been living rather quietly at Metcalfe Farm. I rent it from Helen and William Petherstone."

"Oh yes, I know the place," said the captain. "And I'd heard they'd let it at last—to you, as it turns out! Well, the word was, the new tenant was a frail widow, but . . ."

He stopped, looking disconcerted. Clarissa dismissed his embarrassment with a laugh. "But I'm disgustingly robust, you were about to say?" she asked teasingly.

"Disgusting is hardly the word I'd use," said the captain, a sudden warmth in the straightforward look he shot Clarissa. "Permit me to say that you're a most fortunate addition to our rather secluded society."

"You're too kind," Clarissa said weakly, wondering how in the world she had painted herself into this conversational corner.

"No, I'm not being kind," said the captain, who no doubt would have said a great deal more, had a deep, distinctly cool voice not intruded.

"Your pardon, Battlebourne," said Sir Jeremy. "But if that's your intent, allow someone else a few moments with your charming partner."

Looking up with surprise and anger, Clarissa caught her breath at the sight of Sir Jeremy towering over her, elegant but decidedly imposing in impeccably tailored black, against which his waistcoat of rich oyster satin and crisp white linen were thrown into stark relief. His black hair, neatly clubbed back with a black satin riband, he had left unpowdered, as had most of the younger men present. Squarely, she met his grey-green eyes, which at the moment were distinctly stormy.

"I think it's quite evident the captain was speaking in jest," she said, her voice dangerously quiet.

"Of course," said Sir Jeremy with insufferable irony, bringing the captain to his feet and into the fray.

"It's most good of you, Mrs. Wyndham, but I need no defending," he said quietly. "Nor, I believe, need I explain a private conversation to you, sir. Unless you're in the habit of such intrusions?"

He had his reward in the sudden cold anger that leaped into his adversary's eyes. "Do I intrude, then? My apologies—I'd no notion our staid social affairs had become home to such cozy tête-à-têtes."

"Stop this instant!" Barely containing the urge to stamp her foot, Clarissa interrupted them with a furious whisper. "Can you not see you're making a scene, the two of you?"

In the embarrassed silence that ensued, Battle-bourne recovered first. Clearing his throat, he bowed stiffly. "My sincerest apologies, Mrs. Wynd-ham. That surely was not my intention. Since it's my understanding Sir Jeremy is an acquaintance of yours"—he paused for a pointed moment—"I'll leave you to your conversation. Unless I may be of further service?"

"Please don't let me detain you further," Clarissa said, the warmth of her tone belying the polite phrase. "You've been everything that's kind this evening."

"The pleasure was all mine," said Captain Bat-tlebourne, raising her outstretched hand to his lips. With a curt nod at Sir Jeremy, he was on his way.

Clarissa started to rise from her chair, a few choice words for Sir Jeremy on the tip of her tongue. But he forestalled her by dropping easily into Battlebourne's vacant seat.

"Don't, I beg you, stalk off in high dudgeon," he said. "If you're anxious to avoid a scene, that would never do."

Inwardly fuming, Clarissa settled back into her chair. The music had stopped momentarily, and a few couples were drifting to the center of the room in preparation for the next dance.

"Why?" she asked bluntly.

He did not pretend ignorance. "Why not? You wanted to be rid of him yourself."

She found herself suddenly at a loss; the truth of his statement was impossible to deny.

"Just so," he said quietly. "You were worried; I could see it in your eyes."

She opened her fan, noting with satisfied detachment the steadiness of her hand, the small, definitive snap of ivory sticks and silk. The movement calmed her.

"You have keen eyes, sir," she said. "But you're mistaken about my expression. If I looked troubled, it was only because the captain was being far too flattering."

"No doubt he was, fiend seize him," said Sir Jeremy unemotionally. He reached out to intercept her wrist, stopping cold the restless movement of her fan, letting go an instant later. "But I think you were disturbed beyond the usual exasperation at that kind of gallantry."

"How kind of you to take pity on me, Sir Jeremy." Clarissa took refuge in tartness, trying to ignore his nearness, the unbidden rush of excitement that coursed through her at the warm touch of his fingers. "I'd no notion you could be so chivalrous."

"My knight-errant days are far in the past, believe me," he said dryly. "Nevertheless, it was clear you were upset."

"I can only marvel that a rescue party was not formed to bear me away."

"Oh, never fear, it wasn't noticeable to everyone," said Sir Jeremy, giving her a crooked smile that did the strangest things to the pit of her stomach. "But I could see."

She glanced down at her fan again, saying in a low voice, "You refine too much upon the matter, sir. But since you've ridden to my rescue, what next?"

She would have guessed an acerbic retort or a polite good night. He startled her by laughing in the carefree, unaffected way she had heard him use with Susannah and—just once, in his study—with her.

"What next?" He rose, taking her by the hand and sweeping her, in her surprise, to her feet as well. "Why, I ask you to dance with me, of course."

Of course, she thought dazedly, moving with him to the dance floor, where the set was nearly formed. The evening had taken a mad turn—but what a sweet madness it was, she told herself defiantly, sinking in a whisper of velvet to curtsey to his bow. Moving within the circle of his arm through the opening figure, she glanced upward and caught her breath at the expression on his face, for once unguarded as his eyes raked over her, as if to drink in everything about her. She wondered whether there was an answering hunger in her own gaze, and laughed inwardly. As if she could hide it from a man who could read her face from across a crowded ballroom!

The dance was a reel, fast-paced and lively, and they spent little of it actually together. But the moments they did have seemed to hang suspended and exquisite—when his hands, warm and strong, clasped hers to swing her down the clapping, laughing row of dancers; when she brushed against him, ever so lightly, as she twirled around him in a figure. Above all, the moment in which the dance stopped and she swept a final curtsey to him, raising a face alight with laughter to his. And the answering blaze that leapt into his hazel eyes.

Wordlessly he took her by the hand, leading her swiftly away from the noisy throng of dancers, toward a doorway she had not noticed before. They hurried through it, into a small, deserted parlor.

For a breathless moment they stared at each other, the laughter wiped from their faces. Sir Jeremy broke the tense silence at last.

"I must be mad," he murmured, taking Clarissa by the shoulders. Blindly she tilted her face toward his. "You've made me mad...."

"Madness, yes," she whispered, drawing nearer, her arms reaching upward. "But—"

Her words were stopped as his mouth descended upon hers, demanding and hungry, as he slowly swept his fingers through her hair, combing through the silken strands. After an eternity, he raised his head.

"I've wanted to do that all evening," he said with a ragged laugh. "And this..."

He kissed her again, his hands softly caressing her waist through the velvet of her gown, then crushing her urgently toward him as he rained light kisses over her collarbone, the hollow at the base of her throat, the swell of her breasts above the lacy décolletage.

With a hoarse gasp Clarissa cupped his face in her hands, reveling in the warm, silky feeling of his dark hair, his sharp, clean scent. She raised herself on tiptoe, her lips slightly parted, drawing him down to her again even as some tiny, still-sane corner of her mind cried out in consternation. They clung together, unseeing and uncaring of the world beyond the parlor.

After what could have been minutes or years, a light voice spoke dangerously close by. "Must we leave just now, Mama?"

They froze; Sir Jeremy lifted his head abruptly.

"I so wanted to bid Sir Jeremy good night," said the voice, unmistakably belonging to Miss Amabel Stafford. "He's been so very charming, and we never did fix the time for our ride next week."

Jeremy looked down at Clarissa with a wry smile that died abruptly as he saw the sudden hostility in her eyes.

She drew away from him, almost violently.

"It seems you have other obligations," she said, her voice tight and cold. "I bid you good night, Sir Jeremy."

"What the devil—" He reached out a hand to stop her, but she was far too swift.

"Pray don't concern yourself," she said, fighting back tears, wondering how she could have forgotten, even for a moment, his particular attentions to Amabel Stafford. Clarissa turned on her heel and fled, not daring to slow her steps, not daring to look back.

8

The first week of January

C larissa winced and darted a hasty glance
around in search of a graceful path of retreat,
but there was no help for it: Sir Jeremy was crunch-
ing his way toward her, down the snowy drive of
Thornbeck House, the capes of his greatcoat flap-
ping in the brisk wind, which brought tears to her
eyes.

She inclined her head stiffly as he stopped before
her.

"Good morning, Mrs. Wyndham," he said, with
a courtesy nearly as chill as the air around them.

"Good day, Sir Jeremy. You are about early this
morning."

"A matter at one of the farms requires my attention. No help for it, I'm afraid."

An awkward silence fell. Clarissa shifted her basket to her other hand; Sir Jeremy directed an inquiring look toward it.

"These are some home remedies I promised
Cook," Clarissa said diffidently.

He frowned. "I wish you would be reasonable

and allow me to send the gig for you, Mrs. Wyndham. It's cold to be walking far."

"Oh, no, it's—"

"No trouble. I know." Abruptly, he raised his hat to her. "I must be going."

"Please don't let me detain you," she muttered as he stalked away.

Oh, Lord, it was all she needed that day, an encounter with Sir Jeremy to cut up her peace, reminding her that it was as if the extraordinary moments at the Christmas assembly had never been.

What had it meant to him? she wondered. For herself, it had been no idle flirtation. She—not a green girl, but a widow, with a little experience of the world—had been shaken by the power of the encounter.

He, on the other hand, seemed perfectly capable of paying court to two women at once. Thinking of Miss Stafford, Clarissa felt anew the rage and shame that had overwhelmed her as she left the assembly rooms that night.

None of this mattered now, she thought gloomily. Sir Jeremy appeared determined to treat her with a cool correctness she found worse than his temper. Oh, the man was impossible, and she was extremely wise to avoid him!

Even if she could not stop thinking about him.

With a sigh she turned toward the house, where Mickle, at least, had a kind word for her. "Come in, come in, mistress," he said, hurrying her into the hall. "You must be fair starved with the cold!"

"That I am," Clarissa agreed, following Mickle gratefully into the breakfast room, where a fire was laid. "Has Miss Susannah eaten?"

"Indeed, ma'am, she's finishing breakfast in the schoolroom now. Would you like some tea before you go up? It'd be no trouble."

"Yes, thank you very much," she said. The smile she gave Mickle—as he reported to Cook, upon fetching the tea from the kitchen—would have made a body happy to oblige her least wish. "But that's Mistress Clary for you," he told Cook. "I'm always that glad to see her coming up the drive."

"Pity the master don't feel the same, Mr. Mickle," Cook said.

"That's an impertinent thought, Mrs. Crowerby, and I'm surprised at thee," said Mickle, taking the tea tray from Cook with dignity, privately agreeing with her every word. He'd seen from the doorway with his own eyes how mightily displeased Sir Jeremy looked with the widow. Such a pity. Why, for a little while, he'd almost hoped . . . But no use crying over spilt milk, was there?

Her tea disposed of ten minutes later, Clarissa made her way up to the schoolroom, where she found Susannah concentrating on a copybook and Nurse tatting by the fire.

"Good morning," Clarissa said.

"Hello, Mrs. Wyndham!" Susannah jumped up, nearly upsetting her chair.

"Mind thy manners, Miss Susannah," admonished Nurse. "Good morning to thee, mistress. Tha didn't freeze on th' walk, I see?"

"No, indeed," said Clarissa, unable to shake the conviction that Nurse found this a disappointment. "How are you?"

"Well enough, well enough, mistress," said Nurse, setting aside her tatting and gathering up her workbag. "Tha'll be shut of me in a moment, and can start teaching our highty-tighty young miss here, if she heeds thee."

Clarissa knew better than to pick a quarrel with Nurse over this last sardonic aside, but her lips compressed into an angry line, which did not pass unnoticed.

"Ay, tha knows better, I see," said Nurse, with a gleam in her eyes Clarissa found hard to interpret.

"Susannah," Clarissa said quietly, "run to your room and fetch yourself a shawl. It's a little chilly in here today."

Susannah hurried from the room.

"I wish you would not speak that way in front of Susannah, Nurse," Clarissa said, keeping a firm rein on her temper. "First of all, she is not at all *highty-tighty*, and second, if she should be, it is my concern, after all."

"And powerful concerned tha must be, mistress," agreed Nurse, with a contrition Clarissa did not for a minute believe. "I beg thy pardon—it were fair stupid of me to speak such nonsense. But if tha wouldn't take amiss an old woman's advice—watch young miss well or she'll fall to the temptations of the evil one."

Clarissa asked impatiently, "Whatever are you talking about, Nurse?"

"Bad blood, mistress," Nurse said simply.

"I'm sorry, but I can't see what you mean," Clarissa said, endeavoring to keep incredulity from her voice. "The Sutcliffes—"

"Not Sutcliffes!" Nurse was scandalized. " 'Tis young miss's *mother* I mean, and a bad piece of work she was, too. And like mother, like daughter, they say—"

"Well, that is too bad of you, Nurse!" said Clarissa, aware that this conversation was imprudent but much too upset to care. "I've no idea what sort of person Lady Sutcliffe might have been, but I do know it is most unjust to visit the sins of a dead mother upon a mere child!"

Nurse looked sharply at Clarissa. But she said only, "Is that what tha thinks, mistress?"

"It most certainly is," said Clarissa sternly. "And

I don't believe we should speak of this again."

"Oh, we won't, mistress. Never heed me, I'm old and I blather on too much." Nurse got up with an effort, and picked up Susannah's breakfast tray. "Tha knows best, of course. But"—the odd gleam was back in her faded old eyes—"tha mayn't know everything. I'll be getting this out of thy way, then."

Clarissa watched Nurse's painstaking progress from the room, a faint frown lingering on her brow long after the door had closed. It seemed the past few weeks of winter had been particularly hard on Nurse's rheumatism, but the fierce old lady refused to accept any expressions of concern. Perhaps her ill temper was simply a result of the pain.

Nevertheless, such outbursts really couldn't be tolerated. Perhaps, Clarissa thought, she should consult Sir Jeremy . . . but good God, how could she?

A small noise made Clarissa glance down at Susannah, who had slipped back into the schoolroom.

"Are you all right, Mrs. Wyndham?" Susannah asked. "You look as if you have the headache."

"Not at all," Clarissa said brightly. "Let us start with your recitation, shall we?"

Lady Anne Talmadge to Mrs. Clarissa Wyndham

7 January 1789
Berkeley Square

My dear Clarissa,

I hope this finds you in good health and that you made as merry as could be this Christmastide. I myself am well enough, as is Talmadge, tho' both of us a trifle pulled about from a Yuletide spent with Talmadge's sister and her brood. Lovely children, of course, but must there be *six* of them?

Speaking of children, your last letter was most entertaining. Your little Susannah sounds fascinating.

You will notice I do not urge you to write. Much as I long to hear from you, I fear it may be imprudent for you to send a letter to me. I believe a certain party has not abandoned his efforts to trace you—and I fear very much he suspects me. He thinks that I know where you are, and seems to be watching me rather closely. Whether he would have the audacity to intercept my correspondence, I do not know. But I fear it is best to be careful for a bit.

Stay well, dear friend, and keep busy. An excellent antidote to worry, is it not? Perhaps your employer (how delightful to think of you as a governess) will give you some manuscript to copy. He sounds a veritable taskmaster.

Courage, dear, and only consider—in a very short time all will be resolved, and we can have a comfortable gossip about this adventure.

All my love,
Anne

York, two days later

Emerging rather abstractedly from his solicitor's office in Walmgate, Sir Jeremy was wrapping his muffler round his neck when he nearly collided with Captain Battlebourne, who was hurrying down the busy street.

"Beg pardon!" said the captain, looking not at all sorry.

"Don't think of it," replied Sir Jeremy. "Good to see you, Battlebourne."

They shook hands unenthusiastically. Nathaniel Battlebourne was aware of his own discomfort. Stiffly, he inquired after the health of Sir Jeremy's household.

"Oh, all's well," Sir Jeremy said. "What brings you into the city?"

Momentarily forgetting his annoyance, the captain grinned ruefully. "What doesn't? No sooner had I said I might take a fancy to call upon my old school friend here, when everyone from my father to my fourteen-year-old sister hits upon an errand for me! Right now I'm on my way to the Receiving Office to call for a parcel. Dress goods, I believe my mother said."

Sir Jeremy's smile became genuine. "Let us hope it's nothing more objectionable. You have my sincerest sympathy."

"Thank you," said the captain. "By the bye, is Mrs. Wyndham in good health?

Presumptuous puppy, thought Sir Jeremy, his smile fading. "In perfect health, when last I saw her."

The edge to his voice was not lost upon the captain, who looked Sir Jeremy over in a measured way before saying: "Give her my respects when next you see her, will you, Sutcliffe? I understand she's still teaching Miss Susannah?"

"She is; we seldom meet."

This forbidding pronouncement failed to intimidate the captain. "A pity. She's a delightful woman. One hopes to see her more about in society."

"Mrs. Wyndham is recently widowed, I believe,"

said Sir Jeremy coldly, feeling unaccountably annoyed.

"Well, she's put off her blacks, so she don't seem all that recent a widow to me," the captain pointed out reasonably. "At all events, it's no business of ours whether she chooses to go about, now, is it?"

"Hardly," Sir Jeremy said, with awful politeness.

The captain smiled. "Just so. Well, as I said, give her my respectful regards if you should see her, Sutcliffe. Safe journey home."

"Safe journey," Sir Jeremy replied, treating himself to a pleasant vision of the captain's gig overturned in any of the numerous ditches between York and Thorndale.

They shook hands again, with painstaking civility, and went their separate ways.

Charles Bennett, Esq., solicitor, to His Grace of Belfort

9 January 1789

Enclosed please find copies of the latest dispatches from Mr. Travers in Yorkshire, which appear to be of particular interest. More inquiries will, of course, be needed to discover whether this information is indeed helpful in the matter Your Grace is pursuing. I await Your Grace's instructions upon how next to proceed.

I remain Your Grace's humble servant,
Charles Bennett

A smile of pleasure lighting her face, Helen hurried into the drawing room of Aysgarth Manor, shaking a shawl about her shoulders as she went.

"Clarissa, dear, how splendid that you could come this morning! Is that fire warming you? Was it any trouble?"

"The fire is lovely, and no, it wasn't any trouble whatsoever." Her visitor laughed, unraveling the meaning of Mrs. Petherstone's speech with impressive skill.

"Well, I'm so pleased Susannah could spare you," Helen said, with a twinkle. "It seems an age since we had a comfortable coze. Then, too, I have some books I think you'll find amusing—a few novels, and a collection of Mr. Sheridan's plays."

Clarissa's face lit up. "That's very kind of you, ma'am! You must be a mind reader, for I was thinking just yesterday how much I needed something new to occupy me." Indeed she did, for Lady Anne's letter had caused her a sleepless night and much worry.

"Well, I don't know about mind reading, but it stands to reason that anyone whiling away one of our Yorkshire winters needs a diversion," Helen said. "Of course, if you were to take up tatting, like Nurse—"

"Pray, don't think about it!" said Clarissa, laughing. "I couldn't hope to match Nurse at tatting, and if I could, I'd probably fill the farmhouse with it by March."

"A horrible prospect," agreed Helen. "How is Nurse keeping herself?"

Clarissa, her laughter dying away, gave a tactful but truthful assessment of matters at Thornbeck House.

"Well," said Helen, when she had heard her out, "you're quite right, Clarissa, dear—it's a most delicate situation. These old retainers! Nevertheless, perhaps I can contrive to drop a word in Jeremy's ear. Of course, it will have to wait until he returns from Scotland—"

"Scotland!"

Helen, though keenly interested by the note in her young friend's voice, remained casual. "Why, yes. How shatterbrained of me. Of course you wouldn't have heard; you haven't been to Thornbeck House yet! It seems Sir Jeremy's great-aunt has passed on and left him her house near Ayr—or is it Prestwick? I can't remember. The letter came yesterday, and since the poor old soul hadn't any closer relatives, he must post up there instantly to sort out her affairs, which are in a sad tangle. I expect you'll learn all about it this afternoon."

"I'm not certain of that, ma'am," said Clarissa dryly. "Sir Jeremy's affairs are none of my concern, after all."

"Oh, don't be so—so regal, I beg you!" implored Mrs. Petherstone. "It quite puts me out of countenance."

A reluctant smile quirked Clarissa's lips. "Forgive me, ma'am. I only meant that I've no wish to presume, to—to imply . . ." She subsided into embarrassed silence.

"Never mind," said Helen, taking pity upon her. "Forgive me, my dear; I don't mean to pry. But it did seem to me at the assembly rooms last month that you and Jeremy were in such wonderful accord; I would not want there to be a misunderstanding over this journey of his."

Remembering just how wonderful their accord had been, and what had shattered it, Clarissa hardly knew whether to laugh or to cry. She chose, instead, to beg her hostess's forgiveness again for being silly, and to declare that she really, really should be on her way. Helen made a spirited attempt to coax her into another cup of tea, but in the end wisely let her take her leave.

"For," as she later confided to the interested Mr. Petherstone, "it was obvious the poor girl was beside herself! Whatever could it all mean?"

"What a rhetorical question," murmured William. "As if you hadn't at least three theories on the subject."

"Wretch!" said his wife, sailing off to consult with Mrs. Ivesby about dinner.

Clarissa, meanwhile, continued on to Thornbeck House, teaching an afternoon's worth of lessons to Susannah in a rather distracted state. At length she noticed that her pupil looked woeful and subdued, and Clarissa put her own cares aside.

"What's the matter, dear?" she asked gently.

Heaving a sigh, Susannah glanced up from the map of the Americas she was dutifully reproducing. "Papa is going away, did you hear, Mrs. Wyndham?"

"Yes, I had heard that."

"I know he has to, because of Aunt Eustacia," Susannah said. "But I hate it. There's no one to tell things to."

"Well, that's vexing. But do you know, he won't be away terribly long, I expect. I think you can be brave and make do with me in the meantime—if it isn't too terrible to think of!"

"Oh, I'm glad you're here, Mrs. Wyndham," Susannah said shyly. "It will be hard without Papa, though."

A knock sounded on the schoolroom door. "Come in," called Clarissa, expecting Nurse.

Sir Jeremy entered the room, looking harried and not particularly pleased to be there. Evidently he had been out with Stainewick on the estate, for he was still in riding dress.

"Mrs. Wyndham." He bowed stiffly toward Clarissa as Susannah twisted round in her chair.

"Hello, Papa," Susannah said. "It's kind of you to call today."

"Good God." Despite himself, Sir Jeremy shot an amused glance at Clarissa, who was struggling not to laugh. "You're rather formal, mouse."

"Mrs. Wyndham says that's what you say to callers."

"Well, strictly speaking, I am not a caller, mouse. You need not stand on ceremony with me."

"Stand on ceremony—what does that mean, Papa?"

"I'll explain later; I must speak with Mrs. Wyndham for a bit. Run along and see Nurse, now."

Susannah left reluctantly. Sir Jeremy regarded Clarissa in the sudden silence, making her unaccountably sorry she was wearing nothing more elegant than her everyday dress of dark blue wool, with its modest sleeve ruffles and plain white collar.

"So my little daughter is showing an interest in the social niceties," Sir Jeremy said after a moment. "You're to be congratulated, Mrs. Wyndham."

"Thank you, but it was easy enough to encourage her," Clarissa said. "Nurse, to her credit, has not spoiled Susannah into one of those odious little nursery tyrants."

"Spoken with feeling." Sir Jeremy's mouth quirked engagingly. "Have you a particular tyrant in mind?"

Clarissa could recall several horrid pupils of her father's, in fact, and nearly said so before recollecting herself. Why must the man always take her off her guard?

"None in particular, I'm afraid," she said, more crisply than she intended. "I understand you must journey to Scotland, sir."

The smile died from his eyes. "Yes," he returned, his manner coolly polite again. "I'm leaving on the morrow, and will be gone several weeks, I believe. It's why I wished to speak to you."

Ah, the lord of the manor had instructions for his retainer. "How may I be of service?" Clarissa asked.

"If you would continue Susannah's lessons as before, I should be most grateful."

As if she would have cried off in his absence! Clarissa bit back a sarcastic retort. "But of course, Sir Jeremy."

He frowned. "What the devil have I said to make you glare at me?"

"I am not glaring," Clarissa snapped, losing her fragile hold on her temper. "Or at least, if I was, it was at your utter arrogance!"

"My arrogance?" His tone was distinctly dangerous. "What are you talking about?"

"I should think it would be obvious," Clarissa said, stacking books and clearing away papers from the schoolroom table with unnecessary vigor. "But give me leave to tell you, sir, that I don't need your condescension, and I shan't be abandoning Susannah the instant your back is turned! Just because you are going to Scotland without—without—"

She clamped her lips together tightly, cursing her unruly tongue.

"Without what, Mrs. Wyndham?" Sir Jeremy asked.

Without a word to me! she cried out inwardly, despising herself for the thought. She collected herself and spoke with dignity.

"I was speaking out of turn, Sir Jeremy. I beg your pardon." She expected a stinging setdown in return, but when he spoke, he sounded merely thoughtful.

"Apology accepted. And I beg *your* pardon, for giving offense." He looked searchingly at her. "None was intended, I assure you."

"Of course not," she said, dropping her gaze to the table and gathering papers into a neat pile. "You need not apologize, sir."

"Nevertheless, I do." Lightly, he laid a hand on

one of hers, bringing her work to an abrupt halt. "I've another request," he said casually, his arm dropping to his side again. "I should like you to write regularly—regarding Susannah's progress, naturally."

"Oh. Naturally. I should be happy to," Clarissa said, swallowing past a sudden lump in her throat. "You may depend on me, Sir Jeremy."

"I know that," he said. They stood in silence for a moment.

"Well," Clarissa said awkwardly at last. "I wish you a safe journey, Sir Jeremy."

"Thank you." In a gesture as swift as it was surprising, he raised her hand to his lips. "Stay well, Mrs. Wyndham."

And then he was gone. She stood absolutely still for several minutes, before turning back to the table and slowly resuming her task of tidying up.

Mrs. Clarissa Wyndham to Sir Jeremy Sutcliffe

18 January 1789
Metcalfe Farm

Sir Jeremy,

As you requested, I am happy to forward reports on Miss Sutcliffe's progress. I trust you will find all in order.

I must also report, I am afraid, that there was a minor accident in the study on Wednesday last. Gilly managed to enter while the maids were going in to dust, and she upset an inkwell on yr. desk, fouling some of the papers thereon. Fortunately they did not appear to be of great consequence. But to avoid future distress I am taking the liberty of sorting thro' the disorder and putting safely away anything of importance. The rest, I feel, can be burned, as so much dust is not healthy for the lungs. I am sure you will see the necessity of so doing.

Allow me to express once more my condolences on the loss of your aunt. I hope your business at her estate proceeds well.

Respectfully yours,
Clarissa Wyndham

Sir Jeremy Sutcliffe to Mrs. Clarissa Wyndham

29 January 1789
Sutherland Hall, Ayrshire

My dear Mrs. Wyndham,

By the time you receive this I have no doubt you will have already made free with my desk, so I will not waste ink directing you in that regard. I am sorry indeed to learn that the field of education offers so little scope for your energies. However, if you wish to take up the duties of librarian and clerk as well, I can have no objection.

Your report of the 18th was most interesting—especially yr. comments upon reading material for young girls. I wish you well in replacing the insipid with the inspiring, but have the goodness to stay clear of Gothic horrors. Perhaps Miss Burney's novels will do instead—in time, since Susannah is rather young yet for such matters (if a father may be permitted his humble opinion).

I trust you are in good health.

Yr. obedient servant,
Jeremy Sutcliffe

The Hon. William Petherstone to Sir Jeremy Sutcliffe

11 February 1789
Aysgarth Manor

My dear friend,

Today, as you directed, I called at Thornbeck House. All was well—Miss Susannah looking hale & hearty & minding Mrs. Wyndham nicely. I am told a poem is in progress & will serenade you upon yr. triumphant return to our humble district. (Pray do not tell Susannah I betrayed her secret. I inform you only that you might keep a suitable countenance during the recitation.)

Speaking of our humble district, I am afraid I have not much interesting news of Thorndale. Helen and I made up a party to go to York for the new comic play at the Theatre Royal—Lady Selina was there, and Mrs. Wyndham and Captain Battlebourne—all most congenial, tho' the play wanted wit, in my opinion.

Mindful of your other request, I have peeped into your study to inspect the desk & its contents—all well there—surprisingly neat, in fact. The arrangement of materials according to subject matter and chronology is most efficient. Did you set it in order before you left?

Have you heard any news from Edinburgh? Such a stimulating lot of thinkers there, tho' the place was always too blue-nosed for my taste.

I keep busy with my reading. The latest journals from London arrived here two days since, full of news from France—all gloom and uncertainty. I hope there are happier events to relate soon. I remain, dear friend,

Your devoted servant,
William Petherstone

Mrs. Clarissa Wyndham to Sir Jeremy Sutcliffe

20 February 1789
Thornbeck House

Dear Sir Jeremy,

Your letter was most welcome.

First, to set your mind at ease, I have not discarded or burned anything from yr. desk, tho' I may have exaggerated slightly when I last wrote.

Your further comments upon light reading were most illuminating—of course I have read *Evelina* & think it far more interesting than modish Gothic horror tales. I also recall your expressing admiration for the novels of Mr. Richardson, which I too have enjoyed immensely, tho' I find his view of humanity rather dark. How has this struck you, sir?

Now, regarding the direction of this letter: Susannah has been a little affected by a cold, & I have stayed for a few days to bear her company, since she would have me. You must not be alarmed for her health, however. Dr. Tolliver has been twice to see her & declares she is perfectly sound.

She should be restored in no time at all, & when Dr. Tolliver says the word I shall return to the farm; I shall not trespass upon yr. kind hospitality (tho' in absentia) longer than necessary. I remain, sir,

Your servant,
Clarissa Wyndham

From a letter by Sir Jeremy Sutcliffe to Mrs. Clarissa Wyndham

6 March 1789
Sutherland Hall

...I must hope by these words you may appreciate the depth of my concern. Should my daughter ever again fall ill in my absence, have the goodness to state so directly, not at the end of a babble of tidbits on elocution & grammar.

How stands the case now? Write immediately—the business here proceeds slowly, but I *will come home* at first necessity.

Sutcliffe

From a letter by Mrs. Clarissa Wyndham to Sir Jeremy Sutcliffe

16 March 1789
Metcalfe Farm

...As to my letter, you have yourself proven the validity of my apprehensions regarding yr. ability to consider my news calmly and sensibly. There *was no* grave illness—she is much improved & seems indeed more vigorous than ever.

I wrote as I did so as not to distress you— I see it was useless. You *will* be vexed, and there is nothing to be done to change yr. unreasonable disposition.

I do not know whether you will listen to advice from anyone, least of all myself, but I must again say: Please do not put aside yr. business & obligations on this account. Susannah is wonderfully well...

From a letter by Mrs. Helen Petherstone to Sir Jeremy Sutcliffe

28 March 1789
Aysgarth Manor

... Mrs. Wyndham has been rather poorly, & bids me to convey her apologies for not remitting her promised scholastick report. Dr. Tolliver said she was afflicted with the influenza, & rather seriously, too—I confess I was worried because the fever was very high & for two days she did not know Martha or myself, or anything else, for that matter.

But she is very strong & managed to recover nicely, tho' she must have her rest. I visit every day, and am happy to report that many of our neighbors share my concerns and have been marvelously kind. Captain Battlebourne brought a lovely basket of fruit to the farm yesterday. A very thoughtful gesture, I must say ...

Mrs. Clarissa Wyndham to Sir Jeremy Sutcliffe

7 April 1789
Metcalfe Farm

Dear Sir Jeremy,

Your letter was very kind, but please do not worry on my account; I am much better, & it is a tonic to have Susannah's company. Please say she may continue calling. I have attended to the reports left undone over the last few weeks & hope you will find all satisfactory.

Lastly I must write how much pleasure yr. thoughtful gift of Mr. Boswell's book has afforded me. His journeying to the Scottish isles

awakens such a curiosity in me—have you
seen similar sights in your travels? This volume has made many a tedious hour fly
quickly by!

I trust you are well & can soon return to us.

Your servant,
Clarissa Wyndham

Sir Jeremy Sutcliffe to Mrs. Clarissa Wyndham

10 April 1789
Sutherland House

My dear Mrs. Wyndham,

I am happy you like the book. It is little
enough, but it is the best I could do from this
distance to help ease the tedium of your sick-
bed. I am sorry I could not be there to do
more.

But there is good news from Scotland—the
business here is at last concluded, & I depart
for Yorkshire in a few days. I expect to be at
Thornbeck House by Sunday. I hope I may
call on you when I arrive. There is much we
need to say to each other.

Your obedient servant,
Jeremy Sutcliffe

Mr. Charles Bennett to Philip Higby, Esq., Harrogate

8 April 1789
London

Sir,

Your assistance in this matter is vastly
appreciated. Pray *do not* approach the

lady—her nervous state is most delicate, &
she must be treated with great care, as indeed her loving family is most anxious to
do. The draft enclosed should defray yr. ex-
penses & remit yr. fee. If all is not in order
pray inform me.

Bennett

Mr. Charles Bennett to His Grace of Belfort

8 April 1789
Belfort House—To be delivered directly to
His Grace's hand

Your Grace—

She is found. What is to be done now? And
what am I to do regarding the gentleman (I
use the term loosely) Mr. Travers?

Bennett

A note to Mr. Charles Bennett

12 April 1789
Belfort House

Bennett—

Say nothing. Do nothing. I will send word,
should I require anything. As for Travers, pay
him off & pack him off. His part in this is at
an end.

B.

Metcalfe Farm

Clarissa sat in a wing chair by the front-room
window, Sir Jeremy's latest letter in her lap, her

gaze straying to the sky outside, a troubled jumble
of restless, pale grey clouds.

There is much we need to say . . .

A wry smile tugged at her mouth. *Oh, I should
think so.* The problem would be where to begin. Or
would they begin? It seemed to Clarissa that rea-
soned discussion was hardly their forte. Dagger
drawing, yes. In a pinch, the occasional tart, intel-
lectual debate.

And kisses. Remembering, Clarissa felt the heat
rise in her cheeks again. She could no longer pretend indifference. She was in the grip of emotions
for which even her marriage had not prepared her.
She had always known her feelings toward her
husband had been cut more from respect and affection than from passion, and if she had sometimes wondered what passion felt like, she had
resolutely squelched the thought.

Now she was beginning to understand, and
found it exhilarating and terrifying at once.

But it was not entirely passion that preyed upon
her peace, she admitted with some reluctance. So
much else contrived to keep Sir Jeremy in her
mind—his deadly accurate sense of humor; his patient amusement and genuine sense of discovery at
Susannah's emerging personality; the excitement
that gripped his voice as he talked about his work,
or of journeys to faraway places. She found to her
pained surprise that, for all his maddening ways,
she was dreadfully lonely without him.

In fact, had someone at that very moment demanded the truth from her at the point of a sword,
she would have had to confess she was in love.

A small commotion in the dooryard recalled Clarissa to the present, but, uncharacteristically, she did
not get up to investigate. She had not bounced back
with her customary careless good health from the

influenza; Dr. Tolliver had told her bluntly that she was working too hard. And it *had* been a strain, managing the chores at the farm and keeping up with her duties at Thornbeck House, where Nurse had at last taken to her bed, and the staff seemed rather forlorn without Sir Jeremy's presence.

Clarissa had hesitated at first when Mickle and Cook had asked for advice on household matters. She did not, after all, live at Thornbeck House, for all the time she increasingly spent there. But somehow her most casual observations received eager attention from the servants, particularly Mickle. And to her embarrrassed amusement, he had acted upon some of them—as in the matter of the hangings in the great hall, and one or two other details. She hoped Sir Jeremy wouldn't take offense, although in all likelihood, he would, Clarissa reflected gloomily. . . .

Martha opened the door a bit, and peered round it at her mistress.

"Miss Stafford to see you, madam," she said, carefully correct.

"Oh!" Clarissa glanced down at her grey muslin skirts and worn but warm woolen shawl. Well, they couldn't be helped. "Please, show her in right away."

Amabel, exquisite in a riding habit of simply tailored forest green broadcloth, did not so much enter the room as bestow herself upon it. Her dashingly plumed hat and brown embroidered leather gloves were in one hand, a small wrapped parcel in the other.

"No, pray don't rise, dear ma'am," she said, all gentle concern. "You must recover your strength."

"I'm really much better," said Clarissa, with a touch of asperity. "How kind of you to risk a chill yourself to visit me."

"Oh, it's fine outside," said Amabel, flicking her

skirts as she settled into a chair. "A trifle blustery, but I expect spring weather will really, truly be here in time for Mama's party. You are coming, aren't you?"

"Oh, yes."

"I'm so glad," said Amabel. For a moment, she looked Clarissa up and down with a disconcertingly neutral expression. "Mama will be, too. She's taken one of her fancies to you."

"I'm happy to hear it," Clarissa said. "Actually, I find Lady Stafford excellent company myself."

Smiling gaily, Amabel sprang to her feet and strolled toward the window, which Clarissa had unlatched and left slightly open to capture the cool, bracing April breeze.

"What a lovely room," Amabel said. "And how charming you've made it. Of course, I've never actually been inside this house before."

I should rather think not, Clarissa said to herself, surveying her humble surroundings. "Thank you." She smiled. "I confess I like it, too. Will you take a glass of sherry?"

"Delightful!" said Amabel promptly. As Clarissa rose to pour it from the decanter set out upon a delicate ebony-inlaid table, Amabel seated herself again, watching.

"What a lovely piece," Amabel said casually.

"Oh—" Clarissa paused, disconcerted. "The table, you mean."

"Yes, that. I'm sure it didn't belong to old Riggs."

"No, indeed; it's mine," Clarissa said carefully. She handed Amabel her sherry and took a sip of her own.

"Then the clock must be yours, too! What exquisite workmanship. Papa would be enchanted."

"Thank you. It—it was a gift from my husband."

"How clumsy of me," said Amabel warmly. "I'm sure I didn't mean to distress you."

"No, no," Clarissa said hastily.

"Oh, I am glad you aren't offended. I wondered whether you'd mind, to tell the truth." She took another delicate sip. "Captain Battlebourne says you are most mysterious about yourself, you know. Of course, I told him he was being nonsensical— you simply didn't care to be reminded of your loss. For myself I find it shameful, and simply *vulgar*, the curiosity of some people—"

With an effort, Clarissa held her peace at the implied slur of the poor captain.

"—Why, just the other day, my maid, Parkins— the saucy creature—was chattering on about some stranger asking in the village about you. Shocking, isn't it?" Amabel's cool green eyes opened wide. "Of course, Parkins heard this from one of the servants at Thornbeck House, who had it from heaven knows where. Now, whyever would a stranger be asking questions about you?"

"I've no idea," Clarissa said faintly, taking a fortifying swallow of sherry.

The knock on the door seemed like the trumpet call of a rescuing army. Entering, Martha bobbed a curtsey. "Your pardon, madam, Miss Stafford, but would you be requiring anything? Some tea, perhaps?"

"What a good idea!" Clarissa said. "Miss Stafford?"

"It's most kind, but I fear I must decline," said Amabel. "I must be going in a little while."

What a pity, thought Clarissa. "Well, you must take tea some other time with me. That will be all, Martha."

Martha withdrew, with a speaking glance at her mistress.

"Heavens, how rag-mannered of me," Amabel

said suddenly, reaching for the parcel she had placed in her lap. "This is from Mama, with her very best wishes for your continued recovery."

Clarissa undid the parcel, which turned out to be a finely woven scarf of gold wool, accompanied by a forcefully scrawled note advising Clarissa to mind the doctor, avoid all drafts, and recover her strength in time for the ball.

"You must give your mama my most sincere thanks," said Clarissa, feeling real warmth for the first time in this vexing visit. "And tell her that I wouldn't miss her ball for the world."

"Wonderful," Amabel said. "Simply everyone from the county will be there. The Battlebournes, the Petherstones, Lady Kendall, of course—oh! And Sir Jeremy."

"How nice; I take it he'll be back from Scotland in time," said Clarissa casually.

"Oh, yes. I suppose you hadn't heard. He wrote Mama to tell her particularly that he would be in attendance. It will be marvelous to see him again— he dances so divinely, though he doesn't care to do so often, the provoking creature."

"You are well acquainted with Sir Jeremy?" Clarissa asked, wishing she could stop herself.

"Heavens, yes," Amabel replied carelessly. "I've known him since I was small, though you may be sure he no longer calls me 'little poppet'!"

"I should think not."

"No, no." Amabel smiled sweetly, and cast her eyes modestly downward. "Of course, there have been . . . discussions . . . in that direction since I was in the cradle, if you understand me—"

"I believe I do," said Clarissa, remembering Lady Stafford's words in the churchyard, and feeling rather ill. "It seems an eminently suitable match to me."

"My, you certainly sound like my mama!" Amabel gave a tinkling little laugh. "But yes, I think it will make all of us very, very happy. Of course, I'm still supposed to have a Season, though I find the very thought tiresome, and all is so nearly arranged—but Mama will insist upon my making my curtsey. You know how it is."

"Indeed," Clarissa murmured, wishing herself a thousand miles away, and wistfully envisioning Sir Jeremy splattered with boiling oil, or set upon by wolves.

Fortunately, Amabel at last permitted herself a glance at Clarissa's ormolu clock. "Heavens, the time! I must fly. And you need your rest! I'll see myself out, dear Mrs. Wyndham. Do take especial care of yourself. It has been a delightful visit."

With a whisper of her skirts Amabel was gone, a scent of verbena in her wake. Clarissa sat unnaturally still for a few minutes, listening to the prosaic sounds of her departure.

Then, most deliberately, she rose, picked up the delicately stemmed crystal glass Amabel had set down, and dashed it to pieces in the grate. Casting herself back into her wing chair, she sat by the window once more, watching with wide, tearless eyes as the bright afternoon sunlight gave way to shadows and dusk.

London

The gambling hell was, appropriately enough, smoky and crowded and blazing with the glitter of several vulgar chandeliers. The duke knew he was supposed to find Antoinette's beneath him, not for the gaming—a pastime to which most of his fellow peers were addicted—but for the garishness. The overblown opulence of the place extended to its hostess, a fiftyish woman whose ample curves were swathed that night in a low-cut gown of purple silk, her brassily auburn hair peeping from beneath a flowered satin turban. She affected the title "Madame," along with a carefully cultivated French accent, though more often than not the Billingsgate profanity of her youth slipped through her pretentious armor.

The duke found all that amusing, and he liked Antoinette's disinclination to ask questions about her patrons' transactions, pleasurable or otherwise—a discretion that grew each time her palm was greased.

Of course, the duke was not alone in his affection for Antoinette's. The crowd that night was the typical clutch of aristocrats: some, like himself, indulging in a taste for the low, others skidding to the end of a run of bad luck and unpaid debts that left them personae non grata at the better establishments.

Idiots, thought the duke, turning contemptuously from the main parlor. At his elbow, Antoinette tilted her head to one side in what, no doubt, she considered a Gallic gesture.

"What would monseigneur require?" she asked. "The play is not to your liking tonight? Perhaps another diversion—a round of piquet in a private room . . . and a lady . . ."

"Not tonight, Tony," Belfort said curtly, hitting unerringly upon the diminutive she most despised.

"As you wish, milor'. More champagne, perhaps?"

"Save it for someone a bit more desperate, my dear. No, what I require tonight is very simple."

"Only say the word, dear monseigneur."

"An introduction to the gentleman in the corner."

"That one!" Madame grimaced. "The little north country sprig? You will find scant sport there, milor'. He hasn't a feather to fly with, and he's bosky to boot—that is to say, a trifle disguised."

"I don't recall asking your opinion of the gentleman's condition, financial or otherwise. Introduce us, Tony."

"Of course," Madame said coldly, shrugging.

The object of his attention was a thin, fair-haired young man on the fringes of the crowd gathered about a lively EO game. The young gentleman's nattily tailored blue coat bespoke aspirations to high fashion; the disconsolate droop of his mouth betrayed his foul run of luck at Madame Antoinette's. Madame greeted him, wreathed in smiles.

"Oh, M'sieur Battlebourne, why the long face? Surely Milady Fortune will return before the night is done! Allow me to present a fellow admirer of the games of chance—monseigneur the duc of Belfort."

For Mr. Charles Battlebourne, just arrived from Oxford, the arrival of a genuine duke was as dazzling as a sudden shower of fireworks. It took hardly any persuasion of Belfort's to spirit the young gentleman into one of the private card rooms, where Mr. Battlebourne proceeded to lose an obscene sum to his new acquaintance.

"Another rubber?" Belfort asked smoothly, shuffling the deck and observing the nervous fidgeting and pale, furrowed brow of his companion.

"I—ah—well, I'd be honored, Duke, but it's monstrous late . . . must be abroad early tomorrow—"

"A pity. Ah, well, shall we tot up the damages?"

Mr. Battlebourne gulped. "I've had some devilish rotten luck tonight, sir. But only name the sum and I'll take care of it straightaway."

After a few swift calculations, Belfort complied. If possible Charles grew paler still, but managed, creditably, to maintain enough composure to straighten his shoulders, clear his throat, and declare: "I'm afraid I don't have such a sum with me, sir, but I will wait upon you tomorrow." He reached across to study the vowels, but the duke forestalled him.

"My dear boy," Belfort said lazily, "there's no hurry in the world between gentlemen. Take as much time as you want. In fact"—he paused, appearing to be struck by a fortunate thought—"if you can see your way clear to assisting me in a rather, er, delicate situation, we can safely call our scores settled."

"A-assist you, sir?" echoed Mr. Battlebourne, very hazy from overindulging in cheap champagne.

"If you would," Belfort said. "Your people have property near Castle Stafford, I believe you said?"

Had he said that? Mr. Battlebourne supposed he must have. He gave his head a shake to clear it. "Yes, Your Grace, but what—"

"Then I presume your family attends the Staffords' spring ball."

"Yes, yes, they have for years, cursed inconvenient affair that it is, but what does this say to the purpose, sir?"

"I've"—Belfort paused again, then leaned forward confidentially—"I've an interest in a certain young lady, lately in town, who's been 'curst difficult to run to earth. You don't know her, but I happen to know she'll be in attendance at this affair, and I can see her there. The rub is, I need an introduction to the Staffords; we aren't acquainted, unfortunately. You'll take pity on a man in, er— Cupid's snare?"

With a frank, just slightly rueful smile, the duke looked across the table at Mr. Battlebourne in the candlelight, and Mr. Battlebourne was swept with an overwhelming sense of flattery that such a grand personage needed his assistance.

He was swept, as well, with relief. The sum he had lost was so very large, and he had already visited the moneylenders twice in the past six months.

"Entirely at your sh-service, Duke," he said. Belfort smiled, and tore the vowels across.

Having settled the tipsy Mr. Battlebourne into a hack, Belfort gave a sigh of satisfaction and headed back into the main parlor. With the first faint streaks of dawn lightening the sky outside, the crowd had thinned, but a respectable number of hardened cases remained, intent upon the play. Antoinette presided over them, her affability and Frenchness a little ragged by that point in the evening. A flicker of interest lit her eyes at the duke's reappearance.

"So, monseigneur, did all proceed to your satisfaction?"

Belfort carelessly flicked open an exquisite gold-and-crystal snuffbox, taking a pinch and snapping it shut before replying. "Oh, all was most satisfactory," he said. "I've one more challenge for you— though I think it's well within your talents, Tony, dear."

"And what is that?"

"Three weeks hence I will be requiring an accommodation for a lady."

"A lady, monseigneur?"

"Yes, and not as you understand the term, my dear, so stop smirking in that vulgar fashion."

"How might I help you, milor'?" asked Antoinette, poker-faced.

"I need to know of a house frequented by the lively sort of young woman with whom you and your friends are so . . . profitably acquainted."

"To lodge a *lady* there?"

"Most astute."

"This lady." Madame cast a shrewd glance at the duke. "She is agreeable to this arrangement?"

"Would it shock you, dear Tony, if I said no?"

"No, monseigneur," Antoinette said frankly. "Only, in that case it will be more expensive."

The duke laughed, and the sound sent a prickle down even Antoinette's toughened spine. He flipped a gold sovereign upward, caught it, and tossed it to Antoinette, who nipped it neatly from the air with her right hand and tucked it safely into her ample bodice.

"That," said the duke, "for surety. The rest when the business is finished. I have every faith in you, Tony."

"I am happy to please, I'm sure, monseigneur," said Madame demurely.

The dawn glowed in a low, pinkish line above the chimney pots as Belfort strolled homeward, disdaining a chair, contemptuously dismissing a ragged linkboy. Other gentlemen might fear dark alleys and footpads, but not Belfort. He rather welcomed the prospect of a little excitement. But the streets were quiet this dawn, and he battled his ennui with delightful contemplation of his dear cousin by marriage cozily ensconced in a house of whores.

Where you belong, my dear, he thought. *You'll see what folly it was to run from me.*

Thornbeck House, the end of April

Sir Jeremy's homecoming at Thornbeck House was chaotic but sweet, with two great shaggy sheep dogs, the ostler, Mickle, Stainewick, and—last but hardly least—Susannah swarming into the drive as the chaise drew up, all relentlessly demanding his undivided attention.

"Hold!" Sir Jeremy finally bellowed. The troops fell silent; Sir Jeremy regarded them all, grinning, his hands on his hips. "Now then. Stainewick, I'll meet with you in two hours. Ned, see to the horses. Mickle, there's a pile of bags and packages to get inside; get a couple of the footmen out here, and then you can give me the news. And *you*, mouse"—he swung a delighted, giggling Susannah up and spun her in a circle—"inside with me, and tell me what you've been up to while I've been away."

She had been up to a great deal, she told him, once they had settled down in the study. She and Mrs. Wyndham were doing lessons about the Sun King. Mrs. Wyndham had shown her pictures of the beautiful palace of Versailles—could they go there and visit? Mrs. Wyndham had been.

"Been to Versailles, has she?" Sir Jeremy said thoughtfully.

"Yes, and she says the Petit Trianon is the most charming place—though *very* extravagant," Susannah added conscientiously. "It would be nice to visit, wouldn't it?"

"Yes, pet, but not at present; I'm afraid things in France are a bit tense at the moment."

"Mrs. Wyndham said that, too," Susannah said morosely.

Sir Jeremy could not resist a smile. "Cheer up, poppet; perhaps they'll sort themselves out at that meeting of their Estates-General, and then we'll see."

"What's the Estates-General?"

"Never mind," he said hastily. "You've been obeying Mrs. Wyndham, I hope?"

"Of course," Susannah said, with a scornful look. "We've been ever so busy. We've been doing history, and the globes, and penmanship, and all that. And I've been learning to cook. I wanted to for ever so long. Then I had to get the new dresses—"

"New dresses?"

"Well, I was too big for the old ones. We got my

blue muslin out, and the sleeves were—"

"We? Who was 'we'?"

"Me and Mrs. Wyndham," Susannah said patiently. "She measured me, and we found some lengths of dress goods in the attic, and Mary Lovell in the village did the sewing. This is one of them. Isn't it nice?"

Sir Jeremy duly admired the green-sprigged muslin, which did indeed set off his daughter's flying dark curls and bright eyes to a nicety. "It was most kind of Mrs. Wyndham to see to it," he said.

"Yes, it's been ever so much fun, except for just now, of course, since she's been ill. But Dr. Tolliver has fixed her up."

"I'm glad to hear that."

"She'll be back to give me lessons soon, she says." Susannah swung one foot to and fro, then spoke hesitantly. "Could she be my governess always, do you think?"

Sir Jeremy fiddled with one of the quills in the rack on the desk.

"Well, pet, she really isn't supposed to be, you know."

"But why? Doesn't she like it here?"

"It isn't a question of that, Susannah. Mrs. Wyndham isn't a governess; she's just very kindly taking on those duties for a while until someone comes to replace Miss Harte. One way or the other, she won't be teaching you forever, sweetheart."

"One way or the other? What other way?"

Sir Jeremy was rescued from a reply by Mickle, who presented himself as required, now that the luggage was safely stowed away. Sending his mutinous daughter off to work some sums before supper, Jeremy turned with some relief to his butler.

"So, Mickle! How is the household faring?"

"Very well, very well indeed, Sir Jeremy, saving your absence, of course." Mickle beamed. "I trust you find all to your satisfaction."

"I'm more than satisfied, Mickle. I hardly recognize the place. The Great Hall is transformed, for one thing. You've been busy."

"Ah well, 'twas just a matter of a good spring cleaning and replacing the hangings—"

"The hangings! That's the difference," Sir Jeremy said. "I haven't seen those hunting tapestries since my father's time."

"Well, Betty noticed them in the attics when she and Miss Clary were looking for lengths for Miss Susannah's new dresses. 'Why, these are very fine,' Betty says. I wasn't sure myself, but Miss Clary said they'd do very well with an airing and a good brushing, and she had it right."

"Hm," said his employer.

"Well, sir, the red velvet hangings *were* getting a bit worn," Mickle said, after a moment of uncompromising silence.

"No doubt. Tell me, what other domestic arrangements did Mrs. Wyndham so kindly make in my absence?"

Sir Jeremy did not seem angry, but Mickle eyed him uncertainly before going on. "Why, she didn't *arrange*, sir. Very nice-mannered, Mrs. Wyndham is. It's just that when we were in the attic, we found some other things for the hall—the silver candlesticks and that nice old carved wooden screen. But we didn't change much else, really. Except . . . the books here, sir."

"My books." Jeremy tapped his fingers in a considering way upon the leather arm of his chair, looking at the bookshelves as intently as if he had never seen them before. And in a way, he had not. The idiosyncratic jumble had been replaced by neat, dusted rows arranged by topic. His eye fell upon a grouping of histories; they appeared to be set in chronological order.

Jeremy got up from his chair.

"Are you going out, sir?" Mickle asked.

"Yes, indeed," Jeremy said. "Tell Ned to saddle up the roan. I'm paying a call at Metcalfe Farm."

9

April, thought Helen, was fading on a glorious note. She strolled along the paths of Aysgarth's flower and herb gardens, Coll the gardener's lad beside her. They surveyed with delight the final burst of daffodils and crocuses, busily taking notes on the spring planting to be done now that all chance of chilliness at long last seemed past.

The afternoon sun felt pleasantly warm upon her shoulders as Helen turned form her work for a brief, appreciative look across the slopes of the dale, which rolled away from the south end of her garden in obliging splendor.

Suddenly, her gaze became more intent as a horseman drew in sight over the horizon's farthest rise.

"I wonder—" she said, half aloud, resignedly reflecting that her vision was no longer as keen as she would have liked. Coll noticed her fixed attention and came to stand beside her.

"It looks fair like Sir Jeremy, missus," he observed helpfully.

"Oh, doesn't it? I know he was to be back yesterday evening—" The rider dipped out of view momentarily, then crested another rise, and Helen was certain. Plucking the straw chip hat from her head, she waved it with fine abandon.

"Jeremy!"

The horseman reined in, waved back, and began cantering toward them.

"Splendid!" Helen cried. "Coll, run to the house, do, and tell Ivesby to let Mr. Petherstone know!"

Coll had scarcely bounded off when the great roan and its travel-stained rider clattered up the old packhorse track to the low stone wall of the garden, upon which Helen was leaning, grinning from ear to ear.

Sir Jeremy drew in and grinned back. "Mrs. Petherstone, what a pleasure."

"Likewise, sir!" Helen laughed, retying the strings of her hat. "Oh, dear boy, you are a sight for sore eyes."

"That's a marvel," he replied, swinging down from the roan, "when you consider the abominable stuff that passed for food in Scotland. My aunt's housekeeper was the most amiable woman imaginable, but cooking, I'm afraid, was not among her skills."

"How dreadful for you, poor thing." Helen frowned. "We must have you in for some refreshment. I believe Mrs. Ivesby baked a seed cake this morning—"

"Good God, Helen, I wasn't cadging a meal!" Jeremy laughed, looping the roan's reins about the gatepost and letting himself into the garden. "Let me greet you properly before you begin badgering me about food."

"Jeremy, lad!" They turned to see William hurrying toward them. "Back at last, eh? How was the journey?"

"Smooth as could be, except for a damnable rut just south of Carlisle that cost the chaise a wheel. I lost a day there."

"Good Lord, man, come inside and rest a bit," urged William. "Mrs. Ivesby'll kill the fatted calf."

Sir Jeremy hesitated, looking, to Helen's interested eye, positively diffident. But he spoke nonchalantly enough.

"That's good of you both, but actually I must be on my way. I've a call to pay at Metcalfe Farm, and I'd best hurry if I'm to be back home by dark."

The swift, astonished gaze exchanged by Helen and William did wonders for Sir Jeremy's sangfroid. Cocking a mischievous smile at them, he doffed his hat, untying the roan and swinging back up into the saddle.

"You'll accept my apologies?" he asked.

William recovered first.

"By all means, dear boy," he said. "But you must take tea with us tomorrow, hey, and tell us all the news?"

Sir Jeremy's grin broadened. "Depend upon it." He set his heels to the horse's sides and trotted off, watched thoughtfully by William, and in loaded silence by Helen.

"Well!" she said at last.

"Well?"

"Just—just *well*." She turned an accusing look upon her spouse. "And don't act as if you aren't surprised in the least, because I won't be gammoned."

"Perish the thought," said William, taking her arm as they walked back to the house. "Of course I find it most interesting."

"Interesting? Is that all?"

"Very well—intriguing." William paused. "My dear?"

"Yes?"

"Don't meddle."

Helen shook her head impatiently. "Don't be

gooseish, love. Of course I'll be quiet as a mouse. Only—"

She paused in her turn, looking over her shoulder at the solitary horseman rapidly becoming a blur in the distance.

"Only, I do so hope it turns out splendidly for them."

The sun glowed richly across the dale as Jeremy continued toward the farm, a smile still playing about his mouth at the memory of the Petherstones' curious faces. Giving in to a wayward urge, he set his heels to the roan's sides, urging him to a gallop through the fine spring afternoon. The roan sped across a narrow green meadow, past a scattering of sheep that looked up in mild annoyance, rejoined the packhorse track for a few twists and turns up a hill, then swung off again through a thickly tangled copse and over a tiny, twisting beck, which the roan leapt easily across. They raced toward one of the low stone walls marking the boundary of Metcalfe Farm, clearing it with barely a break in stride.

They were on another strip of grazing land, a green, gently sloping meadow rising up beyond the east side of the farmhouse, and empty but for a scattering of primrose and meadow cranesbill. The weathered grey walls of the farmhouse came into view; Sir Jeremy slowed the roan to a trot and circled round to get a better view of the kitchen yard. He was rewarded with the sight of a slender figure hurrying to an outbuilding, head down, a basket swinging from one hand, the purposeful walk familiar. Even from that distance, he did not need to see the gleam of sunlight on coppery curls to know who it was. He laughed, and urged the roan forward.

Martha looked him up and down when she

opened the front door.

"Happy to see you safe home, sir," she said.

"You don't sound very happy, Martha."

"It's not my place to be happy or sad," she retorted, a martial gleam in her dark eyes. "Miss Clary will be happy to see you, I think."

"Will she? I trust all's been well here?"

"Yes, sir. All's *been* well."

He raised a sardonic brow at her. "Any reason to expect a change in that, Martha?"

"None that I can think of, I'm sure," she said, chin set stubbornly. "But I'm keeping my fingers crossed, all the same. Miss Clary's seeing to the hens, if you want to speak to her, sir."

He heard her voice through the open hen-house door as he approached with deliberate quietness.

"There, there, now, my angel, you sweet thing," she was saying. "No need to worry. Just let your Aunt Clarissa see if you've any eggs for us today. That's right. That's—Oh, you wretched beast!"

He reached the doorway in time to see Clarissa snatch her hand from the nest, squeezing a painfully pecked thumb in the folds of her apron. He leaned a shoulder against the doorway to watch her, shamelessly admiring the way in which her neatly tied apron tapes accentuated her trim waist. Her dress, a cream-colored muslin sprigged with blue flowers, looked rather old but irresistibly charming. She had not bothered to dress her hair, which hung in rich profusion down her back, secured by a blue ribbon. Her basket, with its disappointingly small stock of eggs, waited at her feet.

"Oh, don't fret, dearest," she was saying, bravely entering the ring again. "I don't mean to harm you the tiniest bit; I just need an egg or two." Cautiously she reached toward the nest again, inching her hand further into the straw underneath the af-

fronted hen, who decided with disconcerting swiftness to dive once more toward Clarissa.

"You . . . harpy!" she cried out, leaping back at
the same instant Sir Jeremy swiftly intervened,
grabbing the outraged hen, quite impervious to its
assaults upon his leather riding gloves.

"That's putting it mildly," he said. "Well, are
you going to check the nest or no?"

Clarissa, finding her mouth hanging open, rec-
ollected herself and briskly searched through the
straw. "Nothing," she said disgustedly. "And now
you've upset her so, she'll probably not lay for another two days."

"My apologies. I'll send some eggs over from
Thornbeck House." To the accompaniment of a
tuneless chorus of squawks, Sir Jeremy deposited
the hen in a ruffled heap upon its nest. "Come outside, please," he said, taking Clarissa by the hand
with equal lack of ceremony.

"Well—really!" she burst out, following him hig-
gledy-piggledy into the yard, barely managing to
rescue her basket along the way. "What in the
world do you mean, creeping up on me in such a
fashion?"

"Thank you, Mrs. Wyndham," he said, bowing
low. "Yes, indeed, I find it good to be safe home."

"Don't skirt the issue! Of course I'm happy to
see you back, but what was amiss with our front
door, may I ask?"

Infuriatingly, he was smiling at her. "My dear
Mrs. Wyndham," he said softly, "how glad I am to
find you so recovered."

She blushed, but refused to let the smile—or the
disturbingly warm expression in his eyes—distract
her. "Thank you. Now, in answer to my question—"

"In answer to your question, your front door is

functioning splendidly, as is your admirable Martha, who told me where to find you."

"Oh."

"Now that we have disposed of that point of etiquette, I have a question or two for you, Mrs. Wyndham."

"Such as?" she asked, a little breathlessly, as he advanced upon her. She took a step back.

"Such as how the devil it is you've managed to twist my household staff around your little finger—"

"I never meant to presume," she began, taking another step back.

"—plundering my attics," he went on, as though she hadn't spoken.

"Now, that I can explain—"

"—turning my Great Hall upside down—"

"That was only a spring cleaning; it *certainly* needed it, and there wasn't any harm done—"

"—inciting my daughter to go chasing off to the Continent—"

"I never suggested such a thing!" Clarissa felt the stone garden wall against her back.

"—invading my study," he said relentlessly, planting himself squarely in front of her, his hands braced against the wall on either side of her. "And scattering my books hither and yon."

"Hither and yon?" said Clarissa, in her indignation, momentarily forgetting her precarious position. "Why, it took me weeks to bring some semblance of order to your wretched study!"

"Just so. You've been very busy, Mrs. Wyndham. The staff sings your praises. Susannah quotes you with a reverence rightly reserved for Socrates. In fact"—he took her chin in one hand, tilting her half-alarmed, half-furious face up to his—"I very nearly wonder how we ever managed before you happened along."

"Don't—there is no need to make fun of me in this way, sir," Clarissa said, torn between laughter and weeping. "If I seemed to be interfering, I'm sorry. Perhaps it's best I stop visiting Thornbeck House, if it pleases you."

"Ah, but that doesn't please me," Sir Jeremy said softly, taking the egg basket from her limp fingers and setting it down on the ground. Taking her hands in his, he raised, first one, then the other, to his lips. "It doesn't please me to be in debt, as a rule, either. And I am very much in your debt, Mrs. Wyndham."

She stared up at him through a sudden blur of tears, her voice caught in her throat.

"Will you come riding with me two days from now?" he asked.

The question was so unexpected, she only blinked at him.

"You do ride?" he asked. She nodded. "There's an interesting site not far from here," continued Sir Jeremy, "an old Briton camp from the days of the Roman occupation, or so most of the folk around here believe. It would make a pleasant ride, and we would have a chance to talk at leisure. Will you come?"

"Yes," she said slowly. "Yes, I'll come."

"That's settled, then," he said, an unexpected grin lightening his face. He let go her hands and gave her back the basket. "Now that I've made sure of you, I'd best be back to Thornbeck House."

"*Made sure* of me?" Clarissa repeated, outrage flaring anew. But in two strides he had reached the horse and was out of earshot. She watched, a dangerous gleam in her eyes, as he swung himself into the saddle, saluted her jauntily, and cantered away.

It was sunny enough when they started out in the morning of the appointed day, although Clarissa cast a wary glance upward at the clouds gathering in the western sky.

But she refused to let anything dampen her enjoyment of the outing, giving herself up to the pleasure of being in the saddle again, on a beautiful, dainty black mare from the Thornbeck House stables. "Coo-eee, Starlight!" she whispered to the horse, which, exquisitely responsive, quickened its gait immediately. Clarissa laughed delightedly and turned to smile at Sir Jeremy, trotting up behind her on his roan.

"She's a treasure," she exclaimed.

"One of our own. A half sister to this great brute, if you can believe it. I suppose I should have sold her—she's too small for me, and Susannah's far too young to ride her—but I couldn't part with her, when it came to it."

"Well, I'm fortunate indeed you did not." Clarissa turned her attention back to the terrain, which was getting trickier. He watched her, slim and erect in a dashingly severe habit of royal blue, the ruffled white stock providing the only splash of contrast. He was not surprised to see that she was an elegant and excellent rider, her hands light, her seat good. Odd how much she reminded him of accredited beauties, of Caroline and her set, and yet how little. For one thing, he could never have imagined Caroline setting foot in a hen house.

The very thought surprised a laugh from him, and Clarissa glanced curiously his way.

"Never mind," he said. "We're nearly there."

They had come to the lip of a steep slope, the hill falling sharply away from the side of the track. Running along the base of the hill was a smoothly worn groove in the grassy earth, its contours clearly too regular to be an occurrence of nature. The shadowed line ran intermittently through the valley, parts of it worn down, but much of it still visible for hundreds of yards. They dismounted and tethered the horses to a tree, wandering down the track to look more closely.

"A fortification? Whose?" Clarissa asked.

"Ours," Sir Jeremy replied. "Well, Brigante tribesmen, to be precise. The idea was to hold the hills against the Romans, you see."

"I suppose it was folly to imagine they could overcome the legions." Clarissa paused thoughtfully. "Or maybe not. There must have been tremendous effort and skill involved in building that dike. They can't have been an ignorant lot."

"That's been my point exactly," said Sir Jeremy warmly. "We've been taking the word of the Romans on these things, but whose side, after all, were they on?" He stopped, somewhat abashed. "Your pardon. It's a particular hobbyhorse of mine, I'm afraid."

"Not at all. I've always thought the Romans a dreadful lot of snobs."

He laughed, and offered her his arm. "We can walk along the ridge a short way, and then we'll reach a footpath down to the valley. It's not very difficult, and there's a stone circle a little way south of here: an old Celtic monument, the local folk say. I've always found it rather mysterious. But you should see for yourself."

Both of them were accustomed to long walks; the path did not prove difficult. It snaked down the hillside, affording a magnificent view of the valley cupped in the bowl of the newly green hills. More clouds and mist were materializing to the west; the fine sunlight of the morning was fast fading away. They paused at the bottom to catch their breath. Sir Jeremy looked rueful. "Not precisely a fashionable outing, I'm afraid."

"That would be a pity, had I been interested in a fashionable outing."

"Aren't you?" he asked, looking at her speculatively. "I shouldn't be surprised."

"Much as I hate to disappoint you, I lost my taste for such things a long time ago."

"Really? And how did that come about?"

She concentrated for a moment on negotiating the path. "I placed my trust unwisely," she said finally. "I had met some of what you would probably call the fashionable set, and I thought they were amusing but harmless. I'd no idea it was possible to be both amusing and harmful, you see."

"It seems you were unfortunate in your choice of friends, Mrs. Wyndham."

"I had only one friend in London," Clarissa said flatly. "The rest were a series of social arrangements."

"And your husband?"

She pulled herself with an effort from her memories, and spoke cautiously. "My husband was an invalid for much of the time we spent in London. When he was well, he liked town life immensely. I suppose he thought I would also. It wasn't his fault that I was . . . unsuited to fashionable pursuits." She looked up at him. "It's odd. As a girl in the country I dreamed of going to London—seeing the sights, reading all the books I'd like, going to the theatre any night I chose. And then I arrived and discovered that the sights were for bumpkins, books were for bluestockings, and one went to the theatre to be seen, never to see."

The words had come out in a rush; now she looked away toward the hills, embarrassed at her candor.

His voice cut across her thoughts, a reflective, almost uncertain note in it.

"You've got it almost exactly right, Clarissa. Amusement is all-important there—only, it must be taken in the prescribed fashion." He broke off on a harsh laugh. "As you've probably guessed, I speak from experience."

By now they had reached the circle, a broken line of low, weather-beaten stones whose silhouette had been etched before them against the greying sky as they made their way up the valley. Sir Jeremy stepped inside the circlet of rocks; Clarissa followed, a trifle hesitantly.

He looked over his shoulder and smiled. "You're superstitious?"

"Not exactly," she hedged. "But I've read enough about such places to be properly respectful."

"Well, I think any baleful Druid spirits were laid to rest a long time ago." He indicated one smoothly worn stone for her to sit upon, and seated himself beside her. "Sometimes I wonder," he said thoughtfully, "if you've any idea how unusual you are."

Clarissa looked down at her hands, suddenly shy. "I'm not so amazing," she said. "I just had the opportunity to read more than most girls. My great-aunt said it quite spoilt me, in fact."

"Did she? I suppose she thought the only ideas you required in your head concerned dance cards and dress patterns. She'd have been well pleased with my wife." At Clarissa's startled look of inquiry, he gave a rueful laugh.

"You talked, before, about speaking from experience," she said carefully. "Is that indeed the case? Did you find London—" She stopped. "Oh, never mind."

"How uncharacteristically poor-spirited of you, Mrs. Wyndham," he drawled, stretching his long legs out before him. "It was a fair question. Yes, I too found life in London disagreeable, much to the dismay of my wife. I don't want to be unjust to Caroline, mind. She was never empty-headed, only single-minded in her social ambition. Our marriage conveyed her a number of advantages: the title, the family lineage, the venerable country manor. The only drawback was me."

He had begun in a level, dispassionate voice, but as he continued, a bitter, familiar irony crept into his words. "I was bored to tears chasing round with her from soiree to soiree; she was bored to tears with politics and philosophy. It was a disaster from the start." Another pause. "Well, not quite from the start. We began wildly in love; we were both very young and therefore convinced everything could be smoothed over with a little effort. But as time went on, we quarreled more often; by the time Susannah was born, we had as modish a marriage as one could wish for. Caroline had her social pursuits; I had my translating work—"

"Susannah told me you were with the Foreign Office," Clarissa ventured.

"Yes. An old school friend of my father's secured me the position—very minor but interesting enough, translating and summarizing dispatches from Spain and Portugal."

"So you do speak Portuguese. I saw the grammar in your study." Clarissa was diverted momentarily.

"Portuguese," Jeremy said, "French as well, of course, and Spanish—that only passably. Languages and history were always what I liked best."

"Had you thought of living abroad?" she asked.

"Oh, it certainly crossed my mind; the opportunity no doubt would have come in time. But Caroline was loth to leave London, so I let it lie. We were content enough, once we'd decided to lead separate lives."

His bleak expression saddened her more than his prosaic words as he continued.

"After she—well, afterward, the most sensible

thing seemed to be to come back here. There wasn't any point to remaining in London."

"But your work mattered, surely?" Clarissa felt a need to break the awkward silence that ensued.

"At the time, nothing mattered except closing that particular chapter." His tone brooked no further questions. As if sensing her startled discomfort, he added, "Then, too, I had obligations here. My father had died shortly after I married Caroline; the estate was crying out for closer supervision. And it seemed a good place for Susannah to grow up." He sighed. "Sometimes I've wondered if I could have done things differently with Caroline; tried harder to keep her happy, to understand her—"

"Oh, no doubt you drove her to distraction," Clarissa said with deliberate lightness, wondering yet again about the circumstances of Caroline's demise, but sensing a barrier as strong as it was invisible. "But I don't think one can ever accomplish much with wondering how to do things differently. We are all of us so much wiser about our old mistakes—even as we stumble ahead making new ones."

He laughed at that, but his expression turned serious as he studied Clarissa. "Don't we, though!" he said. "Are you my next mistake, I wonder?"

She searched for a suitable reply, and found nothing.

"I've told you more in the last ten minutes than I've told anyone in the last eight years," he said, his eyes narrowed thoughtfully upon her. "And you're still a mystery to me. Who you are, where you come from—I know these things, yet I don't know them; or at least, they don't seem to add up. You've the bearing of a countess and a bluestocking's education; you dance as though you belong at Versailles—which, I hear, you've visited. What in God's name, I wonder, are you doing on a small and not particularly productive farm in the dales of Yorkshire?"

So little had escaped his notice, all those weeks. She longed to trust him, but could not. She had come so far, and was so close to her freedom; should she not simply keep her secret to herself for the short time remaining? And once she was free to tell him, would he understand? He had heard—and believed—every notorious tale about the duchess of Belfort. Would he believe the duchess herself? She dared not put it to the test until she could face him as a woman of independent means, not as a helpless fugitive.

"There is no mystery," she said slowly. "I know that's how it appears, but there are explanations for everything that vexes you so. It will be resolved soon, and then I can tell you everything. In the meantime"—she raised her head and looked him in the eye—"I can say that I have neither meant nor done any harm by coming here as I did and living here as I have. And I have never been so happy as I have been these past few months."

They stared at each other in silence, and it seemed the world around them had turned very still, but for the wind that played about them, whipping a strand of hair across Clarissa's cheek. He reached out and tucked it back into place.

"Nor I," he said, breaking the silence at last and gathering her into his arms. For a long moment they clung together on their perch on the ancient stone.

"Are you a witch, I wonder?" he said, raising his head after a while. "You make me forget all my resolutions. You've only to look at me with those great eyes of yours and I don't care a whit what I know or don't know—good God, how I remember the way you looked at me the day we met! You were trying so hard to be polite, but one look into your eyes and I knew the truth. You could cheerfully have murdered me."

"I was so angry." She laughed shakily, resting her head in the hollow of his shoulder. "I thought you rude, overbearing—"

"Overbearing? Me? When you were ruthlessly cataloguing my faults and ordering me to change my ways?"

"If only you knew how many times I cursed my horrid temper," she replied. "It was bad of me to be so harsh with you that day. I spoke out of turn."

"No, you did not," he said soberly. "You only spoke the truth. Which was why I had to be so abominable to you, of course."

"Of course!" she said with mock indignation. "Then all the time you were so . . ."

"Arrogant? Brusque? Autocratic?" he suggested helpfully.

"All of those things—and worse! Were you really just acting out of pique?"

"No," he said unexpectedly. "I was falling in love with you."

And as she looked up at him, her mouth suddenly dry, the first raindrops began to pelt them, and the restless winds ushered in what turned out to be a truly momentous downpour.

They took shelter a mile northward, having scrambled up the ridge, retrieved the unsettled horses, and made all possible speed through violent sheets of rain and wind to an abandoned farmhouse. To Clarissa's eyes, it seemed a doubtful refuge. The main portion of the house was built in the resolute grey stone rectangle so common in the north; a wing had been added at some point, and its roof had begun to crumble. The doors hung drunkenly on worn hinges.

To her relief, the main part of the house was reasonably solid, if coated by the dust of the ages. It was also dry, something she could not have said of herself. Sir Jeremy was in somewhat better case, having been afforded a degree of protection by his greatcoat. As he went to see to the horses, Clarissa stood for a moment by the door, disconsolately watching rivulets of rainwater flow from her sodden jacket into puddles at her feet. She gave herself a mental shake, shrugged out of her jacket, and removed her hat, by now a dripping ruin. At least her white linen shirtwaist was reasonably dry. Her damp skirts spread about her in a dark blue pool as she sank, exhausted, to sit on the floor, her back propped against the wall.

Sir Jeremy, having made the horses as secure as possible in the last solid corner of the tumbledown wing, strode back into the main room and, after a glance at Clarissa, muttered, "We have to do something about getting you warm."

Clarissa restrained a tart inquiry as to just how he proposed to do that—fortunately, as it turned out, for Sir Jeremy was not without resources. He discarded his coat, drew flint and tinder from his saddlebags, and went briskly to a corner of the room, where kindling and logs lay neatly stacked against the wall.

"What in the world is that doing there?" she asked in astonishment.

"I put it there," he replied with annoying nonchalance, as if collecting firewood in derelict farmhouses was a cherished pastime.

"That's fortunate indeed, but why?"

"I often ride this way," he said, not looking up from his task. "It's come in handy once or twice."

All at once, he seemed to have become once more the brusque master of Thornbeck House, and she fell silent. But before long he had a blazing fire going in the hearth, and Clarissa, by now thoroughly chilled, drew closer to its warmth as Sir Jeremy began searching again through the saddlebags.

She lifted her hands to her damp chignon, yanking the pins from her hair and letting it tumble over her shoulders. Lacking a comb, she raked her fingers through it, hoping the fire's warmth would dry it before long. *Lord, what a sight I must look*, she thought ruefully, huddling on the floor, and resting her chin on her knees as she gazed into the flames.

Something in the quality of the silence caused her to look up after a few moments. Sir Jeremy was looking at her, and the unguarded hunger in his eyes caused her breath to catch in her throat. The firelight threw flickering shadows over the strong planes of his face; without the folds of greatcoat and jacket, his shirtsleeves and riding breeches only emphasized the lean power of his frame. She found herself put in mind of a panther as she met his gaze—all that lazy coiled grace and those eyes, those striking eyes gleaming in the firelight . . .

His voice wrenched her out of her spell.

"I'm going into the other room. He got abruptly to his feet. "Call out if there's anything you need, though we probably won't have to stay here long—"

"Why are you going?" she asked.

He paused in buckling the saddlebags shut to stare down at her. "You know why," he said.

"Perhaps I don't," she said, amazed at her own words. "Perhaps I should like to hear you tell me."

In a heartbeat, so swiftly she had no time to react, he dropped the saddlebags and knelt before her, gripping her shoulders painfully. "Do you want the words?" he said harshly. "How politely do you want them, my beautiful widow? Shall I explain—at your leisure, of course—how the sight of you with your hair down in the firelight is driving me stark, raving mad? Shall I say, 'Your pardon, Mrs. Wyndham, but if I remain any longer I'll be tempted to take you right here and now'? Is that what you would like me to tell you?''

His hands were warm and hard against the thin lawn of her shirtwaist; she could barely hear her own voice through the pounding of her heart. But she spoke steadily. "I wanted the truth."

"The truth?" he echoed—and with a sound that was half laugh, half groan, he crushed his mouth to hers. The violence of his embrace rocked her back upon her heels; as she flung her head back, he rained hard, urgent kisses down her throat, making her gasp aloud in mingled shock and pleasure. He raised his head to look down at her. "Is that truthful enough?" he demanded.

Wordlessly she stretched out her arms to him. With a muffled groan, he pulled her to him again. Slowly, as if by doing so he could memorize her features, he traced his lips over her temple, cheekbone, the corner of her mouth, and finally reclaimed her lips in a searing kiss, his hands buried in her thick hair. She wrapped her arms tightly round his waist to hug him closer, feeling the muscled warmth of him through his linen shirt. In the warm, dim light that formed an island for them in the shadowed room, she looked up into his lean, dark face and saw that the urbanely cynical gentleman had utterly vanished, replaced with this fierce and mysterious stranger.

"You've had fair warning," he said hoarsely, holding her slightly away from him with a fierce, desperate resolve.

"Too late for warnings," she murmured, cupping his face in her hands, feeling the silkiness of his hair between her fingers.

She heard a ghost of a laugh, felt his arms tighten around her again. "It probably is, at that," he said.

"It seems you have the soul of a gambler instead of a governess, Mrs. Wyndham."

"Perhaps I do," she replied, half to herself, thinking of the secret that still lay between them. She began to pull away, but his hold did not relax.

"Faintheart," he said, the tenderness in his voice belying the mockery of the word. Slowly, she leaned back upon the coverlet his coat made for them. His movements followed, his body covering hers but held apart as he raised himself slightly, his arms placed on either side of her.

"Oh, Lord, you're beautiful," he said softly, lowering his mouth to hers again. And it seemed to Clarissa that this moment, unbelievable and unsuitable as it was, made perfect sense; as if the events that had unsettled her life over the past several months had resolved themselves into a final and logical pattern.

This, she thought. *Of course.*

She shivered with delight as his hands caressed her waist and moved upward; with an almost desperate concentration she returned kiss for kiss, lost momentarily to all notion of her surroundings. Anything at all might have happened had not a sudden, blinding flash of lightning illuminated the dusty room, followed swiftly by a deafening crack of thunder that startled them apart.

They stayed that way for a moment, their breathing the only sound aside from the insistent patter of the rain.

"That was a near thing," Clarissa managed at last, shakily.

"Yes," said Sir Jeremy. "And I am not, my love, referring to the lightning." As her cheeks burned with a fiery blush, he shook his head and smiled ruefully at her. "Don't," he said simply. "But I think it really is time I left you alone. You need to rest. In fact, we both could use some rest."

"Yes," she said, standing and trying as discreetly as possible to shake out her skirts. "Yes, I think that would be wise."

He paused. "I'll leave you now." Picking up the greatcoat, he settled it around her, shaking his head at her protest. "I'll do well enough. Try to get some sleep, love."

Dropping a final, swift kiss upon her lips, he disappeared into the other room.

Love. It was only a word, she reminded herself, but she settled back on the floor into the folds of the coat, strangely reassured. The rain continued its monotonous drumming upon the roof, lulling her into drowsiness. With the flames of the fire blurring before her eyes, she gave herself up to sleep at last.

"Oh . . . damn!"

Trying and failing for the third time to do up one of the row of tiny buttons that fastened her riding jacket, Clarissa gave in to her temper. Now that the rain had ceased, anger seemed her safest refuge.

"Trouble?" inquired Sir Jeremy politely, looking up from his task of putting out the fire.

"Not at all; I was being silly," Clarissa said shortly, turning away.

Watching the stiff, defensive line of her back, Sir Jeremy grimaced before bending his attention once more to his task. He gave her a few moments, and when progress was clearly not in the offing, he sighed and crossed over to her, gently turning her to him.

"Love, you're making a hash of that; it won't go any faster with your being stubborn about it. Let me help."

She looked up at the endearment, but dropped her eyes again and stayed silent as he helped to fasten the jacket. A corner of his mouth quirked sardonically at the sight of her bent head, the hair that had earlier tumbled about her like a tawny waterfall now ruthlessly twisted into as severe a knot as she could manage.

When she stepped back swiftly as the task was complete, murmuring a constrained thank you, he decided he'd had enough.

"The saddlebags are by the wall," he said, as casual as if Kit the stableboy were standing there. "Take them outside, will you?"

Color flared in her cheeks. She bit her lip and marched outside with the saddlebags. A distinct *thunk* resounded from the dooryard, and Jeremy grinned.

Clarissa stalked back inside. "Is there anything else?" she said with dangerous meekness.

"Well . . ." He appeared to consider for a moment. "There is one thing, now that I think of it. Will you marry me?"

She stood frozen, and spoke without thinking. "You don't want to do that."

"On the contrary, I want very much to do that."

"Do you?" she flashed, anger sudden and fierce within her. "What would Miss Stafford think, I wonder?"

"Amabel?" He looked thunderstruck. "What are you talking about?" Then his eyes narrowed thoughtfully. "Idiot that I am," he said. "I now begin to understand why you flew into such a rage at the Christmas ball. Just what, my love, do you consider to be the case between the Honorable Amabel and myself?"

Clarissa's temper faded; her shoulders slumped. "It wasn't just the Christmas ball. She visited me a few days ago and gave me to understand congratulations are in order."

"Are they?" Sir Jeremy said wrathfully. "Perhaps they are for Miss Amabel, but any thought that *I* should be included in the celebrations is conjecture on her part. How could you think otherwise?"

"Well," Clarissa said, trying to keep a level head in a swirl of sudden joy, "you have paid particular attention to her—at the Christmas ball especially."

To her indignation, he grinned. "I rather hoped you'd notice that. You were the most maddening woman that night, flitting off with every eligible in the company."

"I wasn't flitting off! And if you think my conduct in any way compared with your shameless flirting with Miss Stafford—"

"Good God!" Sir Jeremy interrupted. "That was why you gave me that setdown!"

"Of course!" sputtered Clarissa. "Between Lady Charlotte's telling me she had high hopes of you and Miss Stafford making a match, and you—you—"

"Never mind; I remember what I did. And how I got my just deserts! But you're right about one thing, love. It was shameless, because it meant nothing—nothing except that you were driving me to distraction. Will you accept my solemn word, Clarissa, that the Honorable Amabel is the daughter of an old friend whom I've known for ages, nothing more or less? For that is all, believe me."

Clarissa looked reluctantly into his face, and what she saw there reassured her.

"I think I do," she said, a smile tugging at her mouth, a happiness she hardly dared acknowledge making her heart beat faster. "Still, I don't think you really want to marry me. I mean, you don't want it for yourself." She swallowed painfully. "You're asking because you feel you ought."

With a sigh, Jeremy drew her toward a dusty settle and sat, pulling her down beside him. "One thing you'll learn about me, love"—he raised a hand as she began to interrupt—"is that I've never taken kindly to doing things I don't want to do."

"But after—" She stopped, blushing fiercely.

"One of the many reasons for my uncharacteristic attempt at nobility an hour ago, dearest, was the probability that you would jump to this very conclusion." He smiled crookedly at her. "You do have a way of overcoming my resolutions."

She answered the pressure of the hands that grasped hers. He was setting her thoughts spinning, but she knew she must try to think clearly. "It is just like you to say that," she managed to say. "But you had no thoughts of marriage an hour ago."

"Didn't I, Madam Mind-reader?" Nothing seemed to shake him. "You've a mighty low opinion of me. What would you say if I told you I wanted to marry you an hour ago, and an hour before that"—he was lowering his face closer to hers—"and any number of hours before that?"

With a sound between a laugh and a sob, she put her hands upon his shoulders, holding him a little distance away. "I should say you'd run mad, especially with some of the rows we've had."

"Well, you might be right," he said with mock thoughtfulness. "I think I started going mad the minute I saw you in that little parlor, looking like a schoolgirl and lecturing me like a schoolmistress. Clarissa"—he suddenly turned serious—"this is a question I never thought to ask again; I am not asking it lightly, or out of mere obligation. I cannot accept your refusing me for a missish scruple." He sighed again. "But if you don't love me, that's something I shall have to understand."

"Oh, stop being an idiot," Clarissa said, sudden hot tears blurring her eyes. "Of course I love you."

That was more than enough for Sir Jeremy, who put a swift end to all conversation.

A while later, her head resting comfortably upon his shoulder, Clarissa reopened the discussion. "You've said you don't know anything about me—"

"I know enough that matters," he replied. "I know you're strong and clever and brave; I know you've a devilish prickly sense of honor; I know you've worn yourself to a shadow worrying about a child who by all rights has no claims upon you." He pulled away to look into her troubled face. "And of course I know you're afraid of something. I wish you'd find it in yourself to trust me, love."

"I do trust you," she began. "But there are others I don't trust. I don't want you drawn into—"

"Drawn into what?"

But she had regained command of herself. "It doesn't matter," she said firmly. "There's nothing to concern you; really, there isn't."

"Where you're involved, I'm very much concerned," he replied. "But I know better than to try persuading you once you've got that look on your face."

"Thank you—I think!" She turned serious. "Only a week or two more, and I'll have everything sorted out. Then we—"

"We? Should I take that as a yes?"

"Yes," she said, fitting easily into his arms once more. It would all work out. It had to. "Oh, yes."

10

The Staffords' spring ball could be called a triumph of will—specifically, Lady Stafford's—over such obstacles as fickle weather, a grumpy husband, and a general belief that the beginning of May was a terrible time for such an affair. But Lady Stafford persevered and prevailed, even triumphed—from the exquisite flower arrangements to the excellent food and wine to the annual bevy of guests, not one of whom could imagine disappointing her.

Not surprisingly, Lady Stafford was difficult company in the days immediately preceding the ball—when her family saw her at all, that is. She would emerge from fraught conferences with her butler and housekeeper, only to bark orders at her husband and daughter. Small wonder the viscount and the Honorable Amabel looked unenthusiastic when Lady Stafford flung open the door to the breakfast room one morning.

Lady Stafford tackled her husband first, without preamble or elaboration.

"Wear the new black coat and all your orders, mind!"

Lord Stafford, whose attire had never varied in

183

fifteen years of May balls, glared at his wife over his newspaper and preserved silence.

"Amabel!" Lady Stafford turned her sights on her daughter, pouring tea from the pot on the sideboard. "What are you wearing, child?"

"I thought my new figured satin; the rose gown."

"Unsuitable." Ignoring her daughter's outraged look, Lady Stafford marched to the window to assess the weather. "Fine day. Pray the weather holds. Now, what are we to do with you?"

"No doubt you'll contrive something, Mama," said Amabel sulkily.

"Not without help from you, miss," replied Lady Stafford, for whom irony had no place three days before a May ball. "I've a feeling the white and silver will do very well."

"Oh, Mama." Amabel reverted to wistful gentleness. "I really thought something stronger, more striking . . ."

"The trouble with you, child, is your refusal to accept that the most striking color can be no color at all. Really, I'm out of patience with you. Leave the jewel-box shades to women like Mrs. Wyndham; now, she can carry it off—"

"Indeed she can," said Lord Stafford, suddenly perking up.

"Hush, Rupert. But a young gel like you oughtn't to go gadding about like a peacock. This fascination with strong colors is positively vulgar. Wear the white and silver."

"Oh, very well."

"And no last-minute changes, mind! I won't be too distracted to notice."

Amabel, with great dignity, ignored her mother and raised her cup delicately to her lips.

Lady Stafford laughed. "Don't put on airs with me, miss! But there, be a good girl and you shall wear my diamonds to the ball. You're a young girl, true, but the set is in excellent taste and I think you can wear them with the proper air. What do you say?"

"Thank you very much, Mama," said Amabel, brightening considerably.

"Well, I must be off. Don't forget; the white and silver."

Off sailed Lady Stafford, leaving her husband and daughter exasperated over cups of cold tea.

Helen looked at her morning caller with pleasure and curiosity.

"You look absolutely radiant, Clarissa," she said. "I wish you would tell me your secret."

Clarissa smiled back as Helen embraced her, thinking that "secret" summed up matters nicely— much against Sir Jeremy's inclinations.

"Wait until after the Staffords' crush to make an announcement?" he had asked with a hint of irritation, during a brief conference in the parlor at Metcalfe Farm. "Is there a significance to the date that escapes me?"

As it happened, the ball fell one day before the date upon which Clarissa expected to have her inheritance restored to her. And she had been seized with a superstitious dread of announcing her happiness before she was absolutely free of Belfort's grasp.

But of course she could not say that. She had embarked upon a rather weak explanation, when Jeremy offered an unexpected lifeline.

"I've an idea, love, that could answer very well. Why not announce it *during* the ball? I'll drop a word that night in Lord Rupert's ear—it'll be just the sort of thing to tickle him. What do you think?"

After a moment's thought, she had decided that she liked that very well, and so they had agreed.

What difference, after all, could one day make?

Now there was Helen, looking at Clarissa quizzically.

"There's no secret, Helen," Clarissa said lightly. "It's the fine Yorkshire air, of course. Haven't you always sung its praises to me?"

"Fiddlesticks, Clary," said Helen, but without real heat. "Don't think to bamboozle me. You look like a cat that's been in the cream, and no mistake, but never mind! If you won't tell, you won't tell. So come inside, do, and describe what you're planning to wear to Castle Stafford."

And, quite comfortable with each other, they made their way to Helen's morning room and some of Mrs. Ivesby's excellent biscuits.

Charles Battlebourne struggled in the grip of a queasiness only partly attributable to the combination of rutted roads and a poor stomach. After all, the duke's traveling chaise was well sprung and commodious, and they had not drunk so very much at the post inn the night before. But Mr. Battlebourne was unsettled by something in the birdlike glitter of his companion's eyes, half concealed by the lazy droop of his eyelids.

Mr. Battlebourne was hardly a deep thinker, as his brother the captain could have attested, but it had occurred to him over the past week that there were few ready explanations for the duke's interest in him. What, after all, did a fashionable nobleman and he have in common? When this thought arose, he would take a nervous swallow from his pocket flask.

He did so now, and held the flask out questioningly toward the duke, who waved it away.

Charles capped the flask and stowed it in his greatcoat pocket.

"Devilish thirsty work, traveling," he offered.

The duke said nothing. Charles took a restless look out the window, wishing for the fiftieth time that he had made better use of his brief sojourn at Oxford. Perhaps then he could have spun some fascinating conversation with which to while away an hour or two. But his reading had been limited to the "Guide to the Turf," and the duke did not seem very interested in horses. Charles repressed a sigh and looked at his companion. The duke appeared to have fallen asleep.

In truth, Belfort was repressing a strong urge to strangle the young clodpole beside him and reflecting pleasurably upon the charming scene of discovery which awaited his cousin-in-law.

He wasn't yet sure how it would be accomplished. Much depended upon the arrangements at Castle Stafford and the size of the guest list. Ever canny, Belfort had advised Battlebourne that in this delicate affair it was best that his identity remain a secret. His unwitting accomplice had obligingly written his family that he was traveling north with his old school friend Mr. Devereaux, and would it be inconvenient for Mr. Devereaux to attend the ball at Castle Stafford?

It was no trouble at all, of course. Mr. Devereaux was, in fact, invited to stay with the Battlebournes for as long as he wished, an offer Belfort was quick to decline. He would put up at the Boar in York, thank you very much, and Battlebourne could return to the bosom of his rustic relatives.

Belfort was well pleased with himself. But with cool calculation, he knew he must not let complacence betray him into a mistake before the game was played out. He would wait until the hour was late enough, the crush large enough, that he could slip in unnoticed. He would find her and watch for a while, and see what dalliances she was permitting herself in this godforsaken hole-in-the-wall.

There had been talk, in his reports, of a country-squire suitor; further inquiry into the gentleman's affairs had yielded some fascinating information. How diverting if madam duchess had cast her affections in that direction! He would see.

But at the last, he would get her to himself, and she would pay. There was a bottle of laudanum in his valise to ensure her cooperation, if need be. . . .

The day before the Castle Stafford ball, Sir Jeremy had just wound up a morning of writing and an hour of business with Stainewick when there came a tap on the study door, followed by Mickle's appearance.

"Oh, I'm sorry, Sir Jeremy! I thought you were done. I'll be back later."

"No need," said Sir Jeremy. "Stainewick and I were about to finish."

"Just so, sir," said Stainewick. "Although there is the matter of that letter to old Wright about raising the fee at the mill."

"Lord, I'd forgotten!" Sir Jeremy grinned suddenly. "You have my authorization to let the matter go to perdition for today."

Stainewick looked surprised, then allowed an answering smile to break across his austere face. "Very good, Sir Jeremy," he said, and took his leave.

That left Sir Jeremy and Mickle, who, characteristically, hesitated over what he had to say.

"Well, sir, there's been some discussion downstairs," he began.

"Discussion?" repeated his amused employer. "Upon what topic?"

"Upon . . . upon the topic of Miss Clarissa, sir," said Mickle, reddening under Sir Jeremy's interested scrutiny. "While you were away in Scotland, she was most gracious, sir. Kind as could be to

Miss Susannah, and very helpful in general to all of us, very helpful indeed, if I may say so. And—"

"Mickle, what brought this on? Not that I disagree, mind."

"It's—well, it's that we understand Miss Clarissa is leaving us soon—"

"Leaving?"

"Have I spoken out of turn?" Mickle said anxiously. "She mentioned to Cook as how she wouldn't be able to teach Miss Susannah much longer . . ."

So Clary had let that slip, eh? Sir Jeremy relaxed, smiling to himself.

"We got to talking about it, and, sir, we'd like to all give her a present to remember us by, if that wouldn't be too forward."

Sir Jeremy was impressed, touched, and slightly exasperated. This was what came of nonsensical secret engagements, and so he would tell Clarissa the next time he got her alone!

"No, Mickle, I don't think it would be forward at all," he temporized.

"Miss Susannah thought she might like a book. Do you agree, sir?"

"Oh, is my daughter a member of the delegation as well?" Sir Jeremy was secretly proud. "Well, a book would be most appropriate." Mickle continued to eye him hopefully. "And I'd be happy to advise you on selecting one."

"Thank you, Sir Jeremy!" At last Mickle looked reassured. "We're all that grateful."

He hurried from the room, leaving Sir Jeremy to drop his head in his hands and give way to helpless laughter.

Martha had dressed Clarissa for scores of balls, rout parties, and drums. She had combed out coiffures, positioned flowers, and pressed out flounces in the opulent suite at Belfort House in London; in the airy, elegant Queen's Room at Belfort Park; in any number of lovely chambers at well-appointed houses.

On the evening of the Castle Stafford ball, Martha and her mistress were making do with a rather small, very old mirror perched upon a chest of drawers; Martha angled the glass this way and that, as the situation demanded, for a better view. Thinking of the tall cheval glass in its polished ebony frame at Belfort House, Martha sighed wistfully. Not that Miss Clary was noticing. Martha could have laid soot and sacking for her to wear that night and Miss Clary wouldn't have blinked an eye, such was the state she was in.

This was not entirely fair to Clarissa. She had given a good deal of thought to what she would wear that night, with a joy and anticipation so strong, she was almost afraid.

Was it dangerous to feel so much happiness? Yet she wouldn't have changed a thing, even if she could have. Jeremy's calm certainty, as much as his tenderness, were irresistible, she thought with a secret half-smile. The sheer audacity of the man, with his matter-of-fact declaration after all those enigmatic weeks!

I had to be so abominable . . . I was falling in love with you.

She laughed aloud at the memory, earning an exasperated look from Martha, who was shaking out the folds of the ball gown draped over the wardrobe door.

"Will you put on your dress now, Miss Clary? We've not much more time."

"Oh, don't fuss, Martha," said Clarissa, but sweetly. Nothing could have upset her that evening. She lifted her arms, to be surrounded by the

soft whispering of silk and gauze. Martha, lacing
the bodice and pinning a simple nosegay of flowers
into the corsage of foamy Dresden lace, looked
sharply at her mistress but held her peace.

When the last adjustments were made, however,
and Clarissa turned to face the awkwardly placed
mirror, Martha was compelled to break her silence.
"My word, Miss Clary!"

The dress was glowing and gossamer, a bright
variation of the simple, flowing muslin gowns
made all the rage by France's queen. A filmy layer
of apricot silk gauze, embroidered in green and
gold, parted to reveal a slip of darker gold satin.
Green ribbons caught back the deep flounces of the
sleeves and trimmed the edging of the overskirt; a
green sash wound about Clarissa's slender waist.
The colors were strong and a touch exotic, and
Martha privately had wondered whether the gown,
ordered just before the old duke's death for a rout
that Clarissa had never attended, was not a bit too
daring. But the warmth and vibrance perfectly
suited her mistress.

"Is something wrong?" Clarissa asked. "I knew
it! You think green is all wrong for the sash, don't
you?"

"No, ma'am," Martha said, clearing her throat.
"Green is perfect. I don't think I've ever seen you
in better looks."

"Why, Martha!" Clarissa turned from the mirror.

"Well, it's true," Martha said, covering her emo-
tional pride with an injured sniff, and bending to
make a quick adjustment to a wayward ribbon on
Clarissa's skirt. Glancing up, she hesitated. "Miss
Clary—"

"Yes?"

Martha looked down again. "Never mind,
ma'am. I think I hear the Petherstones' carriage.
We'd best get you downstairs, ma'am."

It was not her place to ask questions, Martha reminded herself, having seen her mistress into the carriage, securely wrapped in a taffeta cloak, with gloves and reticule at the ready. Not that Martha really had to ask what ailed Miss Clary—not after John Fothergill had reported a similar state of affairs at Thornbeck House.

"My sister's girl is th' third housemaid there," he had explained to Martha. "Says they haven't seen the master so merry in years! Happen you know why that's so, Martha?"

"Happen I don't," Martha had replied tartly, in as close to a setdown as she ever had dealt to the abashed Mr. Fothergill, who quickly begged pardon. Not even to him would she gossip about Miss Clary.

Something had been in the air for several weeks, and it seemed to be coming on to the boil that night. Well, in all likelihood it was foolish to worry so. If only she could have put from her mind that other tale John Fothergill had told—about the strange man in the village asking after Miss Clary a few weeks before. Surely John had got it wrong.

All the same, Martha hoped Miss Clary knew what she was about that night.

Whatever one's state of mind upon arrival at the Castle Stafford ball, no guest remained immune to the effect experienced when one swept up the shallow, elegantly proportioned staircase and stopped . . . to overlook the great ballroom, whose polished inlaid floor winked back at the blazing chandeliers, its black-and-white squares like some gigantic, fanciful chessboard upon which the brilliantly clad figures of the guests played out a graceful match.

It was a sight to take one's breath away, and Clarissa, who had long considered herself jaded in such matters, was no exception. Taking the obligatory pause upon entering, she gasped and, quite unconsciously, clutched Helen Petherstone's arm.

"Good heavens!" was all she could manage.

"Lovely, isn't it?" said Helen, a veteran of Lady Stafford's balls and therefore considerably better at rational conversation. "Charlotte really does know what she's doing, for all that she seems so engrossed in horses and hunting."

"There is the matter of the architecture," murmured William.

"Well, of course," Helen conceded, "though it wouldn't matter a fig if one went about things in the wrong way. But not Lady Stafford. Everything is perfect."

Clarissa, surveying the silver bowls trailing delicate sprays of hothouse roses of pale pink and white, the graceful apple-green hangings at the Palladian windows, and the cunningly disported arrangements of comfortable seats for those who wished to forgo the dancing, could only nod dumbly.

They had reached the Staffords' receiving line. Lady Stafford, resplendent in puce satin, greeted her guests with a combination of imperial bearing and hunt-field exuberance. Even the viscount, now that the annual uproar was nearly behind him, was in fine humor. Beside them, a graceful sprite in white and silver, the Honorable Amabel regarded the latest guests with her usual calm inscrutability. If her glance flickered a trifle longer over Clarissa, nobody noticed—least of all Clarissa.

"Mrs. Wyndham! Capital to see you!" boomed Lady Stafford, in first-rate fettle. "And looking delightful, too. Helen, William, how d'ye do?"

"Splendidly, and impatient to begin dancing," replied William promptly, if untruthfully. "You've outdone yourself, my lady."

"Pshaw, you say that every year, you rogue! And

then you sneak off to drink claret with Rupert."

"I beg your pardon," said William, gulping but brave. "The viscount *has* mentioned something about a burgundy he'd like me to try—"

"Ha!" Lady Stafford was delighted. "I knew it! You'll find Rupert will have our best for your inspection in the Red Saloon. You see, I try to amuse the gentlemen! But later, mind. Some proprieties must be observed."

She turned to Helen and Clarissa. "Men! Well, go on, my dears, and enjoy the dancing. Which reminds me, Mrs. Wyndham, Sir Jeremy was inquiring after you. Ah, I see he's seen you."

And there, all of a sudden, was Jeremy, bowing low over the hand of Clarissa, whose face, to Helen's interested gaze, lit up with a sudden blaze of utterly unguarded joy.

"Have you saved the first dance for me?" he asked Clarissa without preamble, as they moved away from the receiving line.

"Of course," she said, smiling up at him. "And I believe the set is forming now."

"So it is. Helen, William, you'll excuse us?"

"Of course," Helen said promptly and unnecessarily. Watching them make their way to the dancers, oblivious to everything and everyone save each other, she turned to William with a triumphant smile.

"Did you *see* that?"

"Most certainly," William said, adjusting his spectacles upon his nose so he could see it even more clearly.

"I was right all along," Helen said, so excited that she forgot her usual caution in proclaiming a matchmaking victory before the banns were posted. "They were meant for each other!"

"So it would seem," said William. "So it would seem, indeed."

*   *   *

Mr. Charles Battlebourne and "Mr. Richard Devereaux" hesitated upon the threshold of the ballroom. They were rather late; the dancing was in full force.

"Maybe Lady Stafford can find you a partner; there's a set forming now," said Mr. Battlebourne, helpful as always.

"I thank you, no," said the duke with considerable fervor.

"But it's a dashed ball," objected Mr. Battlebourne. "Must dance at a ball."

"How ill-informed you are, my young friend," replied the duke dryly. "One *must* do nothing of the sort. Now, go along and enjoy yourself. I shall do very well on my own."

Startled and rather suspicious of this sudden breeziness, Mr. Battlebourne took himself off. He was determined to avoid his parents and his older brother the captain, who had been asking far too many uncomfortable questions lately about Mr. Battlebourne's adventures in London.

The duke watched Mr. Battlebourne disappear into the throng, then headed for the staircase that led to the second-floor gallery, which ran the length of the ballroom. He was familiar enough with houses of this design, and had no doubt that somewhere this gallery would afford him a comfortable, hidden observation post with an excellent view of the assembly.

He intended, for the moment, simply to watch.

"Mrs. Wyndham, you are a vision tonight!"

A trifle breathless from the lively figure they were dancing, Clarissa smiled up at Captain Battlebourne. "Fine feathers only, sir!"

To reply, the captain had to wait until the dance brought them together again. "No, I think it's something else," he said under cover of the music as the dance whirled to a close. "Your face looks as bright as a candle. And I don't think I've ever seen you so happy."

She looked up at him, full of joy and good feeling for everyone in the ballroom, in the world—even sulky little Amabel Stafford. And in just a few hours, after the banqueting, everyone would know why.

"I can't stand this much longer," Jeremy had growled under his breath as they left the floor after their first dance. "If I hadn't already promised, I'd announce our engagement right now."

"So impatient?" She had not been able to keep herself from laughing.

"Laugh if you will, madam," Jeremy had said sternly, "but you are not being monitored by Lady Stafford as a potential partner for any one of her hopeful protégés."

"Oh, poor Jeremy!" she had said tragically. "Beset by lovely young maidens at every turn!"

"I might have known I'd find no sympathy in this quarter. When we're married, I hope you keep a more civil tongue in your head."

"Oh, I'll always be civil, never fear. But truthful."

"That's what worries me." As he looked down at her, his expression had changed into one she knew rather well, making her heart race. "Clarissa, it really does seem a long time to wait..."

"—don't you think?"

With a start, she recalled herself to the present and Captain Battlebourne's amused smile.

"I beg your pardon?" she said, flustered.

"Pardon refused, Mrs. Wyndham! You were quite shamelessly not attending!" But his grin deepened, depriving the words of their sting. "As penance, you must join me for a glass of ratafia."

"Gladly," Clarissa said, regaining her equilibrium. "Although I fear yours will be the greater penance! Ratafia, indeed."

The captain not only procured Clarissa a glass of the innocuous stuff; he also heroically swallowed a glass of his own. In recognition of this deed, Clarissa sought to make amends. "I'm so sorry I didn't listen properly before. I believe you mentioned your brother was here tonight?"

"Yes, he is," said the captain, a shadow darkening his face. "What a scapegrace he is! I don't know what he's been up to in London, but I'm very much afraid it wasn't to the good, for he's been uncommonly closemouthed about his visit."

"Is that such a terrible thing?" Clarissa asked lightly.

"If you knew my brother, ma'am, you'd never ask! Normally the problem is persuading him to stay quiet. When he suddenly becomes silent and grave, beware—most likely he's in some sort of muddle."

"Which you, as a kind older brother, must help him out of?" Clarissa said, with a laugh.

"So I suppose," the captain admitted gloomily. "No doubt I'll be untangling something before long."

They were interrupted by the arrival of Sir Jeremy, who conscientiously informed Clarissa that the third set for which they were engaged was now forming. As had the Petherstones before him, the captain regarded Clarissa and Jeremy thoughtfully as they crossed the ballroom.

His reverie, however, was rudely broken by a sharp, short, and decidedly feminine laugh that came from the far side of the pillar upon which the captain was leaning.

"A third dance! How shameless!"

The voice was unfamiliar. With automatic politeness he began to stir, to let the speaker understand she was being overheard. The next part of the conversation, however, froze him where he stood.

"Well, it's not surprising, I'm afraid. Mrs. Wyndham has not always displayed the greatest delicacy of behavior." *That* voice the captain knew very well.

"I wonder that your mama invited her, Amabel!"

"Well—" A pause, perhaps for a shrug. "One must. She is an acquaintance of the Petherstones', after all."

"And of Sir Jeremy's, too!" A distinctly nasty titter followed.

"Yes," said Amabel, and even from behind the pillar, the captain could hear the wealth of meaning in that one syllable. "I have heard they are very . . . *close* . . . acquaintances."

"No!" There was a scandalized, delighted laugh.

And just when the captain had determined, whatever the social consequences, to confront this pair of underhanded gossips, the two conversationalists began to move away. Their words drifted away with them.

"Well, after all!" was the last snatch of conversation to reach captain's ears. "A widow—"

An hour later, Amabel Stafford concluded that if there had been a more miserable evening in her life, she certainly couldn't remember it. A reasonable girl would have consoled herself with memories of the full dance card, the approving pride of her hard-to-please mama, the disarming compliments of a dozen gallants. But Amabel was hardly a reasonable girl. Three developments in particular displeased her:

Mrs. Wyndham had appeared in a gown that could fairly be said to rival Amabel's own.

Sir Jeremy had greeted Amabel with a perfunctory kiss of her hand and a teasing, avuncular: "Lord, aren't you fine as fivepence, miss!"

Captain Nathaniel Battlebourne had treated her with the manners of a pig.

Unquestionably, number three had been the final straw. She had endured two and one with ever-growing ill grace, watching Sir Jeremy and Clarissa circle the dance floor, listening to Mama say thoughtfully, "Now there's a case! Well, well!" She had summoned a wintry but credible smile as Lady Selina Kendall had remarked what a lovely couple dear Sir Jeremy and charming Mrs. Wyndham made. She had fobbed off a dance partner with a fictional torn flounce, hoping to maneuver Sir Jeremy onto the dance floor, only to see him otherwise engaged—in procuring Mrs. Wyndham some punch.

Then she had found herself in a tedious country dance with Captain Battlebourne, a man who had always struck her as insufferably arrogant, and whom she had accepted as a partner only at her mother's insistence. Realizing that Captain Battlebourne had no great wish to dance with her either was too much to endure.

And then he had had the iniquity to notice when she missed a step.

"You'll take a half turn to the left in the next figure," he had reminded her dryly, deftly adjusting to cover her mistake. "Do be careful. I'd hate to take a tumble in front of all these good people next time you're making sheep's eyes at Sutcliffe again."

In a white-lipped rage, she had finished the dance in silence, turning upon him before the last chord had died away. "Pray explain yourself, Captain!"

"Need I?"

"I was not making—making sheep's eyes at anyone!"

Incredibly, Captain Battlebourne had laughed straight into her outraged face.

"How *dare* you! My father—"

"Won't be hearing a word of this, will he? This tale don't burnish your reputation, I fear."

"What would you know about reputation, you lying blackguard?"

Captain Battlebourne had wandered from the dance floor, a furious Amabel keeping pace with him. Since both would have dearly loved to shout but could not, the conversation was conducted in hissing whispers. At length the captain, always an expert at reconnaissance, spotted a charming little alcove before which a cluster of large potted ferns was conveniently planted. Taking Amabel unceremoniously by the hand, he had stepped quickly into this shelter, tugging her beside him, so that they were concealed.

Glad of this opportunity to speak her mind, Amabel had prepared to launch a fresh assault— until her enemy had spiked the guns by clapping his hand over her mouth. As her green eyes grew huge with rage, he had addressed her thusly:

"First, little Miss Termagant, nobody—*nobody, do you hear me?*—casts such slurs in my face without answering for it! Were you a man, I'd cheerfully put a bullet through you. But you're not, more's the pity, so that brings me to point number two. Don't think you can play me for a fool, the way you've done with most of the other poor sapskulls here tonight. I've seen you casting out your lures for Sutcliffe, and I've seen you all but drumming your heels upon the floor because he's got too much sense to nibble. And I've even caught a whiff of the poisonous gossip you've been spreading about Mrs. Wyndham—"

Panting, Amabel had seized his wrist and wrenched his hand away. "Gossip, you say? I shouldn't have thought you'd stoop to listen."

"My ears are quite acute where Mrs. Wyndham is concerned. She's a good woman and deserves better than your childish, spiteful games. So stop it."

Something in the set of his jaw had given Amabel pause, but she had tossed her head all the same. " 'Stop it'?" she mimicked. "Just like that? What if I tell you to go to the devil?"

"Well, then," he had said calmly, "I should be forced—regretfully, you understand—to resort to rumor-mongering myself. I should let it be known that you flung yourself at my head—unsuccessfully, of course—and this mischief-making with Sutcliffe and Mrs. Wyndham is a childish attempt to soothe your bruised pride."

"You'd never *dare!* And—and even if you did, no one would believe you! It's nonsensical!"

The captain had shrugged. "Some would believe; some would not. But everyone would be talking about it. It makes a rare story, you must admit."

Amabel had instantly seen that the captain, devil take his black soul, was right.

"I will never—*never*—forgive you," she had choked out, fairly paralyzed with rage.

"That suits me admirably," the captain had replied, and with a militarily correct bow had left her.

Amabel had retreated to the terrace, where she sat in furious, bitter seclusion.

A delicate cough shattered the silence.

"Your pardon," said a low, cultured voice. "I'd not realized someone was here."

"Someone is," said Amabel crossly, far beyond politeness or flirtation. "Please go away."

But the intruder declined to take the hint, stepping through the arched doorway and onto the terrace. "Forgive me," he said, "but you seem rather upset. Is there any way I may assist?"

"No."

The stranger laughed, lacerating Amabel's tattered nerves still further, but he held up a hand to stop her angry retort. "Come, now. You're far too pretty, and it's far too fine a night, for the sulks. Besides, I've a notion as to what upsets you."

"Do you?" Intrigued, Amabel turned to study her unwelcome guest. His exquisitely tailored evening clothes pointed unmistakably to London, though he clearly scorned foppish affectation—not a patch or wayward ruffle to be seen, and his only jewelry was a plain, heavy gold signet ring. His fair, unpowdered hair was nipped back with a sapphire-blue riband; his silver-grey eyes held a malicious sparkle that made Amabel both speculative and wary.

"Well, I'm hardly well acquainted with this neighborhood," said the gentleman, leaning an elbow negligently upon the garden wall, "but it seems to me that you're not very well pleased with this young widow, this Mrs. Winfield—"

"Wyndham," corrected Amabel swiftly.

"Yes. She's being shockingly forward, don't you agree? You're quite right to be put out."

Amabel felt instantly, gratifyingly understood. "Exactly! She is the most forward, impudent—" Suspiciously, she glanced up at him through her lashes. "What business is that of yours?"

The gentleman smiled slightly. "Your feelings? None whatsoever. The widow, on the other hand, is very much my business. You might say she owes me a debt that's yet unpaid."

"Really?" This was a most improper conversation, Amabel realized. Most improper . . .

She averted her face. "I fail to see what concern that is of mine."

"None at all, I'm sure," the stranger said smoothly. "And it's shocking of me to impose upon you at such a difficult moment, but I thought perhaps it might distract you to lend me a bit of assistance."

She should have terminated their conversation instantly, Amabel knew. She had no business talking, unchaperoned, with a total stranger—

—who seemed to have a score to settle with Mrs. Wyndham.

Amabel swung back to face her companion.

"How may I help you, sir?" she asked.

He began to chuckle softly.

"Just the person to help me!" Sir Jeremy exclaimed gratefully, finding Helen Petherstone engaged in an agreeable gossip with Lady Kendall. He was about to inform Lord Rupert of the announcement he wished to make, but he had to find Clarissa first. "Have you seen Mrs. Wyndham, ma'am?"

"Why, no, not in the last quarter hour, I think," Helen replied, startled. "Is something the matter?"

"Nothing. But it's odd of her to slip away just at this—" He stopped himself. "Never mind! My apologies for disturbing you, ladies." He sketched a bow and hurried off.

"Dear Sir Jeremy seemed rather abrupt, I should say," Lady Kendall remarked with vague disapproval.

Helen, for her part, looked after him with a sense of uneasiness, though where on earth it came from she could not say.

Feeling pleasantly wicked, Clarissa slipped quietly onto the terrace, with one more glance over her shoulder at the ballroom, a mosaic of music, color, and soft laughter. She had been rather surprised to receive Jeremy's summons from Amabel, but there had been nothing in Miss Stafford's offhanded courtesy to awaken distrust.

The night was cool and clear, with only a sliver of a moon to see by. The bright blaze of the ballroom's chandeliers glowed through the tall windows opening onto the terrace, casting squares of golden light upon the flagstones. But the terrace itself was deserted. Clarissa crossed it, and, seeing no one immediately, descended the shallow steps that gave out onto the sweep of lawn leading to Castle Stafford's gardens. She hesitated, a hand on the carved stone balustrade. "Jeremy?"

Behind her came a footstep; she smiled to herself. Without turning, she inquired, "Is this sufficiently cloak-and-dagger for you, my dear?"

"I'm devastated to disappoint you," replied a voice that froze her to the marrow. "But as you perceive, I'm not Jeremy."

Having left Amabel, Captain Battlebourne was seeking to calm his agitated spirits with a tot of excellent brandy obtained from the pocket flask of a fellow military man—really a fine fellow, for all that he was a guardsman and a London lagger. Sipping from an innocent-looking punch cup, the captain struggled for his usual good-natured composure. He had withdrawn to the small but exquisitely furnished Red Saloon off the ballroom, which Lady Stafford had fitted out as a combination cardroom and conversational retreat.

As he savored the last of his brandy and wondered whether he could decently manage to slip off for a quiet pipe, his brother Charles burst in.

"Nat! Devil take it, where have you been?"

"I might ask the same of you," said the captain,

eyeing his younger sibling with disfavor. "Haven't you managed to find a breakneck game of dice somewhere yet?"

The irony sailed cleanly over the younger Battlebourne's disheveled head. "No, what a curst slow crowd the Staffords always get! I wish to Hades I'd never come, that I'd never got myself talked into . . . Nat!" He grabbed his brother's arm. "That's what I meant to tell you—"

"What? What are you talking about?" asked the captain irritably, disengaging himself.

Now that the captain came to think of it, his brother was looking rather haggard. He also was looking rather guilty, in a way the captain remembered very well.

"Charles," said the captain, his tone newly sharp, "what have you got yourself into?"

A few minutes later, seated in a secluded corner of the saloon and rubbing his forehead in pained disbelief, the captain shot his younger brother a withering glare. "Even for you," he said slowly, "it's a hash of an affair. And this Belfort sounds like a rogue, duke or no duke. But other than the fact that you've made an utter cake of yourself, what's to do?"

Charles muttered something.

"Speak up, for God's sake!"

"I said, I thought it was just a curst lovers' tangle!" Charles said sullenly. "But now I don't know, what with this talk of drugging the lady . . ."

"*What?*"

"I heard them, I tell you! His Grace's menservants. I was stealing out into the gardens for a quiet smoke—you know how high in the instep the Staffords are—and there they were. I recognized the voices. We traveled all the way north with them, and a deuced queer pair they were, too."

"What—did—you—hear?" asked the captain,

exerting a careful hold on his fraying temper.

Charles tried hard to collect his scattered thoughts. "Something about how the lady might be 'difficult'; that's what one of them said. And the other just laughed and said, well, His Grace would slip her a dose of something that would knock her out cold! I didn't wait to hear any more."

"Good God!" The captain was aghast. "We could damned well be seeing a kidnapping tonight! If only you knew who this lady is—"

"But I do," said Charles, pleased to be useful at last. "They were talking about how pretty she was and how striking that reddish hair of hers looks. It's the widow—what is her name?—Mrs. Wyndham."

Clarissa had the oddest sense that if only she remained absolutely still, the figure before her would vanish, like the bad dream she believed him to be.

He took a single step nearer, then stopped, smiling faintly. "Well met, Your Grace," the familiar, drawling voice said. "Or should I say Madam Wyndham? Or perhaps simply . . . my dear?"

Clarissa's dry lips trembled a moment, but no sound emerged. Her second try was more successful. "What do you want?"

"How unoriginal," murmured the duke. "But forthright."

Her wits were returning, along with her powers of observation. As unobtrusively as possible, she mapped her surroundings. They were standing below the terrace, just beyond sight of the great ballroom windows, sheltered by the parapet that ran the length of the terrace. A few steps away was the path that led to the formal gardens. In the distance, shadowed by one of the Staffords' neatly groomed box hedges, were two more figures, who were impossible to discern in detail. She rather thought they were no friends of hers.

Shock had driven off all but an icy calm. Her voice was rock-steady as she reminded him, "You haven't answered my question."

"Isn't it obvious? When last I saw you we were discussing a matter of business, I believe."

"Were we? I suppose you considered it so," Clarissa said coolly.

Could she outrun him? Not likely, with her elaborate and heavy skirts. Nor did it seem likely that she could slip around him and regain the terrace. "How much trouble you have taken," she said aloud.

"I do so hate unresolved questions," the duke replied. Her still watchfulness annoyed him; he much preferred tears and pleading. Ah, well, those would assuredly come later. "And you never have responded to my . . . proposal."

The anger that shot into her blood stiffened her spine and brought hot words flying to her lips—but she checked herself. Time; she needed time. Even if she could outmaneuver the duke, there was the question of the pair in the gardens. Until she could think of a way to even the odds, she must have time. Involuntarily, she clenched her fingers over the bunch of primroses fastened to the lace of her corsage . . . and felt the pearl head of the long, sharp pin Martha had used to fix them there.

The duke had noticed her nervous gesture, and his smile grew thinner, more satisfied. "You're so quiet, Cousin," he said. "Of course, you never were a woman of many words—for me, at least. But I did hope for a warmer greeting after a most inconvenient journey."

"Then I suppose you should have gone where you are welcome, sir," she said tranquilly, keeping her hand upon the flowers, watching him carefully in case his eyes slipped away from her.

Sooner or later, something would distract him, she told herself with desperate conviction. Then she would get the sharp pin free, and . . . What would happen next, she had no idea.

But she was certain of one thing. Whatever the duke had in mind, she had no intention of submitting tamely.

Jeremy, making his way toward the supper room, started at the urgent hand on his coat sleeve. He swung round to find Captain Battlebourne, whose blue eyes were intent and anxious.

"Sutcliffe! Have you seen Mrs. Wyndham, man?"

"No. Why do you ask?" Sir Jeremy's voice was cold.

"It's extremely important," said the captain, too busy scanning the ballroom to fully appreciate the anger in Sir Jeremy's question.

"Oh? And just why is that?" Sir Jeremy, hardly a man of violence, was fast changing his ways.

"Because—" Belatedly, the captain heard and understood the dangerous quietness of Sir Jeremy's voice. "Blast it, man! Don't cut up at me; there's no time! Mrs. Wyndham may be in danger."

Sir Jeremy stared hard at the captain. "What are you talking about?"

"I'll explain as much as I can; I'm not sure myself just what's afoot. It may be just a harmless prank, but I just don't like the sound of things, Sutcliffe. We'd best hurry and try to find her; I'll tell you what I know on the way."

The faint glimmer of light from the ballroom set Belfort's features in an eerie cast. Clarissa fought not to think too hard about her fear as a slight breeze played softly with the end of her gauzy sash. If she gave free rein to fright, it would become a monster, devouring all that remained of common sense.

Her one advantage at the moment was Belfort's apparent—and chilling—desire to chat.

"You're looking very well, Cousin." She responded with a slight nod. "I understand you have been occupying yourself with useful employment. How industrious of you."

She remained silent.

"Of course, I find it difficult to picture you as a governess, though you were always a bit of a bluestocking. Still, you're far too pretty. No sane lady of the manor would tolerate it, I think. But"—he paused delicately—"I forgot. There *is* no mistress at Thornbeck House, is there? A sad situation."

"Sir Jeremy is a widower. You appear to be well informed," she replied politely.

"Thank you. I try. Of course, it was difficult to find where you decided to take your little rest cure, but once I understood where you had gone, I made it my business to discover your doings. Your welfare is most important to me, Clarissa, dear."

"Have you known for a long time, then?"

"Only the last few weeks," Belfort said modestly. "But long enough to discover many fascinating things about your tenure as governess to the tyke at Thornbeck House, who appears to be motherless, at the moment. Now, *that's* a most interesting story, I gather. . . . Had you aspirations in that direction, cousin? It hardly seems your style."

"Whatever my aspirations are, I do not consider them to be of interest to you," she said icily.

"You underestimate me."

"I have never done that," she said, unable to keep the bitterness from her voice.

"You're a wise woman, then, my dear." Belfort moved a step closer; reaching out, he brushed the back of one hand against Clarissa's hair. "Let me explain to you the delightful program I have devised for us this evening."

Sir Jeremy and the captain had checked the ballroom and the various salons. They had also glanced through the tall glass doors that gave out onto the terrace. But as that area was plainly deserted, they troubled themselves with it no more.

The captain had given Sir Jeremy a terse summary of his brother's muddled tale. Now he offered an apology. "Had I any idea what a mess the young idiot was in—but there's no time now to cry over spilt milk. Mrs. Wyndham's nowhere to be seen among the guests, and I don't like that, not at all."

"Nor do I," said Jeremy grimly. "We'll search the gardens now."

"Have you any idea who would wish her ill?" the captain asked as they slipped out a side door. "Has anyone made threats against her, or been bothering her in any way?"

"Not a soul. If there's a better-liked person in Thorndale I'd wish to hear about it," Sir Jeremy said heatedly. "Could this person be trying to get his hands on some money?"

"I wondered that myself, but why?" said the captain. "She hardly lives in grand style. Of course, that doesn't necessarily mean anything. We really know so little about her."

Sir Jeremy shot a sharp look at him.

"Calm down. I think she's a fine woman. But I confess I've always wondered what brought her here—"

He bit his words off abruptly, and they both stopped in their tracks, having rounded a corner of the great house and seen, at the same time, the two figures standing at the base of the steps leading down from the terrace. Sir Jeremy started forward, but the captain forestalled him, pulling him along as he backed soundlessly behind the corner of the building again.

"What the devil—"

"Have you forgotten the two fellows my brother told me about?" the captain whispered. "They're here too. Look over there, where the yew hedge begins. Fortunately no one's seen us yet."

Sir Jeremy examined the scene himself, and saw that all was as the captain had said. He shrugged impatiently. "Two against three; the odds aren't so bad."

"Not unless one of them has a pistol," the captain said dryly. He watched emotions flicker across his companion's face, as Sir Jeremy concluded that this possibility was too risky to deny.

"And we, of course, have no way of knowing, at the moment," Sir Jeremy said, rubbing his chin thoughtfully. "Battlebourne, have you the means to even the odds?"

"In my carriage. One never knows what one might encounter on a journey."

"No, one doesn't," said Jeremy, never taking his eyes from Clarissa. He was too far away and the light too poor to see her face, but the tension of her bearing spoke volumes. "I think you'd better fetch your pistols, Battlebourne," he said. "Can you do it quickly?"

"Yes, but what about you?"

"I'll keep an eye on our friend, here." Sir Jeremy smiled mirthlessly. "He seems to be in no hurry; we can say that for him."

"You are quite mad," Clarissa said faintly, but with conviction. "I had my suspicions in the past, but now—"

"Spare me your concerns, my dear; I'm quite

sane," Belfort said. "You'll admit it's a superb plan."

"It is an odious plan, and if I may remind you, it happens to be illegal! Kidnapping generally is considered so, I believe, and rest assured, kidnapping is what you're proposing, for I would never consent willingly to this."

"Your consent is, well . . . immaterial, Cousin, dear," said Belfort.

"Oh, you mean your footpads in the garden? I've seen them already," said Clarissa scornfully. She was past fear and caution now, and in the grip of a white-hot rage. "You could have a hundred of them there, Belfort; it will do you no good. I shall scream and fight until every one of the Staffords' guests is out here wondering what in the world is going on. And I shall tell them exactly what you planned to do here tonight, *my lord duke*."

"Dear me," Belfort said, his eyes traveling her face appreciatively. "Rustication has done nothing, I see, to mellow that temper of yours."

"You may joke as much as you please. I mean every word. And may I also remind you," said Clarissa with fierce satisfaction, "that in just another hour you will have no claims whatsoever upon me, legal or otherwise. Have you forgotten what day it is, Belfort?"

Belfort's affable mask dropped; his face contorted in a spasm of ugly anger so sudden and intense that Clarissa stepped back involuntarily.

"Oh, you're so clever," he spat out. "How very clever you must be thinking yourself, little cousin, hiding away until you had the inheritance—and the means to leave me. But it doesn't matter, don't you see? The money doesn't matter a damn, and never did. *You* were what mattered."

Her heart was beating so loudly she thought she would faint; her fingers tightened around the posy at her neckline, crushing the flowers, clenching the pearl handle of the pin. She kept her eyes, wide with fear and desperately attentive, upon his face, much as she wanted to look away.

"You could have a thousand inheritances, and it wouldn't make any difference!" The soft venom in his voice was worse than a scream. "You talk of claims and legal rights; to hell with that! How far will your talk of legal rights get you in the brothel where I'm taking you? And when I'm done with you," he added with a cold half-smile, "no man in the world will want you, not for all the inheritances in England."

Her knees felt suddenly weak; she fought to master herself. "You forget," she said swiftly, retreating another step as he relentlessly closed toward her. "I am not going anywhere."

"You'll go," he said. "If I see the first sign of so much as a whimper, I will take this flask of laudanum, which I took very good care to bring with me, and toss the entire contents down your pretty throat. In just a minute or two, you will be quite unable to lift a finger."

There was no place left to run. The stone wall of the parapet was at her back; the gardens stretched ahead of her, dark and mysterious, and within them, the shadows of the two henchmen waited. Above her, from the brightly lit house, she could hear the music and voices from the ballroom, so heartbreakingly near. Oh, God, if she could only send some sign!

"Which way is it to be?" His ragged breath fanned her neck; she twisted away. He laughed. "I don't care for myself . . ."

There was no more time for anything but action. As Belfort's hands closed over her shoulders, she let her knees buckle, let a trembling sigh escape her, as if she were fainting. His momentary hesitation was her chance. Swiftly she jerked the pearl-headed pin from the lace of her gown and brought it blindly up in a lightning motion, scoring a thin red rip across Belfort's left cheek. She opened her mouth to scream; with a curse, he closed his hands around her throat.

Dimly, through the blood thudding in her ears, she thought she heard footsteps racing along the gravel path; that was surely Belfort's helpers. Dear God, help her . . .

"Get your hands off her, you cur, or I'll make damned sure you're sorry!"

The crushing weight at her throat was abruptly lifted; she heard a curse from Belfort, the thud of his body hitting the ground. Clarissa staggered back, shaking her head to clear it. "Oh, Jeremy, thank God," she whispered, hardly daring to believe he was there.

"Are you hurt?" he demanded, grasping her shoulders urgently.

"No, but you came just in time—oh, dear heaven!"

For Belfort, only momentarily dazed from the blow Jeremy had dealt him, was on his feet again, his sword drawn. Swiftly Jeremy turned to face him, putting himself between Belfort and Clarissa. But before any of them could make a move, a cool voice drawled from the shadows behind them: "Drawing a weapon on an unarmed man? It seems to be your style, but I'd really think better of it, if I were you."

Captain Battlebourne stood on the gravel path, holding a very efficient-looking pistol in a steady grip. Seeing Belfort's eyes dart over his shoulder at the gardens, Battlebourne gave a grim laugh. "Your associates discovered they had business elsewhere. I had a word with them just a minute ago."

Belfort sheathed his sword. The captain nodded

approvingly. "But you'll understand, I'm sure, when I keep this in sight for a while longer," he went on. "Just until you leave. Which I think had better be soon, don't you agree, Sutcliffe?"

The duke gave a polite nod. An oddly humorous smile spread across his face as his eyes went from Jeremy to Clarissa and back. Watching him, Clarissa felt her relief fade into uneasiness; the hairs at the back of her neck began to prickle.

Belfort shook his head at her reprovingly. "The game is not played out yet, my dear," he said.

"I think it is," Sir Jeremy interposed. "Except that it would create embarrassment for the Staffords, it would give me great pleasure to eject you from the grounds with the most force possible. As it is, do the healthful thing—get out of here and stop bothering this lady."

"Lady!" Belfort bit the word out on a harsh laugh. He sketched a deep, mocking bow. "Very well, I'll take my leave. But not before I enlighten you upon a few important points. Beginning with the idea that *this*"—he swept a contemptuous hand toward Clarissa—"is a lady."

"Get out," said Jeremy coldly. "And take your foul-mouthed lies about Mrs. Wyndham with you."

But Belfort only laughed again, his eyes alight with unholy amusement. "Ask her!" he said. "Ask dear 'Mrs. Wyndham' who she really is. Ask how she married a doddering old fool three times her age and made herself the spectacle of London. Ask why her name is currency in the betting books in every club in St. James Street!" He looked with satisfaction at the three faces turned toward him; two thunderstruck, one frozen in horror.

"I see you haven't been introduced properly," Belfort said. "May I present Clarissa Harcourt, the dowager duchess of Belfort. My esteemed cousin-in-law."

"What in God's name is he talking about?" Battlebourne burst out, to no one in particular. Sir Jeremy was silent, but his eyes fastened upon Clarissa with a terrible intensity as she turned a beseeching face to him.

"That is my name," she said quietly.

"Dear me, you really didn't know!" Belfort said chattily. "Apparently poor Clarissa came north, needing a bit of a holiday from her suitors, and from me in particular—"

"You disgust me," she said, her voice low and shaking with contempt.

"Do I? You never used to be so particular, darling," Belfort said. "She's quite famous, you know," he added to the others. "They call her Titania. The hair, you see."

Sir Jeremy did not appear to be listening; his eyes were still riveted upon Clarissa. "You," he said. "You're the young duchess of Belfort."

He spoke with a chill remoteness that stabbed at Clarissa's heart. As if he were talking about an unsavory stranger. *Well, isn't he?* she thought, quelling a hysterical giggle. *Please, dear God, let this be a nightmare; let me wake up.*

"Not quite the simple little widow, as you see." Belfort's drawl cut across the suddenly charged silence.

"Get out," Sir Jeremy said again, softly but with acid harshness. Battlebourne took a step toward Belfort, pistol at the ready.

"No need for that," Belfort said scornfully. "I'll take my leave in a moment. I must say, after such an unpromising beginning, this interlude has turned out to be quite agreeable. Even piquant. Mistaken identities, and all that. Each lover hiding behind a little mask . . ." He paused theatrically, enjoying Clarissa's startled look, Jeremy's sudden vigilance. "Oh, I see I've been indiscreet again."

A wave of fresh wariness pierced the fog of misery that shrouded Clarissa; her eyes narrowed. "What do you mean?"

Belfort shook his head, smiling. "Only that you, too, have been a dupe, my sweet. You seem to believe our friend, here, is a widower. But Lady Sutcliffe isn't dead. She's really quite alive and living in some comfort on the Continent—though not, precisely speaking, Lady Sutcliffe any more."

Clarissa tried, and failed, to find words. Instead, she looked at Sir Jeremy, whose turn it was to go pale.

"You are a complete bastard," said Captain Battlebourne.

"Do you know what he's talking about?" Clarissa whirled to face him.

The captain's silence was her answer. She laughed shortly; the sound was ugly to her own ears.

"I'm sure he does," Belfort said. "Why, even I was able to find out about you, Sutcliffe. Odd how history repeats itself, isn't it? It seems that once more you've encountered a lady who is not exactly what she appears. Of course, you're luckier this time. Clarissa really *is* a widow. No messy prior entanglements to sort through—legitimate ones, anyway . . ."

"Jeremy," said Clarissa with quiet implacability, "what is this about, please?"

"Only that Sir Jeremy, in his salad days, unfortunately wed a lady who was already promised," Belfort said, with a mischievous look at Sir Jeremy's grim face. "Quite married, in fact—though she managed to keep it secret for a while. But only for a while."

Captain Battlebourne had heard enough. He ad-

vanced purposefully upon Belfort, the evenness of
his voice, more than the pistol, conveying the se-
riousness of his resolve. "You've spread enough
poison here tonight. You're beyond contempt, you
blackhearted bastard. Get out before I put a hole
through you."

"Oh, I'm truly going now, never fear." Belfort
bowed to them all. "A most pleasant good evening."

He melted into the garden shadows.

The captain looked after him as one might regard
a particularly low species of rodent. "I'm going after him to make sure he's off the grounds," he said
tonelessly. "And the two ruffians he brought with
him."

With that, he, too, vanished down the path, leaving Sir Jeremy and Clarissa alone on the sweep of
manicured lawn, ink-colored in the darkness. In the
pallid light from the ballroom, Clarissa could see
Sir Jeremy's stony face, the grim, angry set of his
jaw. She knew as surely as she stood there that the
anger was not directed entirely at Belfort.

"So," she said, "that is all? You've tried and con-
demned me on Belfort's word?"

"No," he said, and the coldness in his voice was
unmistakable. "What about *your* word, Your Grace
of Belfort? Who are you? Or would it be too much
to ask, letting me in on the little secret you've been
keeping all these months? Were you saving it for a
surprise? Well . . . I'm surprised, darling."

He turned full toward her, and she flinched at
the contempt in his face. "How did my proposal
compare with old Belfort's, Clarissa? I'm sure I
haven't quite the old duke's address—certainly not
half his fortune. Did any of that weigh with you?
How serious were you about accepting me, I wonder?"

Grief swept Clarissa, and a terrible, terrible anger. All the promises, all the hopes, were crumbling into dust. There was nothing left of his trust, she saw . . . and what of *her* trust? Thinking of Jeremy's secret, of all the friends who must have borne silent witness to her ignorance, Clarissa fought to control her temper and, fatally, lost.

"Oh, you've puzzled out exactly who I am," she said passionately. "You know all about me now, don't you, Jeremy? Very well. But now I must ask—who are *you*? How dare you look at me as if I were a criminal, question me like an inquisitor! I never denied I had secrets—"

"No indeed," Sir Jeremy bit out. "And what secrets they were. Even in this backwater we've heard of Titania. What sport you must have had among the rustics!"

"Oh, fine sport indeed!" Clarissa flung at him with furious sarcasm. "But it seems you had your sport, too! It seems to me that a widower whose wife is still alive might be holding a rather large secret, might he not? A secret that everyone in the district likely knows but me! Oh, yes—how much sport must you have had!"

"Damn it, Clarissa—"

"Don't talk to me any more!" She drew away from him, shaking with anger and shock. "Spare me the explanations; they're always so awkward, don't you agree? And in return, why don't I let you return in peace to your—your high-minded seclusion? What a fortunate thing our announcement hasn't been made! Go back to hiding; I'll spare you the inconvenience of an entanglement that's obviously grown repulsive to you. You may consider our engagement at an end."

He did not move or speak. And in his silence, Clarissa heard all she needed to know.

"Good-bye," she said in a whisper.

She picked up her skirts and hurried up the

stairs. Her eyes were dry; she felt empty of everything but a fierce resolve not to break down, to hold her head high for just a little while longer, until she could find the Petherstones and ask them to convey her home.

Sir Jeremy did not turn as she left. He stayed in the garden for a long while after, until the sky began to pale and he realized it was long past time to take his leave.

11

In an uncharacteristically glum mood, Helen drove her pony trap the three miles to Metcalfe Farm. Normally the bright promise of the spring morning would have encouraged her natural tendency to smile at life. That day, however, she had much on her mind.

Martha answered her knock with weary efficiency; Helen's heart sank further at the careworn face before her.

"Will Mrs. Wyndham see me, Martha?" she asked.

"I don't know, ma'am," Martha said. "I think so. Step into the parlor, Mrs. Petherstone, and I'll bring you some tea while I find out."

Following Martha into the parlor, Helen found little to raise her spirits. The household was clearly in the stages of packing up; two trunks sat open and half full in the hallway. The parlor had already been swept bare of all ornaments. Here and there, books were stacked in untidy piles. Helen was shaking her head at the sight when Clarissa came in.

"Hello, Helen," she said, extending a hand.

Helen pressed it warmly, taking in Clarissa's pallor, the circles under her eyes. It was difficult to believe that this was the creature who'd been aglow with dazzling happiness at the Staffords' ball two nights before.

"You're going away?" Helen asked abruptly. "Why?"

"Oh, it's terribly inconvenient, but I've been called away to—to—" Suddenly, Clarissa dropped into the wing chair by the fireplace, overcome by a weariness of spirit too strong to deny. "It's no use, Helen. I can't tell you why. I'm sorry, but I simply have to leave as soon as possible. I shall be careful to leave all in order—"

"Never mind about that. I think I have an idea what the matter is, dear," Helen said gently. "Won't you please let me try to help?"

"Oh, Helen." Clarissa's broken little laugh was almost a sob. "I don't think you can really know; if you did, you'd realize there's nothing to be done."

Helen drew up a chair beside Clarissa's. Her voice was very kind. "You've been carrying a terrible burden. It's time you had a little help . . . Your Grace."

Clarissa stared at her, heartbreak momentarily forgotten. "How long have you known? Oh heavens, did Lady Anne—"

"She most certainly did not say a word," Helen said firmly. "You know Anne would never break a confidence."

"Of course not; I'm sorry," said Clarissa, abashed. "But how?"

"Well, of course she had written about you from time to time; about her friend the young duchess, I should say. Though not about your troubles with that horrid cousin of yours. *That* came to my ears another way, but never mind for now. We never would have had occasion to connect Anne's friend with our Mrs. Wyndham, except for an engraving in one of those blasted journals William is always ordering. . . ." She paused, seeing Clarissa flinch. "No, my dear, it wasn't a very nice picture. The resemblance to you was there, though. And so we wondered."

"If you saw that engraving, others must have," Clarissa said. "Why did no one say anything?"

"First, don't assume such things *always* travel far and wide. Then, too, how could one be sure? William and I knew of your friendship with my sister, so we had more cause to think twice about the likeness. But many would mark it down to a coincidence, and leave you to go about your business. That's the way around here; we let people keep their business to themselves."

"As you do with Jeremy?" It came out before Clarissa could stop herself.

"Ah, yes, Jeremy," Helen said.

"You've heard . . . everything . . . about the ball?" Clarissa asked hesitantly.

"Enough, I think," Helen said, a trifle dryly. "Captain Battlebourne came to see me yesterday—in strict secrecy, I might add. He might not have confided in me at all, had he not been worried about you."

Clarissa took a handkerchief from her pocket and began pleating it aimlessly upon her lap. "You know everything, then," she said in a low voice. "I wonder that you don't despise me."

"Despise you!" Helen shook her head with impatience. "How could I? You've been a dear friend, not only to me, but to any number of other people in the dale. I assure you, no one hereabouts would sit still to hear someone speak ill of you."

"But I don't think Jeremy would agree with you," Clarissa said. "He has quite a different opinion about my character."

The quiet words tugged at Helen's heart; she considered her next words very carefully.

"Clarissa, I can see you've been terribly hurt. But please try to understand that when Jeremy spoke and acted as he did, I truly believe he wasn't talking to you, not really. He was talking to a ghost from his past, and that's a painful past indeed."

Clarissa sat very still. "You'll have to explain the entire truth, I think," she said after a minute. "Otherwise I shall never have a hope of understanding a thing."

Helen nodded. She looked pensive, and rather tired—so different from her usual cheerful briskness. "Of course you wouldn't have heard," she said. "It happened a long time ago, and even the juiciest scandal fades away with the years. Such an ugly, hurtful story—and so very sad. You know, I've never believed it was entirely Caroline's fault, or entirely anyone's fault, for that matter. The closest there is to a villain in the piece was Caroline's father, and even he was to be pitied, in a way."

Clarissa waited, folding her hands.

"You've heard something about how it began," Helen said. "When they met, Jeremy was just establishing himself at the Foreign Office. Caroline was bright and lively and extremely beautiful; Jeremy certainly wasn't the only man to fall in love with her when she entered society. Caroline's mama had died when she was small, and her papa simply doted upon her; and since she was an only child, she was sole heiress to his fortune, which was considerable.

"But that fortune came from trade, and not every gentleman's son was willing to offer Caroline marriage. And that was what her father apparently wanted above all things—a genteel marriage. So when Jeremy proposed, I imagine it was manna from heaven.

"Now, Lady Alice—Jeremy's mama—had died a few years before that, but old Sir Andrew Sutcliffe was still alive, and very much opposed to the match. It wasn't just Caroline's background; Sir Andrew was absolutely sure she was all wrong for Jeremy. Unfortunately, he told Jeremy so in no uncertain terms, and you know how stubborn Jeremy can get once his will is crossed."

"I have an idea," said Clarissa.

"Oh, how foolish it all seems, looking back!" Helen sighed. "Had it been me in Sir Andrew's shoes, I should have agreed to the marriage and insisted upon a long engagement. Then they might have tired of each other, and the thing would have died a natural death. And if it hadn't, well, maybe it was meant to be after all. But there! In any event, they married, for as Jeremy pointed out, he had already come of age."

Helen sighed again, more sharply. "Well, in time old Sir Andrew was proven right about the marriage, though he didn't live to see it. Things soured quite quickly for Jeremy and Caroline, from what I can gather."

"Yes, Jeremy told me about that," Clarissa nodded.

"Did he, dear?" Helen looked keenly at her. "He doesn't speak of it very often, I can assure you. Well, to continue . . . Susannah had just been born, and Jeremy was very pleased about *that*, at least. And no doubt they'd have gone along like so many couples, making the best of things, muddling through the worst. Except one day a stranger came knocking on the door—and swore he was Caroline's husband."

"My helpful cousin Belfort explained that part of the story," Clarissa said grimly. "But how did this come to be?"

"It wasn't such a great mystery in the end," Helen said, wry and sad at once. "The man was a soldier, and Caroline had run off with him when she was barely fifteen—a silly infatuation, but the consequences were serious indeed. Her father was unable to overtake them until the next day, and decided he'd no choice but to consent to their marriage; a very hushed-up affair it was, too. Then the old man bought the fellow a commission, and off the lad went to the colonies. And not long after that, they received word he was lost.

"The trouble was, they knew nothing for sure. One of his comrades wrote to say he'd been killed in a skirmish with Indians. Another told them he might have been captured alive, although the chances were slim. And after two years had passed with no further word, Caroline's father embarked upon a very foolish, irresponsible course: he decided to give the soldier up for dead and launch Caroline in polite society, as he'd always planned. Only, they'd keep her marriage a secret."

Clarissa, whose eyes had been growing bigger and bigger as the tale progressed, belatedly found her voice. "And she *agreed* to this?"

"Oh, it was a wicked thing to do!" Helen said. "And risky. Mind, now, hardly anyone outside of Caroline's own family knew of her marriage—and they did not belong to the circles to which she hoped to gain entree. It was certainly a gamble, but from what I can tell, Caroline was a gambler, and at least as stubborn as her papa. She had come to regret her rash escapade and was anxious to establish herself more splendidly in life."

Helen shrugged as she went on. "To be fair, Caroline's soldier was hardly a model of virtue, either. He *had* been captured—and escaped, wonder of wonders—but afterwards he'd decided to wander about the Americas a bit, rather than return to his obligations. It was only when his pockets were sadly to let that he remembered his wife's father was very rich. And that was how he turned up on Caroline's doorstep."

"But what did Jeremy do?"

"What could he do? The first marriage was absolutely valid, for even though Caroline had been a minor, they'd had her father's consent, and there had been witnesses. Also, this soldier was a prudent rogue: he'd left the marriage lines in safekeeping with a friend here in England before he sailed to America, so there was nothing in dispute. Oh, it was scandalous!"

Clarissa did not reply immediately. She was remembering her last conversation with Jeremy in the garden, with dawning understanding and fresh despair.

"What became of Caroline?" Clarissa asked at last.

"I know she went away with the soldier to the Continent. Where they are now, or even whether they're still living as man and wife, I have no idea. Caroline's papa died not long after that; one could almost feel sorry for him, with all his cherished hopes turned to disaster in an instant!"

"Disaster, indeed," said Clarissa, her eyes dark and troubled. "And disgrace, too."

"Yes . . . disgrace," Helen said thoughtfully. "The disgrace fell upon Caroline and her father, for they had been the deceivers. But derision—that was reserved for the deceived husband. For someone as stubborn and proud as Jeremy, the gossip and finger-pointing were simply intolerable. So he decided to leave London. He threw over his career and came back to Thornbeck House with Susannah."

"Susannah!" Clarissa looked stricken; in following the twists and turns of this strange tale she had forgotten its implications for Jeremy's daughter.

"That was the most painful part of the wretched affair," Helen said. "The idea that the child would be harmed, that the busybodies would make her fair game . . ."

"Oh, no!" Clarissa said involuntarily.

"It was another reason Jeremy decided to live a retired life," Helen said. "Understand that, legally, Susannah is quite safe. Even though her parents' marriage was false, at least one of them undertook it in good faith, which, according to the church and the law, is all that is required to consider the child legitimate. What the gossips think is another matter." She gave a small, proud smile. "Not that Jeremy cared a jot for what anyone might say! He left no doubt where he stood, regarding that child. He wouldn't hear of giving her up to Caroline to raise, although I'm afraid Caroline was not very insistent on that point. And he's done everything possible to provide for Susannah's future."

"But Susannah doesn't know the truth," Clarissa said. "She believes her mother is dead."

"Try not to think too harshly of Jeremy," Helen said. "He was trying to do what seemed to be best in very difficult circumstances. Susannah was barely more than a baby; it was too complicated to explain to her. And as time went by, it just seemed easiest to let her believe Caroline was dead."

"She's growing too old for that," Clarissa said thoughtfully. "She is asking questions, and soon she won't be satisfied with the answers she's given."

"Yes, in time she will have to know." Helen sighed. "It will be a difficult moment for Jeremy—I don't think he has ever gotten over the humiliation of having his marriage blasted apart so publicly, of being made to appear so foolish."

Clarissa was quiet again, thinking of the night in the garden.

"So there it is," Helen said. "Believe me, it is not a story I relish telling—and Jeremy, of course, won't hear it spoken of. We have all known Jeremy since he was a boy, and it hurt deeply to see him so unhappy. . . . But I thought it was important for you to understand. My dear, can't you try to forgive him, at least to talk to him again and try to put matters right?"

"I don't know," Clarissa said frankly. "If you knew what was said, how—how final everything was . . ."

"Well, I don't know anything about that," said Helen. "But I've certainly lived long enough to know words don't last forever. Dear Clarissa, I have wished so much that Jeremy could be happy again. I'd simply given up hope until you and he . . . these last few months . . ." She looked at Clarissa's troubled face, at the fingers clenching the handkerchief. "I've grown quite fond of you, and it's dreadful to see you suffering like this. You and Jeremy are so well suited, it would be positively wicked to part over this misunderstanding."

"Oh, Helen, you're being wonderful and kind," Clarissa burst out. "And I know you mean everything for the best. But this is more than just *my* misunderstanding. Can't you see? That night in the garden, Jeremy—oh, he sees me as some heartless society flirt amusing herself at his expense—"

"And what is the truth, my dear?" Helen asked gently.

"Oh, allow me some pride!" Clarissa said with a rueful laugh. "You've already guessed, anyway. But I can't convince Jeremy, Helen. And I don't think I can try anymore. I don't think I can face that hurt again." She bowed her head. "You'll think me a poor creature."

"I should never think that," Helen said gently. "But, Clary, what do you plan to do?"

"I must go to London and settle matters with my solicitors. I'm a woman of means now, you know," she said with a ghost of a smile. "I have much to do. I'll collect my things at Belfort House and stay with Anne for a little while. Then I shall engage a companion and take a little house in a quiet place—"

"Clarissa, you'd be burying yourself alive!" Helen sounded remarkably like her sister, Lady Talmadge.

"Well, not right away!" Clarissa said in a rallying way. "I intend to travel for a year first."

"Alone?"

"With a duenna. When I find one," she said lightly. Helen still looked dubious.

"Please try to understand," Clarissa said, with quiet firmness.

"Oh, my dear, I want only to see you happy. And if this is what you wish..." Helen gestured helplessly. "You'll come visit William and me before you go? And write faithfully?"

Clarissa assured her that she would, and they parted, each with a moist gleam in her eyes.

A few days later, Jeremy and his daughter wandered the paths of the garden his mother had laid out at Thornbeck House, Susannah naming the emerging plants and pausing every so often to ask if Sir Jeremy could identify some creature that skittered or flew within their sight. She was a good deal more successful with the flora than he with the fauna, prompting Sir Jeremy to exclaim, "Good Lord, mouse, am I raising a botanist?"

She grinned saucily up at him. "Maybe. What's that?"

He smiled back at Susannah, who was dressed to the nines in one of her bright new muslin dresses, with black slippers laced about her ankles and a beribboned straw chip hat protecting her against the sunshine of the lovely spring morning.

"That's a shrewd answer," he said. "A botanist, my prudent little daughter, studies plants."

"Oh, well, that's all right, then!" She paused before another flower bed. "That's what I did with Mrs. Wyndham. She knows ever so much about plants. She said her mama used them to doctor people."

Some of the sun went out of the day for Jeremy. He asked abruptly, "Do you have all the things you mean to take to Metcalfe Farm?"

"Of course, Papa," said Susannah, disconcerted. She tapped the basket at her side. "I have the book, and some of Cook's spiced apple jelly, and a muffler that Betty knitted."

"Well, the Petherstones should be here to collect you at any time now. Let's go round to the front of the house, shall we?"

As they left the garden, Susannah ventured a hesitant look upward at her father. "Are you sure you don't wish to come along, Papa? The Petherstones will have lots of room."

"No, pet, I told you, I've business today."

"But Mrs. Wyndham is going *away*," Susannah persisted.

"Susannah, I have already said I am not going today," Jeremy snapped. "Don't pester me so!"

Susannah's lower lip trembled slightly, but she said nothing. Jeremy looked down at his daughter's bent head, inwardly cursing his sharp words, but maintained his silence.

He did not trust himself to keep his temper on the topic of Mrs. Wyndham—or should he call her the duchess? His thoughts upon that point, and so many others, were still in disorder. Except upon one matter: Clarissa had hidden a truth from him far more complex than anyone could have guessed.

He had supposed her to be a widow alone, too frightened by her nameless enemy to confide in anyone. Well, was that false? She *had* been a widow; there *had* been an enemy. But such a widow, and such an enemy! How could he reconcile that scandalous duchess with the plainspoken, warmhearted tenant of Metcalfe Farm? He just didn't know.

There was one comfort in this mess, at least: Belfort had quit York, as Sir Jeremy and Captain Battlebourne had discovered after inquiring in the city. Presumably, he had taken his employees as well, or they had fled, for of them there was no sign either. Sir Jeremy had written as much to Clarissa in a stiff, awkward note, and received an equally stiff reply, replete with the usual phrases: *I beg you will inconvenience yourself no more on my behalf. . . . I think upon the matter of my cousin you should be easy now. . . . I wish you good health.*

And the signature: Clarissa Belfort.

Belfort . . . there was that name again, mocking him, reminding him of the gap that yawned between their worlds. Sometimes he admitted to himself that he found it hard to believe Clarissa capable of leading him on for sheer amusement. But he equally doubted that the dowager duchess of Belfort could have been content as mistress of Thornbeck House. He had lived such a mistake before.

A clatter of hooves in the drive announced the Petherstones' arrival. "Don't lose your shawl, mind," he said gruffly to Susannah. "It will still get cool later. And behave nicely at the farm."

"Of course I will!" Susannah turned haughty. "It isn't as if I'm a nuisance or anything. And Mrs. Wyndham invited me especially, so I could tell her good-bye." She hesitated. "Should I tell her good-bye from you, too, Papa?"

Helen and William were waving at them from

the open carriage door. Avoiding an answer to his daughter's question, Sir Jeremy took her hand and walked up to greet the Petherstones.

"Good morning!" William said, a touch too heartily. "You're looking well, my boy. And what have we here? Is this fashionable vision really Susannah Sutcliffe?"

Susannah laughed delightedly. "It's my new dress," she confided. "The skirt is yards and yards full. Look!" She twirled to show off a whirl of muslin and petticoats that, much to Sir Jeremy's relief, missed being caught upon a carriage wheel, though barely.

"Very impressive, mouse," he said. "But let's not keep the Petherstones waiting." He lifted her into the carriage. "I'm much obliged to you both," he told Helen and William.

"Not at all, not at all, dear boy," William said, waving off his thanks. "The pleasure's ours. It's a perfect day for a drive."

"Indeed it is," Helen said. "A pity you can't join us, Jeremy."

Jeremy glanced at Susannah, and was taken aback at the level, almost adult look she fixed upon him. Just where had he seen that direct, stubborn gaze before? In his father's face? Caroline's? His own? How fast she was growing up.

"Papa!" said Susannah impetuously. "Shouldn't I tell Mrs. Wyndham good-bye for you?"

An uncomfortable silence descended upon the three adults. William looked thoughtful; Helen was a study in exasperation and despair.

"Shouldn't I, Papa?"

"Yes," Jeremy said awkwardly at last. "Yes, tell her I wish her a safe journey, Susannah."

He handed her basket up and moved forward to close the carriage door. But it was Helen who had the last word, saying so softly, he almost missed the rebuke: "You're being stubborn fools, both of you!"

At Metcalfe Farm, the first sight to greet them was John Fothergill's sturdy wagon, drawn up in the dooryard and loaded for the journey. Martha was already outside, wearing a serviceable traveling cloak and a grim expression.

"So," said William with determined briskness, once the usual greetings were exchanged. "Is Her—" He broke off, glancing at Susannah. "Is Mrs. Wyndham ready to go?"

"Some might say so," Martha said glumly. "She's been up and about for hours. Now that it's time to go, she's decided to look over the house again. You'll find her within."

At that moment the door creaked open, and Clarissa appeared. She was very composed, but there was a sad, withdrawn look in her eyes, and her face was rather pale.

"Oh, my dear," Helen began impulsively, then stopped. In the sudden, awkward silence, Susannah hurried forward.

"Look, Mrs. Wyndham," she said. "Here's a basket of presents to remember us by."

Clarissa knelt to accept the basket, taking a moment, for Susannah's sake, to look over the contents. "It's lovely," she managed to say.

"And there's a box with ever so much food," Susannah chattered on, made nervous by the strained silence of the adults around her. "You won't get hungry on your journey."

"No, I won't," Clarissa agreed. "Thanks to Cook, of course."

"Papa says to wish you a safe journey," Susannah said, a trifle too quickly. Her bright hazel eyes searched Clarissa's face with sudden urgency. "You won't forget us, will you, Mrs. Wyndham?"

Her voice trembled slightly, but she reminded herself sternly of her resolve not to be a baby in front of everyone. "You will write, won't you?"

The tears Clarissa had spent so many days repressing welled up with abrupt force. She could only trust herself to set the basket down and gather Susannah in her arms for a quick, fierce hug.

"I shall write every week," she assured Susannah when her voice was steady enough. "At least. You do the same, mind."

"Yes, Mrs. Wyndham," said Susannah, in a tone so reminiscent of their schoolroom days that Clarissa was surprised into shaky laughter, in which the Petherstones gratefully joined.

"We'll all write," said Helen robustly, hugging Clarissa in her turn. "And remember, you have a place with us at Aysgarth whenever you wish."

"Indeed, yes," said William. "No matter how far you roam." He glanced around the dooryard. "I must say, though, you're not likely to roam very far at this rate. Where *has* Fothergill gone?"

John Fothergill obligingly materialized in the far corner of the yard. "Right here, sir," he said placidly, strolling up to stand beside Martha. "Just checking that the outbuildings were bolted up nice and tight."

"And a fine long time you were doing it!" scolded Martha, with a sizable sniff. It must be the morning breeze, she told herself, making her eyes all teary. "Don't say anything nice," she said to Fothergill in a low voice. "I won't stand for it."

"I won't," he assured her. "But happen we should be on our way now."

All eyes turned toward Clarissa, who straightened her shoulders and gave Susannah a last, swift kiss. Then she turned the big key in the lock of the front door and withdrew it, holding it for a mo-

ment in the palm of her hand before giving it to
William Petherstone.

"Thank you for everything," Clarissa said. "Will
you make my farewells to—to everyone?"

To her intense gratitude, the Petherstones simply
nodded.

"Thank you again, all of you," Clarissa said.
"You've been so very good."

Then, since there seemed to be nothing else to
say or do, she walked over to the wagon. John
Fothergill helped her up, and Martha, then climbed
up himself and snapped the reins.

"Off we go, Sally!" Fothergill told the mare.

In a silence broken only by the creaking of the
wagon and the clopping of the mare's hooves, they
left the farm and the dale behind them.

12

Early August

The afternoon sunlight cast a tranquil glow in Lady Talmadge's upstairs sitting room, a stylishly comfortable retreat decorated in shades of cream and rose. Lady Anne sat at her delicate writing table, the picture of elegant composure in cherry-striped taffeta, a lace-trimmed cap atop her silver-streaked brown curls. Only the swift tapping of her quill against the paper betrayed her.

"Wimbledon!" she said for the second time. "Why not Hans Town, pray?"

Her irony fell flat. "Why not?" asked Clarissa, removing her gloves with ostentatious calm. "Don't be so horrified about Wimbledon, Anne. The house looked charming. It's a pleasant neighborhood."

"Very pleasant! Perfectly dull, too, I might add—do you propose to take up knitting, as well?"

Clarissa, modishly dressed in a walking costume of fawn silk, wandered over to the window. She glanced over her shoulder, a slight smile hovering on her mouth. "Why not?" she asked again.

"You're hopeless," said Anne. She wanted to say much more, but did not. The past several weeks had shown her forcefully that there were certain points upon which Clarissa would brook no discussion. One was her plan to wander abroad; the other was her intention, upon her return, to settle into a secluded life.

In vain had Anne urged her friend to reestablish a London life. No, Clarissa had replied: adventure abroad was the very thing! Her immediate destination was Rome, where she planned to spend the forthcoming winter. After that, who knew? Perhaps France; perhaps Switzerland. Perhaps even New York or Philadelphia.

"Why not Brazil?" Lady Talmadge had asked sardonically.

"Why not?"

"You're becoming flippant, Clary," she had said, exasperated.

So Lady Talmadge, with many a heavenward glance, had composed letters of introduction for Clarissa to a selection of the Talmadges' hospitable acquaintances among the Roman expatriate colony. Clarissa, for her part, had gone serenely and mechanically about the business of booking passage on the Dover packet and closing up her suites at Belfort House and Belfort Park.

In this she was unimpeded by the presence of the duke, who at last report was in Ireland, at the estate of one of his wilder friends. More than that was not known, and remarkably few people cared to ask.

Lady Talmadge regarded her friend with shrewd kindness across her writing desk. She was not entirely certain what had befallen Clarissa in Yorkshire, for her sister Helen took confidences as seriously as did Lady Talmadge. But Lady Talmadge was perfectly capable of reading between the lines, and she found her friend's forced briskness disturbing.

"How do your travel plans proceed, dear?" she asked.

A flicker of animation brightened Clarissa's face. "Very well. My man of business informed me today that he has confirmed the passage. The ship sails in three weeks."

"Goodness, so soon!" Lady Talmadge shook her head. "The summer has simply flown by! I can scarce believe it will soon be time to see you off. Oh, la!"

She glanced at the pretty gilded clock upon the table across the room. "I must find Nell and change. Thank heavens we dine at home. You'll be joining us at the theatre tonight, my dear?"

"No, thank you. I'm tired from all the errands today," Clarissa replied. "I shall rest this evening."

"Of course you must do as you see best," Lady Talmadge said. "But do consider getting out a bit more, Clary. I'm positively besieged with inquiries as to where you've been hiding yourself."

"No doubt," Clarissa said dryly.

"Don't turn sour, dear. It's most unappealing. I believe the inquiries were kindly meant. There was some concern when you vanished from town, you know."

"I find that hard to believe."

"You, my dear, were not here to see how thoroughly unpleasant Belfort made himself during those months," Anne said with a hint of severity. "Bad as it was to encounter him in polite circles, one could not help wondering how much worse it might have been, living under his roof. But there, don't tease yourself about it."

"You're a dear, Anne, and I'm dreadful to be so peevish!" Clarissa bent to place a swift kiss on her cheek. "But truly, I do need to rest for a bit, and you should set about changing, or you shall be late indeed!"

Making her way to her bedchamber, Clarissa let her shoulders slump wearily. It had not been a very good day. Despite the brave face she had assumed for Lady Talmadge, she was unaccountably unhappy with the house shown to her that day. Perhaps it was the nasty dark stairwell, or was it the awkwardly placed kitchen? Come to think of it, no property shown her thus far had appealed to her. How tiring and dispiriting it all was!

But perhaps this odd state of mind was occasioned by the letter from Susannah that had arrived in the morning post.

Reaching her bedchamber, Clarissa crossed to the dressing table, slowly unbuttoning her jacket. She opened a little rosewood box and drew the letter out with a sad smile.

Dear Mrs. Wyndham:

I was not sure how to address you in this letter, so will you please tell me how when you write back? Mrs. Petherstone says you are not really called Mrs. Wyndham, and we are to call you Your Grace instead, because you were really a duchess in secret. I think that is almost as exciting as King Charles escaping the Roundheads in disguise.

I am sorry to say there is not much news here, so my letter will be very dull. Except that Papa almost found me a new governess. She is Miss Bassenthorpe from Harrogate, and she came to Thornbeck House to meet me. But she did not take the post. An inkwell was spilled on her, and she was very upset. Papa apologized, but she said she still would rather not stay.

Everyone misses you very much. Mickle and Cook say to please send their respects and very best wishes for your health. And I say the same.

Very respectfully yours,
Susannah Sutcliffe

Clarissa folded the letter carefully away again. Unpinning her hair, she glanced at the book lying upon the dressing table: *Useful Hints to Those Who Make the Tour to France*. She grinned to herself, picturing her newly engaged chaperone, who had dispatched the volume to her by messenger, with a note firmly adjuring her to read every word.

Mrs. Abigail Silverbridge, who had presented herself as an applicant for the post of companion in response to discreet inquiries by Lord and Lady Talmadge, could be called many things. "Boring" was not among them; neither was "fainthearted." Seated in Lady Talmadge's green saloon, her small, compact form as erect as a soldier's, Mrs. Silverbridge had listened with calm approval as Clarissa outlined her travel plans.

"Capital!" she had said briskly. "Now, the situation in France is odd, to say the least, but one has only to avoid the rabble in Paris and one may be quite comfortable. Of course, the French are all mad for *la mode anglaise* at the moment, so that, at least, is in our favor. And once in Italy, one need hardly stir further. There is so much to capture the interest and enrich the mind in the Italian kingdoms. You have not mentioned Naples, for instance."

Clarissa, striving to maintain dignified composure, acknowledged she had not.

"An unfortunate omission, Your Grace. The volcano Vesuvius! The dreadful, fascinating ruins of Pompeii!"

Abigail Silverbridge's dark eyes sparkled with intelligence and humor; her beautifully arranged hair was snow white, though she could not have been a day over fifty. Her late husband, an army officer, had settled a small sum upon her that Mrs. Silverbridge intended to use for her old age. Which, she said firmly, was quite a few years off yet.

"When I am in my dotage, I shall do very well. But until then . . ." Her remarkable eyes flashed. "One should experience as much of the world as possible! Of course, as women, we are sadly hemmed in. When my dear husband was alive, I liked nothing better than to follow the drum. Now, I should wish above all things to set off to seek my fortune with my pack upon my back, as the songs say, but that would never do. So I must contrive in other ways." She smiled. "My last position, for instance, was as governess to a colonel's family. I accompanied them to Gibraltar. A most edifying journey! I kept a fascinating journal when time permitted. Unfortunately, my employers were stupefyingly seasick the entire way. I trust you don't get seasick, Your Grace?"

Clarissa assured her she did not.

"Providential! Nothing can be more tiresome, I assure you."

Clarissa had said gravely that she did not doubt it, and engaged Mrs. Silverbridge on the spot.

How funny Abigail was, and how wonderful, Clarissa thought, smiling to herself. How William and Helen would have liked her! And how Jeremy would have enjoyed her odd, forceful opinions on the ancient Romans. . . .

Clarissa's happy musings came to an abrupt halt. Although she was quite alone, she could not, for some reason, bear to look at her reflection in the mirror. She stared down at the jumble of pins, combs, and boxes on the dressing table for some time before she felt able to summon Martha to help her dress for dinner.

York, late August

The afternoon shadows slanted low and dark over the old city as Sir Jeremy crossed the cathedral close. But the gracious Minster might as well have been set in the midst of Bedlam, he thought with exasperation. Not only was race week fast approaching, but Their Highnesses the Prince of Wales and the Duke of York planned to bestow their presences that year upon the proceedings. Shopkeepers were feverishly polishing windows and draping bunting; representatives of the municipal corporation prowled about, casting stern eyes upon mucky streets and unswept walkways. Passing by the guildhall, Sir Jeremy had been favored with the energetic efforts of the band that would precede Their Highnesses during their formal procession through the city. Everyone in York, it seemed, could talk of nothing but the visit, and Sir Jeremy was heartily sick of it.

Here by the cathedral, though, the madness faded into a distant hum. The ethereal notes of evensong floated into the air; Sir Jeremy slowed his steps slightly. No matter what his business in York, he always found a way to steal a moment by the Minster, whose soaring majesty exalted and comforted him.

Right now his spirit stood in need of some serenity. Why, he could not exactly have said: Thornbeck House had settled into an almost dull calm these several weeks past. Nurse was ensconced in her own small cottage, an arrangement that pleased her surprisingly well; Stainewick had cannily bargained the miller to a more agreeable price; Betty was dusting his study with punctuality, if not thoroughness. No one rearranged his books, challenged his opinions, or reconsidered the appearance of his manor's great hall.

The only ripple in this tranquillity was the thwarted search for a new governess. Miss Bassenthorpe had seemed as near a solution as any, but then had come the inkwell incident.

"That was bad-mannered and wrong of you," he had told Susannah severely in his study.

"It was an accident," she had insisted, wide-eyed.

"I think, Susannah, you helped this *accident* along a bit."

"We-ell, yes," Susannah had replied reluctantly. Then, raising her chin: "I am not sorry she left! She was not very clever, Papa."

This sally had earned Susannah a long stay in her room, with an admonition to consider well how undutiful children grieved their fathers. But nothing, of course, was really resolved.

Sir Jeremy heaved a vexed sigh. The voices from the cathedral died away; there was no excuse to linger. As he reluctantly picked up his pace, a voice behind him made him pause anew. "Well met, Sutcliffe! It *is* Sutcliffe, is it not?"

Sir Jeremy turned to see Captain Battlebourne hurrying toward him, his hat tucked under one arm and his fair hair rather disordered. "I wasn't sure for a moment," the captain said, shaking Sir Jeremy's hand. "What brings you here? Not the races, surely?"

"Business, and a visit with an old friend of my father's," Sir Jeremy said. "What brings *you* here? The Minster's an odd place for a military man."

"Oh, I wouldn't know about that!" The captain grinned. "Men become mighty godly before a battle, sir, as well you'd guess! But that's not why I'm here. I was paying my respects to my old tutor, who's now one of my lord archbishop's secretaries. Much more rewarding for him than pounding Latin into my thick skull, I assure you! Enough of that—will you join me for a drink? Or must you be hurrying home?"

It developed that neither man had intended to attempt the journey back to Thorndale that day. Sir Jeremy had planned to stay at the home of his old friend; the captain was putting up at the inn to which they repaired. They settled into a corner of the taproom, and Sir Jeremy paid for the ale, over the captain's protests.

"Consider it a payment toward a debt," he told the captain. "It's little enough, God knows."

"The Castle Stafford affair?" The captain raised a quizzical brow. "I did what was necessary, nothing more."

"Nevertheless..." Sir Jeremy said gruffly. "It was a damned chancy tangle. And you made all the difference."

"Well, I'll accept the praise, Sutcliffe, and I'm entirely at your service." Captain Battlebourne paused, watching his companion narrowly. "But why do I have the feeling that my selfless heroism has not produced a happy outcome?"

"Battlebourne, you're the best of good fellows, and I feel sure you'll understand when I tell you to go to the devil."

The captain grinned. "Well, you know how it is with military men. No tact. Terrible, but there it is. So: what in God's name has gone wrong with you and Mrs. Wyndham?"

"If you are referring to Her Grace of Belfort," Sir Jeremy said icily, "I have not had the honor of a letter from her since she departed for London."

"Most impressive setdown, Sutcliffe," the captain said. "Would have been a facer, if I happened to care about such things, which I don't. I've a few questions I want answers to."

"Ask away," said Jeremy with a mirthless laugh. "It's clear nothing I say will stop you."

"See here, Sutcliffe." The captain crossed his arms upon the table, leaning forward. "I'll be receiving new orders soon, probably to Upper Canada, maybe back to India—who knows? All I can say for sure is, I won't be in England much longer. Now, I think Mrs. Wynd—oh, dash it, the duchess—is one fine woman. I'd post off tomorrow to ask her if she'd wait for me, except I know it'd do no good. And not, my friend, because of her fine title."

He looked across at his watchful companion. "Lord knows I tried to fix my interest with her," the captain said with deliberate matter-of-factness. "But it was clear to me almost from the start that she had eyes only for you. And you for her, of course."

Utter silence reigned in their little corner of the taproom.

"Unless I was mistaken," the captain said dryly.

"No, damn it, you were not mistaken!"

"Then what happened?"

"Oh, nothing," said Sir Jeremy, savagely ironic. "A trifling deception, really. You see, I paid my addresses to Mrs. Wyndham, the poor widow. The dowager duchess of Belfort came as a bit of a surprise."

The captain made a rude noise. "Is that her sin, then? She lied to you about who she was?"

"You'll admit it was a considerable lie!"

"Well, yes, she withheld vital information," the captain acknowledged. "That's how an aide-de-camp would put it, I suspect. He might also say she was compelled by strategic necessity."

"Damn it, Battlebourne, this wasn't a campaign plan! She might have trusted me."

"Might she have?" Battlebourne gave Sir Jeremy a very straight look. "But—pardon my bluntness— were you not withholding some vital intelligence of your own?"

The silence at the other end of the table spoke volumes.

"Oh, you have me dead to rights, Battlebourne," Sir Jeremy said at last. "Still, *my* reasons—"

"Reasons!" the captain broke in impatiently. "You had reasons; she had reasons. Maybe you were right, maybe she was, maybe neither of you was. What's that to the purpose? The point is, what do you want to do now?"

He set his tankard down with a little bang. "I'm not a man of learning, as you are," he continued, "but I've learned one damned useful thing in the army: no sense wasting time on this earth. There's not nearly as much of it as you think. You can tell me to go to the devil again, but I'd go talk to Mrs.—to the duchess, if I were you. I wouldn't pay attention to filthy gossip, either. My God, man! As if you couldn't know what she truly is, after all these months! Have some sense and put the poison out of your mind."

"Spoken like a general, sir," said Sir Jeremy sarcastically. "Any further orders?"

"No," said the captain, unfazed. "Just think about it, would you?"

Their tankards empty, they got up from the table, and the captain accompanied Sir Jeremy to the bustling street.

"You'll be in Yorkshire a few weeks yet?" Sir Jeremy asked abruptly.

"A few," the captain said. "Long enough to find out whether you took my advice."

"Oh, let it lie, Battlebourne!" Sir Jeremy said. But he smiled at the captain and held out his hand. "In case we don't have the opportunity to talk again, take care of yourself, wherever they send you," he said. "You're a damned meddlesome fellow, but for some reason I'd hate to hear you'd come to harm."

"Thank you—I think," the captain said.

Over the next few days, Sir Jeremy threw himself into his writing and his estate duties—revising a final chapter, discussing the outlook for the year's wool production with Stainewick, riding the rounds of his tenants' farms. Life at Thornbeck House settled into its usual quiet rhythms, but for once these gave Jeremy no comfort.

On the fourth morning after his trip to York, he woke to grey skies and a dull feeling of inevitability. Making his way to the study, he thought with an inward groan of his newly completed book, of the stack of pages remaining for him to copy out in a neat copperplate suitable for his publishers' eyes. The tumble of papers on his desk, the stacks of books he had neglected to reshelve, did nothing to uplift him. Instead, the captain's words rose up, a mocking echo.

No sense wasting time . . . not nearly as much of it as you think.

He yanked open the drapes and stared out over the moors—until his gaze fastened on a small, familiar figure nearly at the horizon line, wandering down a distant byway toward the farthest end of the dale.

"Mickle," he said sharply to the old servant, who had come in with the breakfast tray. "Look over there."

Mickle set the tray down and obediently joined Sir Jeremy at the window. "Why, it's Miss Susannah," he said. "She's abroad early this morning."

"What are you talking about?" Sir Jeremy's brows snapped together. "What is she doing, wandering off by herself?"

"You've nowt to fear, sir. I'll send Kit out to follow her, as always. He'll make sure she comes to no harm."

"This is a regular occurrence?" His eyes followed the tiny, drifting figure. Again, unbidden, he heard the captain's impatient voice.

The point is, what do you want to do now?

"I wouldn't say regular, no, sir." Mickle spoke cautiously. "But she's taken to doing it now and again, since . . . well, lately. It's not as if she goes owt in particular. We keep an eye out and make sure someone's always within hailing distance— Sir?"

Sir Jeremy was shrugging into his coat. "Never mind sending Kit," he said over his shoulder as he headed for the door. "I'll fetch Miss Susannah myself. And see that my portmanteau is packed and a trunk prepared for — oh, let's say a week's journey. I'll have more to tell you about that after breakfast."

Dover, mid-September

The packet was already two days late in sailing, and, as Mrs. Silverbridge gloomily informed Clarissa after making her daily inquiry of the inn's host, it was highly unlikely to leave any time soon, the winds remaining contrary.

"But when?" Clarissa asked, chagrined.

Mrs. Silverbridge, though a seasoned enough traveler to find this question amusing, resisted the impulse to smile. "I'm afraid we sail when the wind favors us, Duchess. There's nothing for it but to wait it out."

They were putting up at the King's Head, Mrs. Silverbridge having assured Clarissa that it was comfortable, quiet, and accustomed to accommodating persons of quality. Though Lord and Lady Talmadge had offered to see her off, Clarissa had bid them fond but firm farewells in London. She had no longing for drawn-out good-byes, and she knew they were anxious to retire to their property in Lincolnshire, the Season being well and truly over.

Off Clarissa had gone to Dover, with Mrs. Silverbridge, Martha, a footman, a courier, and a quantity of baggage. And here they were at the King's Head, with nothing left to do but wait— "and make that rogue of an innkeeper happy," Martha observed irreverently. "The custom he must get, with all the travelers stuck here!"

Clarissa had taken a fine corner room with a private parlor, and had bespoken a second room for Martha and Mrs. Silverbridge. These spacious quarters, however, proved unequal to Clarissa's restless pacing. On this third afternoon of waiting she prowled about at fitful intervals, wondering aloud whether she had forgotten this or that, until Mrs. Silverbridge at last suggested some exercise.

"A walk would do you good, Duchess. It has a calming effect."

"I am perfectly calm," Clarissa said, rummaging through one of her boxes. "I just wish we could be away!"

"What an odd way to put it." Mrs. Silverbridge looked up from her copy of the *Livre de Poste*, the essential guide to hiring horses in France for a reasonable fee. "One would think we were fleeing the country."

"Of course not," her employer replied. "I meant

I wished I could finally find some sort of distraction. . . ." She trailed off.

"Distraction. Hmmm. That is a common expectation of travelers, Duchess—but, I've found, generally a false one," Mrs. Silverbridge said. "Travel broadens the mind, but cannot be relied upon as a narcotic. Although," she finished delicately, "I'm sure that wasn't your meaning, Duchess."

"Oh, no!" Clarissa said hastily. "I meant—I mean—Do you know, I think I *will* go for that walk you suggested."

"Excellent!" Mrs. Silverbridge said approvingly. "I shall find Martha for you."

Mrs. Silverbridge was therefore left to agreeable peace and quiet in her little room, which she put to good use by recording some interesting reflections in her journal. She was reading her entry over, chewing absently upon the end of her quill, when a knock at the door startled her.

Outside, the innkeeper's daughter waited, all excited curiosity.

"Oh, ma'am, there's a gentleman below, inquiring for Her Grace, and her just gone out! Whatever shall I tell him?"

"A gentleman? Did he state his business?"

"No, ma'am. But very nicely spoken he was," the girl said, with a speculative grin that drew a frown from Mrs. Silverbridge.

"I am not interested in your opinion of his manners, miss," she said with asperity. "Have the goodness to conduct this gentleman to Her Grace's parlor, and I will see him there."

Mrs. Silverbridge was not sure what sort of person she expected to see when she entered the parlor, but she could find nothing objectionable in the gentleman who waited there, aside from his travel-worn appearance. Though clearly she was not what *he* expected, she noted with approval his polite suppression of curiosity. He merely bowed, and waited.

"I am given to understand you have business with Her Grace of Belfort?" Mrs. Silverbridge inquired.

"I do," said the gentleman.

"Her Grace has just gone out. Perhaps I may help you?"

"I'm afraid not. This is rather private business, you see."

"Private?" She raised her brows. "How am I to take that, sir?"

"Calmly, ma'am, I beg of you," the stranger said wearily. "I've come a long way, and I don't think I've the stamina for a storm of outraged virtue."

Mrs. Silverbridge surprised him with a sudden bark of laughter. "Well put, sir! I like a man who doesn't mince his words. I am Abigail Silverbridge, Her Grace's companion."

The visitor bowed. "Sir Jeremy Sutcliffe of Thornbeck House in Yorkshire, at your service."

"Ah!" Mrs. Silverbridge had not heard Sir Jeremy's name before, but the mention of Yorkshire caught her attention. Several other hitherto mystifying bits of information fused in her agile brain, and she smiled beatifically. "I believe you are the answer, sir."

"To what, ma'am?" Sir Jeremy, left in a dangerous temper by many days of breakneck travel, found himself unexpectedly amused.

"To several questions that have crossed my mind of late. Let us examine them in an orderly fashion." Mrs. Silverbridge began ticking off her points upon her fingers. "Sir, I am about to travel across Europe with a delightful lady who is spending a great deal of money and a vast amount of effort upon a journey that should be a wonderful adventure. Yet she goes about looking as if she is on her way to a funeral. What do you think of that?"

"Most strange," said Sir Jeremy, a spark of hope leaping into his eyes.

"Most strange," agreed Mrs. Silverbridge. "Furthermore, whenever one mentions Yorkshire—a tolerable enough place, I have heard—this lady looks distinctly troubled."

Sir Jeremy waited.

"*Furthermore*," concluded Mrs. Silverbridge, "I am now receiving a gentleman from Yorkshire who says he has matters of a private nature to discuss with the duchess. Most interesting."

Sir Jeremy agreed that this was so.

"I see I cannot ask your business, sir," Mrs. Silverbridge said, looking at him keenly. "You clearly mean to keep it to yourself. But I must ask: whatever your errand is, do you mean it kindly?"

The smile that transformed his face reassured Mrs. Silverbridge more than any words. "You are persistent—and most loyal, madam," he said. "Yes, I mean it kindly."

She looked at him a moment more, then nodded briskly. "She has gone walking with her maid. To Robinson's Lane, to look in the shops. There are not so very many of interest; you should be able to find her easily enough."

She extended her hand; Sir Jeremy, to her pleased surprise, raised it to his lips. "Many thanks," he said. "I believe I'll try the bookseller's first."

"You know her well, I see," said Mrs. Silverbridge.

Clarissa had bought two books: one an earnest-looking treatise on education by Miss Edgeworth; the other a memoir of travel through Tuscany, "being the true recollections and observations" of a clergyman from Warwickshire. As she and Martha stepped out into the crowded street, the brightness and noise caused Clarissa to blink momentarily. She looked down to see a small, grimy hand clutching her skirt.

"Penny for an apple, lady?" the little boy rasped.

A stout gentleman passing by admonished Clarissa to send the lad about his business. But Martha had already dug a penny from her pocket, and gave it to the boy, saying sharply, "There, and never mind the apple. Now, go on, and don't fret the lady so!"

"Thanks, and God gi' ye g'day!" the boy replied cheekily. He bit the coin, grinned, and wandered off.

Looking after him, Clarissa could not restrain a laugh.

"Now, Your Grace," Martha admonished her. "You'll only encourage his sort by laughing like that."

"Encourage him? *I'm* not giving him pennies. He seemed harmless enough."

"Well, he isn't, Your Grace, and I ought to know," Martha said. "Why, I've heard—" She broke off, a look of astonishment crossing her face. Clarissa, glancing idly into the window of a milliner's, waited in vain for her to continue.

"Yes, Martha?" she prompted. "What have you heard?" But Martha was still silent. Clarissa turned from the shop window with a mixture of concern and impatience. "Whatever is . . . the . . ."

She saw Sir Jeremy standing before them, and became very still. The shoppers and sailors, costermongers and errand boys jostled around them, parting and breaking like the ripples on a river.

"Hello, Clarissa," he said. She remained silent, studying him. He looked tired, a little out of sorts—and something else that she could not immediately define. His boots were filmed with dust;

his clothes looked vaguely rumpled. His hair had grown longer since she had seen him last, she noted irrelevantly. He raked an impatient hand through it.

"You've come from Thornbeck House?" she asked at last. "Is everyone well?"

"Everyone's well, thank you," he said. "Susannah and the Petherstones send their love."

Jeremy paused for a moment, drinking in the sight of her. Even from the end of the crowded street, he had spotted her instantly: her slender, erect figure, the quick, forthright walk, so familiar. And yet not quite. This Clarissa was every inch the town lady. Her green coat, pearl-grey gloves, and dashing hat, elegant in their almost masculine severity, were a far cry from the woolen shawls and chip bonnets she had worn in the country. And the broad, plumed brim of her hat shaded her features from him.

Martha cleared her throat. "Should I be getting back to the King's Head, Your Grace?"

Clarissa paused a moment, then nodded. "I think so. Yes. Please tell Mrs. Silverbridge I should be back in . . . half hour. Will you be able to escort me back, Sir Jeremy?"

"Of course," he said.

Martha slipped off, and they were alone.

"You're looking very well . . . Your Grace," Sir Jeremy said. At the use of her title, she looked sharply at him, but his face was unreadable. Slowly, they began to walk along the street. "I've had a most pleasant conversation with your Mrs. Silverbridge. A remarkable woman."

Clarissa confined herself to a nod.

"Lovely weather today," Sir Jeremy pursued relentlessly. "Such a pity you have apparently lost your voice."

She glared at him. "I'm sorry if I appear rude. This is a surprise, you see."

"I thought it might be."

"I am going away for a while," Clarissa said. "The packet has been delayed."

"Forgive me, but I was glad to hear of the delay," Sir Jeremy said quietly. "I had hoped to find you still here. The Talmadges told me where to find you, you see."

"Did they?" Clarissa felt her heart beating uncomfortably fast. "I believed them to be in Lincolnshire already."

"They are; I went to see them there, not finding them at home in London," Sir Jeremy said.

"Oh!" Clarissa digested this. "You've—you've certainly been traveling a great deal, Sir Jeremy."

"Not nearly as much as you will be," he said in a perfectly conversational way. "You're bound for Italy, I believe?"

Clarissa nodded. "Florence for a while, and Rome. Venice, too, I think, although we shall see—"

"An ambitious itinerary," he said, his eyes never leaving her face.

"Oh, it's only the beginning, sir," she said quickly. "In the spring I want to visit Munich, and Vienna. Of course France would be lovely, but one must await events there." Her voice, she was uncomfortably aware, had become parrotlike. Had she recited this so very many times? Was he noticing?

He replied mildly, "It sounds like a grand adventure. And challenging. Not many people would undertake it."

Across the street an old woman was selling flowers; her latest customer, a very young and earnest gentleman, seemed to ponder his choice painfully before selecting a twist of yellow blossoms. Clarissa smiled at the sight, and looked up at Sir Jeremy.

"Well, I'm not such a poor creature, sir, as I think I've told you before. I can take care of myself, I believe."

"With the assistance of Mrs. Silverbridge, I should think so. Brigands in every land will tremble," he replied. The thought provoked them both into laughter, but as it faded they lapsed into silence, strolling absently past a chandler's, then a linendraper's. Abruptly, Sir Jeremy stopped.

"Will you come back?" he asked.

She tilted her head to look at him better. The brisk breeze had ruffled his hair; he looked very serious.

"What a question!" she said lightly. "I'm not going into exile, you know. In fact, I've made particular plans for my return; I will be taking a house in Wimbledon. The neighborhood is so peaceful. . . ." She trailed off.

"No doubt," Sir Jeremy said. "The Talmadges had told me of that scheme too, actually."

"Then why did you ask?" Once again, her heartbeat began to race.

"You misunderstood my question. I meant: will you come back to me?"

"*Apples!*" the hoarse little voice shrieked by their side. "Apple for a penny!" Through his tangled brown hair, the urchin squinted up at Clarissa. "Hey! For you it's half a penny!"

"An acquaintance of yours?" Sir Jeremy asked, a look of wicked amusement replacing his scowl of annoyance.

"Don't be nonsensical," Clarissa snapped, blushing. Sir Jeremy shrugged and flipped the boy a penny.

"Be off with you," he told him.

"What, don't you want an apple?" the boy asked, aggrieved.

"No, I do not want an apple, and I'll thank you to go about your business before I call the watch!" Sir Jeremy told him firmly.

The boy scampered off again, muttering something incomprehensible. Sir Jeremy turned to Clarissa and started to speak, but at the same moment a heavy dray clattered by, causing them and the other passersby to leap aside.

"Oh, God, this is all wrong," he said when the danger was past. "If there were a quiet place where we could talk—"

"What difference would that make?" Clarissa broke in, her voice low and sad.

"Don't say that, Clary—"

"No!" She stopped him with a sharp look, an upraised hand. "I don't understand you, Jeremy. I don't understand why you're here, why you're asking me these questions now. For suppose, just suppose, that I said yes. How could I be sure that you wouldn't have second thoughts about allying yourself with the notorious Duchess? I can hardly believe you're bringing yourself to consider it." Her tone had become ironic, cutting. "Or don't you quite remember who I am? Nothing has changed!"

"I remember," he said quietly. "I remember everything that's been said—and everything I *know*," he concluded, with a note in his voice she had never heard before. "And while we're on the subject of pasts, do you not remember everything about mine?"

"Yes," she said baldly, biting her lip. "Oh, Jeremy, why couldn't you have *told* me?"

"For many reasons," he said as they resumed their walk. "But they all added up to just one reason, really. I was afraid."

"Of what, for pity's sake?" Clarissa stopped in her tracks.

"Looking foolish," he said with a crooked smile.

"It's my besetting fear, after all. In fact, in my most honest moments, I knew that was why I was so angry at you that night at Castle Stafford—I felt you made me look ridiculous." He held up a hand. "Oh, I know you didn't mean to! You had compelling reasons for your secret. *My* secret wasn't nearly so logical. It just seemed, well, important that you see me in a certain way. Certainly not as the man who had been duped by Caroline."

"I think," Clarissa said with a hint of sternness, "it is high time you forgave yourself for all that. Especially since it sounds as if you forgave Caroline a long time ago."

"Is that so, Madam Philosopher? Perhaps you're right. But the way things ended with Caroline . . . I felt bitter about that, and about her, for so long that I entirely failed to notice when it had ceased to matter anymore. And it stopped mattering a long time ago."

"That night in the garden, it did not seem so," Clarissa said quietly. She bowed her head, unable to continue.

"Yes," he went on gently. "For just that moment, all of it came back. I acted like an utter fool. I think I must have realized it the moment you left, but my pride wouldn't let me admit that I was hurting you for the sake of something that was over and dead."

He stopped, and faced her squarely. "I'm making a hash of this. Clarissa . . . I can't undo the past, but I don't want to go forward without you. I—I've missed you damnably, and I want you back. I want you for my wife. No matter who you happen to be."

She looked up again, her eyes suspiciously bright, a smile trembling upon her lips. "Even Titania?"

He kept his voice steady and light, not daring to

acknowledge the hope rising within him. "Even Titania."

"Or," she said, mischief returning to her voice, "that scrubby little schoolboy you nearly ran down that first day?"

"Lord, that seems an age ago!"

"Or that interfering, opinionated governess Mrs. Wyndham?" she persisted.

"Oh, my love," he said, gathering her into his arms with fierce tenderness. "Especially she."

Heedless of passersby, they clung together for a long moment.

"Cor!" said an interested, all-too-familiar voice behind them. "Quality, too! Now, that's a sight, that is!"

"On your way, brat!" said Sir Jeremy, loosening his hold on Clarissa momentarily and flipping him another coin.

The boy took it, dazzled. "Not one apple the poorer, neither!" he marveled, speaking to no one in particular as he trotted away. "Thanks, Your Worship!"

"Odious boy!" Clarissa had drawn slightly away from Sir Jeremy, caught between laughter and tears.

"The devil with him! Clarissa, are you saying yes?"

She held him off, her face becoming grave. "Jeremy," she said, hesitantly meeting his watchful look, "do you truly mean it? What's done is done?"

"My dear doubter," he said calmly, "I can see you'll need convincing. And I don't blame you, of course. What a joyless recluse I must have seemed when we first met!"

"I never thought that!"

"*Didn't* you? I seem to recall a lecture upon the selfishness of burying my 'well-informed mind' in seclusion."

Clarissa turned scarlet, and grew quite silent. Jeremy took pity on her with a grin she could only term self-satisfied. "You'll be happy to know I've finally taken your advice to heart," he continued. "Yours weren't the only plans I discussed with Lord and Lady Talmadge."

"Then what else—" She clapped her hands in sudden excitement. "Jeremy! The Foreign Office?"

"I've begun to reestablish my connection with them, but slowly. It's enough, for now, to be back in touch, to spend some time in London each year with some interesting friends and see what develops." He paused. "I'm not inclined to turn my back upon the dale completely, you see. I confess I've grown attached to it for its own sake, and Susannah is so happy there. But later, perhaps, when she is older . . ."

Listening closely, watching his face, she saw his unexpected diffidence. Could that actually be anxiety shading his voice?

"That sounds extremely sensible," Clarissa said with deliberate casualness. "What a splendid idea for the future! Helen and William will be so pleased."

"I'm delighted to hear that, naturally. But I'm most interested in hearing what Her Grace of Belfort thinks about changing her travel plans for this year to Yorkshire, rather than Rome. The dale isn't nearly so agreeable in the winter, as we both well know."

He spoke lightly, but his eyes were scanning her face with intensity.

"Her Grace of Belfort thinks Yorkshire in the winter would be beyond splendid," Clarissa said softly. "There can always be other journeys—"

"Clarissa, does that mean—"

"I think it must," she said, almost wonderingly, reaching up to touch his cheek. "Must mean yes, that is. And—" But her next words were cut off abruptly with another ruthless kiss.

"Jeremy," she said warningly, when at last he released her. "A few more minutes of this, and I won't have a shred of reputation left."

"In that case, we had best be married as soon as possible."

"Is that so? There was something most *peremptory* in that pronouncement—" Suddenly she paused, looking stricken.

"What is it, my love?"

"Lisbon! What am I thinking? Jeremy, there's so much to *do*! The baggage—my passage—Mrs. Silverbridge . . ."

He smiled at her, tucking her hand through his arm as they neared the gaily painted sign of the King's Head inn. "You needn't worry, love, at least about Mrs. Silverbridge. First, I've a notion she won't be at all surprised by our news. Second, I believe I have hit upon the perfect challenge for her—involving a somewhat younger lady. Since Mrs. Abigail seems interested in improving minds . . ."

Clarissa's gaze flew up to his in sudden, delighted agreement. "Of course—she's the perfect governess for Susannah! Now, why didn't I think of it earlier?"

"You could hardly be expected to attend to Susannah," he said, smiling down at her with the warmth that made her momentarily, delightfully dizzy. "You were rather busy keeping her father in order."

Clarissa shook her head at him as they approached the door, but the smile had returned to her face. She laughed impulsively into the companionable silence between them.

"Do you know, Jeremy," she said in response to the inquiring lift of his eyebrow, "I really think everything is going to work out splendidly."

Pausing in the act of handing her over the threshold, Sir Jeremy looked into Clarissa's face, shining in the glow of the autumn sunlight.

"So do I, my love," he said, a sudden catch in his voice. "So do I."

Avon Romantic Treasures

Unforgettable, enthralling love stories,
sparkling with passion and adventure
from Romance's bestselling authors

CAPTIVES OF THE NIGHT *by Loretta Chase*
76648-5/$4.99 US/$5.99 Can

CHEYENNE'S SHADOW *by Deborah Camp*
76739-2/$4.99 US/$5.99 Can

FORTUNE'S BRIDE *by Judith E. French*
76866-6/$4.99 US/$5.99 Can

GABRIEL'S BRIDE *by Samantha James*
77547-6/$4.99 US/$5.99 Can

COMANCHE FLAME *by Genell Dellin*
77524-7/ $4.99 US/ $5.99 Can

WITH ONE LOOK *by Jennifer Horsman*
77596-4/ $4.99 US/ $5.99 Can

LORD OF THUNDER *by Emma Merritt*
77290-6/ $4.99 US/ $5.99 Can

RUNAWAY BRIDE *by Deborah Gordon*
77758-4/$4.99 US/$5.99 Can